Wild Card

Etudes in C#, No. 1

Jamie Wyman

Pajamazon Wordworks
Mesa, AZ USA
www.jamiewyman.com

First Edition November 2013, Entangled Publishing
Second Edition May 2015, Pajamazon Wordworks

Edited by Danielle Poiesz and Double Vision Editorial
Cover design by Nathalia Suellen

Ebook ISBN: 978-0-9903925-3-8
Print ISBN: 978-0-9903925-2-1

Pajamazon Wordworks, Mesa, AZ
Printed in the United States of America

For Ohana.

Family by blood and by choice.

Other works by Jamie Wyman

Etudes in C#

Wild Card

Unveiled

Short Fiction in Anthologies

When the Hero Comes Home 2 (Dragon Moon Press, 2013)

Two Hundred Twenty-One Baker Streets (Abaddon Books, 2014)

CHAPTER ONE
"Nobody Weird Like Me"

I should've known something was wrong with the world that day. On my way to work, I breezed through every single green light like I owned the city. I even found a primo parking spot near the center of the Strip. The promise of the weekend bubbled up before me like primordial awesomeness waiting to be tapped and turned into a brew of good memories.

So, of course, someone had to squash my optimism like an ant under a boot.

As I stomped toward Caesars Palace for my next appointment, my phone rang. *Barracuda* by Heart. I let out the signature sigh of the bone-weary. Nothing good ever came of phone calls from *him*.

Without breaking stride, I rummaged through my bag and retrieved my cell. "This is Cat," I said tersely.

"Catherine, darling," sang the unctuous voice. "What a delight it is to speak with you."

"Marius," I growled. I didn't even attempt to conceal my loathing for the satyr and his smug British accent.

"I can tell by your enthusiasm that you've missed me."

"I've counted every second we've been apart," I sneered. "What do you want?"

"Our mistress wishes to see you," he said.

His smirk nearly blasted through the phone. My knuckles popped as I clenched my fist, imagining the glorious day when I could finally smack that look off his face.

"Marius, I can't play right now. I have to work. You know? The thing mere mortals do to pay the bills?"

"Yes. Tedious, that."

I snorted. "More than a little. I'm on my way to a job right now, Marius. The boss will just have to wait."

"Be that as it may, the Lady expects you in her office in one hour. Ta-ta, love."

I glared at the phone. The goat-legged son of a bitch hung up on me. Stuffing the cell in my bag, I heaved a sigh and thought, *I hate immortals.*

***

When one of the more adept techies in Las Vegas had called the office with server problems, I'd cringed. If Tully reached out for help, it meant he'd probably run into some weird, arcane shit. On the plus side, it also means this girl gets to pay rent.

Like always, I met up with David Tullemore at the registration desk of Caesars Palace. When he strolled into the lobby, he was a sweaty mass of panic. One look at me, though, and Tully's face sagged with relief.

"Thank God, they sent someone competent today."

Since I can say with utmost certainty that God didn't send me that day, I appreciated the compliment for what it was worth. More than once Tully had told me how he'd called up Answers, Inc.—my more mundane employer—and his problems multiplied until they'd handed the reins over to me. Among our tight community of code monkeys and IT gurus, I'd built a bit of a reputation for knowing my craft.

As he escorted me through the winding halls of the casino offices we were a study in opposites. Tully was tall and damn near spherical whereas I was stick straight and short. We were dressed similarly in the unofficial uniforms of our trade—polo shirts and khakis—but while my demeanor was casual, Tully was jittery as a coked up squirrel. We exchanged pleasantries, dropped the mantles of contractor and helpless techie, and melted into the routine of friends.

"So, saved the world today?" he asked as he dabbed perspiration from his forehead.

"Not yet. But I did rewire a celebrity's panic room this morning. Thanks to me she should be able to survive hordes of paparazzi and fanboys."

"If you did the job, she'd survive a zombie apocalypse."

"Well," I said after thinking a moment, "she'll survive if she doesn't trip over her implants."

His round face split with hopeful awe, and his eyes sparkled. "Whose house?"

"If I told you I'd have to kill you, Tully." I chuckled as we rounded a corner. "How's the wife?"

He blew out a tired, dramatic breath, and rolled his eyes. "Fine until a few hours ago. Today, Cat, I am in the doghouse."

"What's going on?"

"This stupid party tonight. Apparently it's been on the books for months, but no one in the whole hotel knew we were hosting a gala tonight! Security is scrambling and management has called all hands. I have to work my regular hours plus the graveyard shift to make sure nothing else goes wrong with the system."

"Can't hand it off to someone lower in the food chain?"

He shook his head. "No. This isn't just some benefit dinner. This is big time. A lot of money will be walking in the door tonight. If a light bulb so much as flickers, my boss will grind me to a pulp and serve me up as tacos on the ten-dollar buffet."

"Easy, Tully," I said, placing a hand on his shoulder. "Before you start smearing salsa all over yourself, why don't we take a look at what you've got for me."

Swiping his card key, Tully accessed the data center, the beating heart of the casino. Cold, dry air blasted me in the face as I stepped in. Everything in Las Vegas depends on one computer system or another. Security, gaming, hotel room lists and reservations, Wi-Fi—you name it.

Walking into the clean, orderly room, the tension left my shoulders, and I felt my limbs relax. As the white noise of massive air conditioners lulled me into a Zen-like peace, I could almost feel my breathing fall into a cadence with the steady rhythm of the machines around me. Rooms like this are my spa. Everything has a purpose. Everything has its place. Here, everything is simple.

If only the rest of my life could be so structured and solid.

Tully rounded a corner and gestured to the worktable. "This is my problem, Cat," he called over the mechanical din. "My domain controller shut down last night, and I can't figure out what the hell is wrong with it."

4

The domain controller is the brain and spinal cord of any casino's systems, the "God server." It ensures that everything runs as one smooth operation. I shuddered. If *Tully* hadn't solved this riddle, what kind of a mess would I find when I took a peek?

My friendly demeanor dropped as I switched into work mode. When I spoke again, my words were clipped, my tone all business. "Backup controller working?"

"Backup is fine, but I want this one online before tonight."

"Understood."

I sat down at the desk and hunched over the server. I opened the case and let my eyes wander over the tangle of cables and cords connecting to circuit boards and processors. Without laying a finger on it, I acquainted myself with the machine's landscape.

I'd often thought peering into the insides of a computer was a lot like reading entrails. Most people thought every hard drive looked like the same ancient riddle, but my trained eyes saw a language, a pattern, a grand design. Whenever I looked into the guts of a machine, I knew things.

As I took out a pair of magnification glasses, Tully slowly paced the room, his bulk rolling with each step.

"Please, God, just make this work," he said. "Make this work and I will do anything."

Without taking my eyes off of the problem in front of me, I blew a stray lock of my copper hair out of my face. "Name's not God, and I don't know Him."

"Sorry, Cat," he said. "I'm nervous."

I pushed the glasses up over my forehead and regarded Tully. "You know what I think is funny? Everyone always wants to believe that some all-powerful deity is watching them and guiding them, but, in reality, deities aren't all that helpful."

5

Tully nodded, his cheeks rippling in a nervous grin. "It's Vegas. What do you expect? Everyone wants the cards to turn their way. Faith and luck are everywhere"

"I guess. But why would they give a damn one way or the other about what goes on in our lives? Oh, that's right. They don't. The gods only care about themselves."

He tilted his head. "You have some wisdom on the matter, Cat?"

Loads, I thought. I've met more deities than most people acknowledge even exist. I'd just gotten off the phone with an actual satyr, and my best friend was a mage who could manipulate machines and electronics. If Tully wanted to wax philosophical I could blow his paranoid, caffeine-soaked mind. But, since I figured he wouldn't want his worldview rocked that day, I refrained from going off on the rant that was bubbling up inside of me.

"My experience? It's when the gods take an interest in you that you should start praying."

His face fell.

I let him chew on that thought and went back to work, gazing deep into the circuitous paths making up the motherboard. Like a map, the lines spread out before me, linking together to form a picture as familiar as my hometown. I found the problem by the conspicuous absence of a simple connection.

"Bingo," I cheered.

"Cat, I've been elbow-deep in that thing for hours, and I couldn't figure out what was wrong. You've been here maybe five minutes."

"Sometimes, it just takes a fresh pair of eyes. Hand me the soldering kit, will ya?"

I exchanged my magnifiers for a set of safety goggles and set to the gentle work of repairing the "God server."

"So," I said, "tell me about this party."

Tully's stress pushed out of him in a long string of words. "The *joyous* rumor is there will be a lot of high-society types. Celebrities, rock stars, models. The works."

"Pricey entrance fee?"

"Invitation only."

"Ooh, fancy."

"Very. Security has extra staff coming in to work the ballroom, and my boss has me doing grunt work so he can try to get in and schmooze."

"If it's any consolation," I said, "I'm on call tonight, too."

"For us?"

"No, standard agency work." *Or whatever random slog through humiliation and death-defying trickery the goddess has planned for me this time*, I grumbled to myself.

"But," I added cheerfully, "at least if something goes to hell tonight and you call for help, you'll probably get me."

"Well, that's a relief. At least I know the work would get done right the first time."

Tully stopped and loomed behind me. Distracted by his presence and the weight of his anticipation, I slid my chin over my shoulder and gave him the slightest of glares. He raised both hands in apology or surrender—or both—and backed away.

I batted my eyelashes in gratitude and went back to my task.

Soldering is delicate work, but fixing a couple of loose connections is cake. There's something relaxing about it, too. Watching molten metal solidify, I can almost feel the links being created beneath my fingertips. It makes me wonder if that's what the world looked like millions of years after the Big Bang—little dots of slag spreading out, quenching in the briny wash of the ocean to form restless continents.

When I finished, I looked over my work with a satisfied smile. "Turn the key and see how she runs."

Tully dragged a thick hand over the greasy fuzz he called hair, then plugged the server into a nearby test strip. Immediately the LED light on the front began to glow. Tully chewed on his lip and watched the monitor, waiting. When the boot sequence began, his fingers clenched into fists. Only when the system was purring and fully functional did Tully let out a hurricane-force sigh of relief.

"See?" I said. "Good as new."

Tully's second chin wobbled a little as he gaped at me. I take that sort of thing as a compliment.

I bowed as Yoda might to Obi-Wan. "My work here is done. Unless you've got something else for me?"

He shook his head. "No, I think we're good."

Good, I thought. *Maybe I can actually be on time meeting the goddess for once.* Her wrath was not one I particularly wanted to meet again.

I handed him a clipboard to sign off on the work I'd completed and set to packing my tools.

As he scribbled, Tully said, "I don't know how you do it."

"Sheer awesomeness," I offered.

"Seriously, Cat, you're the best."

I gave a slight shrug. "It's a gift."

Tully showed me out of the server room, and we began the trip back to the front desk. "Being wasted on contract work, if you ask me," he said. "Someone as brilliant as you should be the IT head of any casino in this town. Where were you when we needed a new one?"

I snorted as Tully hit one of my sore spots. When people ask me questions like this—or worse, ask why I don't work for one of the big names like Google or Microsoft—I have to take a deep breath so I don't stab them with my multi-tool.

"I interviewed for the job to be your boss, Tully. Don't remind me."

"Really? Why didn't you take it?"

"I didn't get the offer."

"Seriously?" Tully said, offended. "But you're the best! And I can totally tell you love what you do. I've heard you hum while you work. You'd be a way better boss than the asshole I deal with everyday."

I nodded along with him. I've danced to this one before.

"No," I said, "I mean I didn't *receive* the offer. My phone ate the message for a week. By the time I'd gotten it, they'd already filled the position."

Tully sagged. "That sucks. Bad luck."

You have no idea.

"Well, maybe you can get work with Apple. I mean, you've got the tattoo."

He pointed down to my left wrist, and my eyes followed.

Any traces of a good mood I may have had vanished at the mention of my mark. The gold tattoo looked exactly like *that* apple—a stylized silhouette with a bite taken out of it. It was a common misconception. A tech nerd fixing computers for twelve hours a day with a freaking apple on her arm? Yeah. Most people associated the tattoo with the brand. It was *a* brand, sure, just not that kind.

The bitch that had etched her symbol on my arm waited for me, and I was running out of time. I had to get the hell out and hoof it down the Strip.

Giving my friend a quick salute, I shouldered my bag. "All right, Tully. I'm out. Good luck tonight." I kicked myself into gear and began the brisk walk back through the casino's labyrinth.

"You, too," he called after me.

Thanks, I thought. *I need all the good luck I can get.*

CHAPTER TWO
"My Friends"

Since I was at Caesars Palace—relatively central on Las Vegas Boulevard—I could walk to the goddess's office without any trouble. Also, walking ensured I didn't lose my epic parking space and further screw up the careful rhythm of the rest of my day. I tucked my head down, shoved my elbows out, and rammed through the foot traffic.

The goddess kept a penthouse on the top floor of one of the more posh casinos in the city. I'd never tell anyone which one, though. I prefer my soul firmly attached to the rest of my body, thank you very much.

Once at the casino, I had to pass through slaughterhouse that is the gaming floor to get to her office. The stench of stale cigarettes, cheap booze, and old-lady perfume formed a thick haze over the green felt tables. My throat tightened, and my eyes began to water. Some things you just don't get used to even after nearly a decade of living in Sin City.

My ears ached from the cacophony around me: croupiers yelling, "Blackjack!"; the jangle of hundreds of slot machines; video poker games calling out their siren song to passersby. I used to look around a casino and think of good times with just the right dash of vice. These days all I see is work. Machines about to break down, cameras on the fritz—another mess I'll have to clean up eventually.

Glancing to one of the black globes in the ceiling, I gave a polite wave to whatever poor schmuck was on shift in the crow's nest.

I shouldered through the throng of gamblers. As I passed a roulette wheel, the marble dropped and a voice called out, "Eight! Black eight!"

Typical. It lands on my number when I'm not betting. Such is the kind of luck I'd lived with for too long.

I turned to take myself away from the pit, keeping my eyes down and fidgeting with my bag. Beside me, a bank of slot machines went wild a blazing chorus of bells and whistles announcing the mother of all jackpots. Jumping in surprise, I jerked to a halt just before ramming into another body.

I looked up to see the familiar, long face of my best friend, Flynn. With a warm smile he chided me, "You should really watch where you're going."

The slot-jockeys around us grumbled. Though the machines—all of them—had rang out in triumph, no coins spilled forth. In fact, as far as I could tell, none of them had even been close to having a winning pull. Flynn beamed with a prankster's pride. And why not? Setting off a whole bank of slots with little more than a blink was pretty damn cool. Ah, the perks of technomancy.

A few of the gamblers resorted to one of my preferred methods of tech support: percussive maintenance. Smacking or kicking the machines, they cursed with some of the more colorful profanities I'd heard in a while.

"Troll," I said to Flynn. I passed him a smile of my own. "You're going to piss people off if you keep making them think they're winning."

"Adrenaline is good for you, right?"

"And heart attacks are just muscle cramps." I pointed to an elderly woman staring at two cherries and a seven. One pincer-like hand clutched a tumbler while the other pressed to her chest. "There! See? Look what you've done," I chastised Flynn. "You've gone and given some poor old lady a heart attack! Shame on you."

His hazel eyes glittered with mercurial charm. "I promise, from now on, I'll only use my powers for good. Forgive me?"

I wagged my finger at him like an angry mom—which probably looked ridiculous since he's at least a foot taller than me. "Fine, but you're grounded, mister. No technomagic for you for a whole week."

"Aw, man!" he whined. Flynn dropped the act and wound his inked, ropy arms around me. "How have you been? Feels like I haven't seen you in months!"

"It's been a week." I laughed into his shoulder. As I pulled away, some of my annoyance at the world disappeared. Flynn's hugs are just that good.

He wore his standard black metal-band T-shirt and black pants with chains dangling from the belt loops. The tattoos along his arms and piercings in his ears, combined with his spiky red hair, gave him an undeniable punk vibe.

Flynn carried himself like a secure man in his thirties. The lines on his face hinted he might be a decade older. His hazel eyes, though, have always given me the impression that he's just watching yet another epoch go by.

At the club he owned, we were often mistaken for siblings. I suppose you could chalk it up to the fact that we're both pale as sin with flame-red hair, but I like to think it's just how we are.

My brother-from-another-mother took in my work clothes and bag. "On a job?"

"Just finishing one, actually," I said. "A God server went down."

"Ouch. I bet that caused more than a few headaches."

I shrugged. "Nothing a bit of soldering couldn't fix. I was in and out in a few minutes."

The technomancer snorted. "Seriously? You soldered? How cute!" He patted me on the head. "So old-fashioned and beneath you."

"That's a new record," I said. "Usually it's at least an hour before you start prodding me to admit I'm a technomage."

"Because you are."

"Not. How many times are we going to do this?"

"Until you quit with the games and just come out with it."

I shook my head. Sadly, I wasn't part of the cool kids club. "I'm sorry to disappoint you. Unlike *some* people I know, I can't just look at a computer and tell it to do my bidding."

"Whatever," he said, rolling his eyes. "Got time for me to buy you lunch?"

"Any other day I'd say yes, but I got a call from the boss lady."

"Ah…" Flynn shuffled his feet and looked to the ceiling. While most people labored under the blissful delusion that myths were just bedtime stories, Flynn knew firsthand that there was so much more to the world. I'd been able to confide in him long ago about my arrangement with a deity. "Her mouth to your ear, eh?"

"Unfortunately. Marius says I need to be there soon. We'll see what fresh torture she has planned for me this time."

"Leave me for a satyr—I see how it is."

"If I were into non-humans, I could do worse, I suppose. Sex and pleasure is what they do, right?"

"From what you've told me about Marius, I think I'd rather see you hooking up with frat boys and Republicans."

I grabbed his wrist and stole a glance at his watch. "Shit. I'm going to be late."

Flynn put an arm around my shoulders and squeezed. "Fine. I'll see you at the club tonight, though, right?"

"I'm on call. If I'm lucky I'll be able to make it, but right now it's looking bleak. Coffee next week?"

He nodded as I gave him a parting wave and took off into the casino again. Behind me the slot machines went up in more jangling clangs of victory. Despite my growing sense of doom and gloom, I grinned. Flynn had odd ways of saying hello and good-bye.

A few seconds later I'd cleared the forest of video poker and made it to the hotel-casino's elevator bank. I got in an open car and pushed the topmost button, ready to visit the harpy who owned a piece of me.

Specifically, my soul.

When the doors slid open, Marius greeted me. "Damn!" he said, snapping his pocket watch closed. "You made it with three minutes to spare."

I passed him a wry grin. "Hoping I'd incur the wrath of our mistress?" Bile rose in my throat as I said the last word.

Smoothing his goatee with slender fingers, he said, "Well, one does hope to break the monotony somehow. There's nothing like a good old-fashioned smiting to raise the heart rate a bit."

Marius straightened the cuffs of his paper-white shirt. Today he appeared crisp and collected in a charcoal-gray suit. A golden ribbon held his long black hair at the nape of his neck. As much as it pained me to admit it, he definitely fit the "tall, dark, and handsome" bill. His olive skin and inky hair spoke of a Mediterranean heritage, but his voice was as smooth as London fog. With his lithe build, clipped goatee, and a lopsided smile that could charm the scales off a snake, he could easily pass for a pirate or some other scoundrel, too.

The illusion was ruined for me long ago, though, the first time he opened his mouth and began spouting about his sexual prowess. The British accent—pleasant on the ears as it may be—couldn't assuage my dislike for him. It was all part of his act, part of the glamour that kept his goat's legs hidden and his bed—and belly—full. Marius was not some traveling scholar, not a millionaire playboy, and he was most certainly not a Time Lord. Marius was a bastard, plain and simple.

I drew in a breath to steel myself against whatever horrors the goddess had planned for me. "Let's get this over with," I said as I began a brisk walk down the hall.

In two quick strides, Marius caught up with me. "I must say, Catherine, you look rather fetching today."

Yeah, right, I thought. I glanced down at my work uniform. The red polo shirt with my company's glyph-like logo hung loosely on my petite form, and the cargo pants looked bulky and boyish. Since I'd seen Marius working his particular brand of smarmy magic on a pair of unsuspecting coeds wearing skimpy leather skirts, I doubted my frumpy outfit seemed "fetching" to him.

"I think," he said, "that is a new scrunchie you're wearing."

I rolled my eyes. "Thanks for noticing."

"Was there a sale at Walmart?"

I raised one hand and extended my middle finger.

"Is that an invitation?" he asked. He jogged ahead of me and blocked the door to our boss's office. Slippery temptation danced in his green eyes. "How about it? I've always thought you had the look of someone who needed a good, thorough shagging."

As is reflex around Marius, my lip curled. "In your dreams."

"I think the lady doth protest too much."

"Sorry, Marius. Unlike your goat-fucker of a father, I stick to humans."

His smile didn't waver as he spread his arms as in false apology. "A satyr's gotta sate."

I pushed him aside and barreled into the office. Before the door closed behind me I heard him call, "Delightful to see you again, as always."

I let out a long breath and went through the motions of forced genuflection. A slight bow and a monotone rumble of, "Hail, Discordia."

And then, I was alone with the architect of the Trojan War. The Goddess of Strife, Eris herself.

CHAPTER THREE
"Soul To Squeeze"

The goddess was a study in angles. Her nose sliced through her hawk-like features, and she had sunken cheeks, skeletal fingers, and sharp elbows, Eris's appearance shouted a warning to keep away. Her skin lay in pasty wrinkles reminding me of Iggy Pop on a bad day. I'd think a divine being would look a little more attractive—or at least eat a damn cheeseburger—but Eris liked to fuck with people's heads.

She rose from her chair and swept around the desk to greet me with open arms. Her eyes, though, held about as much warmth as those of a shark.

"Catherine, my dear! It has been too long."

I let her pull me into a chilly embrace. Repulsed, my stomach quivered. If it upset her that I didn't return the hug, she kept her opinions to herself.

"It's been almost three months," I said. "I was beginning to hope you'd forgotten about me."

She clucked her tongue as if I were a naughty kindergartener then took her seat. In stories, people describe the inner sanctum of a god to be all mist and Corinthian columns or something. I'm no expert but if Eris is any indication, the gods have adapted over time. That day—and every day before it—her office was as barren as winter and just as colorful. No sofas. No wet bar. No chairs, except her own that sat behind a single slab of glass Eris used for a desk. And, of course, a black bowl full of gleaming golden apples sat atop said desk.

Floor-to-ceiling windows offered a panoramic view of the Strip. At night, the dazzling glitter of Vegas put on a show lovely enough to die for. Staring out at the casinos, the goddess could plot all of her schemes and imagine that each flickering light did so at her whim. Each missed bet?

Each card turning up aces that shouldn't have? Blame Eris.

"I've got an appointment in fifteen minutes," I said, "so can we skip the drama and get to why you called?"

Her plum-colored lips split into a leer, showing too-white teeth. "I ask of you a favor," she said, her voice rich with amusement.

"A favor or a job?"

"What is the difference?"

"Easy," I said. "A favor is something I do out of the goodness of my heart to help someone. I expect nothing in return for a favor. I get paid to do a job. Where you're concerned, jobs go toward balancing our books."

She shifted in her chair. Leather squeaked and rumbled under her bony ass. As she brought a manicured hand up to her cheek, she grinned again. "Very well, Catherine. I have a job for you."

Nodding respectfully, I put my hands into my pockets. "What'll it be this time? Hacking into Hermes's email account? Stealing the dreadlocks from the head of a Rastafarian? Hunting down some dragon scales on eBay?"

In the long moment Eris spent staring at me, her gold eyes traced up and down my form, and I felt her judgment. I could see she enjoyed this scrutiny from the way she let her shoe dangle from her toes, the curve of her mouth, her folded hands. Greed radiated from her in such thick waves I thought she might start salivating. After an uncomfortable, pregnant silence, she said, "I want you to go to a party."

I spocked an eyebrow. "That's it?"

"That's all." Her nails traced circles over the glass of her desk.

I tried to find her angle, the way she'd sink in her teeth to make my life hell. Nothing involving Eris is ever that simple. "I just have to go to a party?"

As confirmation, she dipped her chin.

17

"When?"

"Tonight."

Of course. "Tonight? I'm on call at work. I can't go to a party tonight."

"I can assure you that your presence at this gathering will be of more importance than whatever other nonsense those mundane sloths would ask of you. Besides," she added, locking her eyes onto mine, "if you perform well this evening, it may well—how was it you put it?—balance our books."

My heart skipped a few beats. If I agreed to go through with the goddess's plan, I might be free? For eight years I'd danced on her strings and now, just like that, I could be done with her? I didn't dare breathe out of fear it might shatter this beautiful moment. But I had to know.

"All I have to do is show up, right? No pyrotechnics or djinn like the time in Belize?"

She shook her head.

"I go and you'll free me? You'll give me back my soul?"

As if annoyed by my stupidity, Eris took a deep breath. From hooded eyes she glared. "If you go tonight, our arrangement may come to an end."

An end. A way out. I nearly jumped up and down right there at the idea. I tried to keep my calm, though. Pouncing on this would be a colossally bad move.

"Where is it?"

"It's a lovely little soiree at Caesars Palace. Very elegant and quite exclusive. Many of my colleagues will be there."

I growled through clenched teeth. "The gala at Caesars? Seriously?"

"You know of it?"

I nodded. "And what am I supposed to wear? You know I don't make enough money to buy anything elegant. And you sure as hell don't pay me."

"Fear not, Catherine, your faery godmother is expecting you at the salon downstairs. Cinderella will look divine at the ball tonight."

"Oh, no, I'm not putting my soul further into hock with you for a sparkly dress and big, poodle-puff hairdo."

Eris tilted her head. She reminded me of a bird, a gigantic crow with beady eyes that missed nothing. "My treat."

Shifting from foot to foot, I searched her offer for holes. Eris—a tight-ass with money—never offered me so much as a dime for a job. And now she'd reached into her coffers so I could get gussied up and pranced around like her pretty pony?

Being Eris, she had an angle of some sort, some way to wreak havoc in my life. With a trickster deity like her there are no coincidences. There is always a game somewhere. I couldn't see it, though. Something didn't jive, but if these were the last hoops I'd have to jump through….

"Why this party?" I asked. "What am I supposed to do there?"

She pursed her lips. As she lifted her hand, I flinched reflexively. The strike I'd feared did not come. The goddess merely examined her nails.

"It is not your job to ask questions," she said. "It is relevant to my interests—and, therefore, to yours—to attend. That is all you need to know on the matter."

From our history together, I knew this would be her last word about it. If I'd been in the mood for excruciating pain, I could have pressed. I silently mulled over the situation. It was stupid to go into an agreement with Eris with so little information. My freedom lay there for the taking, though. I couldn't refuse.

"Fine," I said. "I'll go."

"Excellent," she said. Her lips pulled back in a wolfish grin as she laced her thin fingers together. "Now, let us not forget that tonight you will be acting as my emissary. Make sure you're on your best behavior. Also, I'm sending Marius as your escort."

I winced. *Great. She's going all out on this last job by forcing me to go on a date with Marius.*

"No need to be so vicious," I grumbled.

"I thought you'd be happy about this assignment, Cat. Here I am, giving you an invitation to one of the premier events in the city, a glamorous night out on the arm of an attractive satyr, and you're turning up your nose." She *tsked* her tongue. "How am I being anything other than gracious to you, dear?"

"You want to be gracious? Give me back my soul."

"While you're still in my debt? I don't think so, Cat. I helped you when you had little more than a string of poor decisions and your name."

Anger rose in my cheeks, and my ears flared with heat. "Yeah, and I have run all over the place for you ever since. Just what do I have to do for you to consider us square?"

"Go to this party. With Marius," she added, her words crisp, "and we'll see. Won't we?"

I hoped it was true. I needed this shit to be over and done with so I could move on with my life.

Eris flicked her fingers as if she could shake me off as easily as dust. "Better hurry along."

Without another word, I turned on my heel and marched toward the door. As my hand touched the knob, Eris called out, "Oh, and Catherine, do be a dear and make sure you don't start any wars on my behalf."

***

Armed with a bullshit excuse, I called my boss—the mortal one who controls my paycheck—to see if the rest of my day could be handed off to other techs. I hate bailing on people who are counting on me, but spending most of a decade in forced servitude to a deity realigns some of your priorities. When the person with a chokehold on your soul says, "Jump," you pack your parachute and hope for a soft landing. Thankfully, it worked out that schedules had cleared, and I could be freed up for the rest of the day to do Eris's bidding.

I made my way down the elevator and into the hotel portion of the casino. The thing about the big places in Vegas is that no one ever has to leave. It's like living in a shopping mall. Food, shows, salons, shops—all of it just an elevator ride away. Thus, the trip to see my "faery godmother," as Eris put it, was a short one.

I shambled into the salon, and Simon, the self-proclaimed God of Hairdos, promptly swallowed me into one of his bear hugs. As his plump, rosy cheeks inflated with a genuine smile—and more dimples than a golf ball—he took my hands as if we were the oldest and dearest of friends. I normally hated dealing with the Fae. I've been burned by their kind before. Never being sure if you like *them* or their glittery glamours and charms doesn't exactly make them super trustworthy.

Simon was different, though. He had the rare gift of making everyone feel equally special. Oh, sure, he shared his kin's penchant for beauty. From the frosted tips of his honey-brown hair, the sparkle in his jewel-bright eyes, Simon could've been on any billboard in the world rather than making other people beautiful in his salon. Maybe that's one of the things that had endeared him to me. I'd had to make use of his talents for another one of Eris's shitty little assignments, and I knew that while he might not be human, he was good people. Simon's was a soul born for laughter, and I let myself enjoy being around him.

"How's my favorite kitten?" he asked.

"Peachy," I droned.

"You're a rotten liar." With a flick of his wrist he motioned for me to sit at his station. "Put your ass in the chair."

I let my messenger bag slide to the floor and took a seat in front of a wall of mirrors.

"Now," he said as he pumped the chair to a more comfortable height, "Eris made your appointment, but she didn't say what we were doing."

I looked at the utterly unremarkable spinster in the glass and let out a breath. "I need you to make me pretty."

"Then you don't have work for me, honey. You are already lovely!" As he said this, he carefully undid my ponytail. My red hair tumbled down past my shoulders in wilted waves. "What's the occasion?"

"Gala at Caesars."

Simon swatted at my arm. "Shut up! You got on the guest list?"

His contagious excitement coaxed me to smile in response. I nodded.

"Well, aren't you just full of surprises?" Standing behind me, he stared into the mirror, assessing me as an artist would a blank canvas. "So, what will it be? Classic updo with some face-framing curls?"

He twisted a plump finger through a lock of my hair and produced a perfect spiral. He narrowed his eyes; something didn't please him. When he tugged at the spring it straightened once more.

"Or maybe..."

Simon chewed at his tongue as he considered the possibilities. His eyes lit up, and he put both hands against my scalp. Dragging his fingers through my hair, he said, "Highlights."

Strands of spun gold glittered where he had parted my tresses.

"Yes," he breathed. "I've got just the thing for you. Come on."

The next few hours passed in a whirlwind of plucking, teasing, shampooing, drying, and, most humiliating, waxing. I did, however, enjoy a relaxing facial that left my skin glowing. I wanted nothing more than to go around handing daisies to people.

As Simon painted my face, he asked, "So, do we have an escort to the ball, princess?"

I groaned. "Eris is making me go with Marius."

Simon pursed his lips. "Oh, he's the centaur, right?"

"Satyr," I corrected.

"Whatever. He may be a half goat, but the rumor mill says he's hung like a horse. I'm a little jealous. He doesn't come around often."

I snorted. "Seriously?"

"Let me put it this way: that one has stellar word of mouth."

"He's a satyr, though. Isn't that part of the gig? You know, wine, women, song, being a good lay?"

"You say that like it's a bad thing. It might be a genetic trait, but apparently Marius is exceptionally talented for his kind. Trust me. If you get a chance to play with him, please do come back and spill it all."

I rolled my eyes. "He's not my type. I prefer my men human."

"Kitten, that hurts," he said, fingers splayed over his heart. "But to each her own. I don't judge you *homo sapiens*."

As one of his underlings walked past, Simon snatched her arm. "Run across the hall to the dress shop. Size six," he barked. "Something shiny. Go!"

He dabbed a make-up brush on his hand, "Still," he mused, "a date with a satyr would be hard to pass up."

"It's not a date," I snapped. That place in my chest where my heart used to live shivered and yawned like a black hole. "I don't do that anymore."

"How long has it been, Cat?" he asked, his voice tender.

I hesitated. I trusted Simon but one answer might lead to more questions. More questions might lead him to scratch the surface of the wound. No, I couldn't answer. He was already tap dancing too close for my comfort.

"Not long enough," I muttered.

He took the hint and finished doing my makeup in silence.

Soon, his employees paraded in with a rack full of dresses. Some gowns offered a modest yet striking cut while others seemed to be little more than glorified dish towels. And all of them had price tags with more zeroes than my weekly salary. The sight of them all lined up on a gilded rack intimidated me. I'm not a fashionista by any means. In fact, if there were a church for those who embrace a life filled with pajama pants and tank tops, I would be their high priestess. I was in Simon's place of worship, however, so I sat patiently while he rattled off a sermon about Vera Wang and Jimmy Choo.

Four hours after I'd arrived, his employees slumped in a corner over the pile of discarded dresses. I stood in a semi-circle of mirrors and looked at the person staring back at me.

As he fluffed my hair over my shoulders he said, "I was right. An updo on you would be a sin. Don't let anyone tell you otherwise."

I had to hand it to him. The faery performed a miracle when he gave me fat, luxurious waves of gold and ginger. Simon called my makeup "simple," but anything more than lip balm is astrophysics to me. My eyes, lined with dark purple and painted with a shimmering lilac, stood out as particularly green. He dusted my skin with soft glitter scented with rose water. He didn't have glass slippers in my size, but the strappy sandals were worth more than my car. Even my toes seemed to shine.

Simon was damn good.

He adjusted the thin strap of my dress—a gold, backless sheath with spangles to cast the light here and there. With a satisfied smile, he said, "My work here is done."

I hardly recognized myself, but I had to admit, I loved what I saw in those mirrors. Words like "elegant" and "vixen" came to mind as I stared at my reflections. Doing this for myself would be too much effort—and I'd botch it anyway—but letting Simon play as if I were a doll once in a while would be more than okay. Maybe I'd let him give it a try sometime when Eris wasn't pulling the strings. If I could afford him.

"You're stunning, Kitten." He put an arm around my shoulder and pulled me close. "This," he said, "is why you are my favorite accessory."

I beamed in response.

"How do you feel?"

"Fantastic," I breathed. "Simon, you are amazing."

"I know," he said with a gentle swat on my arm.

"Good gods of thunder and fire!" a British accent called from behind.

Looking up past my own image, I saw Marius in the mirror. He'd changed his gray suit for one of blackest night. A gold tie drew a line down his pressed black shirt. Our reflections—dressed to the nines in our patron goddess's signature colors—made an attractive couple. We could easily have found ourselves on a red carpet somewhere, paparazzi flashbulbs popping and blinding the world on the sparkles of my dress.

So good was my mood I actually thought he looked quite handsome. Behold the power of a facial. The expression he wore piqued my interest, too. The satyr's eyes bulged like a child's on Christmas morning. The slightest of dimples formed on one cheek.

Marius appraised me, his eyes doing laps of my body. Sure, he'd judged me before in his snarky way, but this was different. For the first time I saw something else in his expression. Was that attraction? His stare—laced with this alien expression—poured a shot of heat through my belly. I swallowed hard, shoving down the desire to know what was behind that look.

Then he was back, eyes narrowed, picking me apart.

I leaned over to Simon. Out of the corner of my mouth I asked, "Is he objectifying me?"

"Enjoy it! Just this once!" Simon hissed.

I sighed, steeling myself beneath the weight of Marius's scrutiny.

"Wow," Marius said slipping his hands into his pockets. "Who knew?"

Fidgety, stomach fluttering now that he'd finished his assessment, I asked, "Who knew what?"

"That you could actually look like a woman?"

Any good feelings for Marius burned to cinders.

I planted a kiss on Simon's cheek. "Thank you," I whispered.

Stalking toward the door, I held Marius's eyes with an arctic stare. He bent forward and turned his cheek toward me.

"Don't I get one, too?"

Lady or no, I can't pass up an opening like that. I hauled my arm back and then smacked him across the face.

"Let's get this over with."

I stomped out of the salon, leaving the satyr to pick his jaw up off the floor.

CHAPTER FOUR
"One Big Mob"

The promise of freedom bolstered my courage as I walked into Caesars with an obnoxious satyr on my arm. For the eight years I'd been on Eris's list of indentured servants, I lived an existence of minimums. I had a small apartment, a day job with no chance of advancement, and with the exception of Flynn, most of the numbers in my cell were business contacts or take-out restaurants. It may be Eris's penchant for sucking the joy out of life, or it may just be that I was born under a bad sign, but things never seemed to go my way. I circled the runway while others flew away on the backs of their dreams. My life had become a monotonous holding pattern.

But now? If Eris let me go? I could change that. I could have the life I wanted. I could apply for the jobs I thought I'd be good for, rather than just the ones with an entry-level salary and flexibility. Maybe even try a relationship again, or leave Vegas. My mind swirled with fantasies of all that my future could hold. I practically skipped at Marius's side as he sauntered into Caesars Palace.

At the door to the ballroom, a ridiculously buff man in a centurion's costume blocked our path with his plastic pike.

"Give unto my lord that which is his due," the soldier ordered.

I stifled a chuckle while Marius reached into the black silk of his coat and pulled out an invitation. Passing the folded parchment to the centurion, he said, "What a lovely skirt you're wearing. Is it Dolce and Gabbana?"

The guard scowled and bent his head over the paper. Finding nothing wrong with our invitation, he straightened his pike and motioned for us to pass.

"Hold on," a voice called.

All eyes flashed to see the speaker and found him strutting toward us.

He was strawberry-blond with features carved out of pale marble and eyes the exact blue of a gas flame. He wore his gray suit well on his lanky frame, but something about the sight seemed wrong. Maybe it was his rakishly spiked hair or the wrinkle at the edge of his smile. This guy wasn't bred to wear a three-piece.

With the strange, otherworldly sense that came with my brand, my arm grew cold, and I realized it wasn't even a man. I'd seen too many shows from behind the wings to believe the glamour. He fit into the category of *other*. But what?

"Let me see his invitation," the blond said, voice ringing with authority.

"Yes, sir."

"Oh, it's you." Marius's mustache twitched. "My employer sends me as her proxy this evening."

"Your employer is rarely invited to events such as this." Blondie passed an ice-pick gaze over the parchment, and it shivered in his fingers. As a spell moved over it, through it, magic distorted the air around his hands.

He nodded, satisfied we hadn't forged our way in. As Blondie returned the invitation to Marius he fixed me with a cool stare. "I know you, satyr, but not your friend. Who is she?"

Before Marius could answer—undoubtedly with something snide—I pushed a step forward and offered him my hand. "Catherine Sharp."

The corner of Blondie's mouth hitched up as he gave me a once-over, his eyes lingering over my brand.

"Catherine," he said. "How interesting."

"Is it?" I asked.

Without a word, Blondie took my hand. I returned his firm grip, grateful he hadn't given me a weak handshake for being a petite girl. I hate that shit. With another nod of approval, Blondie backed away and told the centurion we could pass. After sliding the invitation back into his coat, Marius looped his arm around mine, and we breezed into the ballroom.

Under my breath, I asked, "What the hell was that?"

"Ignore him," Marius said. "That one just likes to cause trouble."

We rounded a corner, and the grandeur of the event came into full view. Every surface seemed to be bathed in amber light. Ice sculptures and champagne flutes cast back glints of perfection like diamonds on a queen's throat. Tables set with silver divided the room. To the right, the dining area and a buffet table. The left half of the room had been cleared for dance floor. On stage, a jazz combo belted out "Luck Be A Lady."

Breathtaking as the décor was, I marveled most at the people. My brand began to itch, to burn and writhe like fire ants were crawling on my skin as I realized every guest—with maybe a handful of exceptions—clearly fell into the category of *other*.

Faeries. Dragons. Demi-gods and deities. Oh, sure, they all looked like perfectly normal humans, but that's easy magic. Even Marius used a glamour to conceal his horns and goat legs. Beneath veils and spells, the true masters of the universe led dates around the dance floor and rubbed elbows with one another at the punch bowl. I recognized some of them from my work with Eris: Guests steered clear of Ares's towering figure. Aphrodite danced with sinuous grace, her mortal companion the envy of all.

Some of the deities, though I didn't know them, were obvious by their appearance. Like the Nubian princess in her gown of pure white feathers was probably Mother Isis. Then Marius confirmed my suspicions about the sanguine man at the bar when he shouted, "Dionysus!" I had to admit, I had been surprised to see them give one another a Bro hug.

Other guests, however, remained a mystery to me. I'm glad of it. It's enough to know the gods exist. I don't need to know them all by sight. And the more guests that arrived, the fewer registered as vanilla human. I was a minority. A very tiny minority in a room filled with cosmically huge beings. I felt so small. So insignificant. My legs seemed to be made not of flesh and bone but pudding.

My face burned hot as August asphalt, and my voice caught in my throat.

"Oh God," I eked out.

"Quite a few, yes," Marius said.

My stomach turned sour, and I whirled in my expensive heels. "I've gotta get out of here."

Marius caught me at the elbow and spun me back toward ballroom. "Easy there. You've got a job to do."

"She said a party," I said breathlessly, "not a fucking gaggle of gods."

"First of all, they're called pantheons. Secondly, do you ever relax and have a good time?"

Leaning on Marius for support filled me with a fresh shame.

"Come on," he said, "she wouldn't have sent you here if she thought you'd fold."

"Was that a compliment?"

"Would it make you feel better if I insulted you? Threw you up on the stage and started a rousing game of Slings and Arrows? This is the right crowd for it. Some of the older ones love stoning you pitiful creatures."

I let out something between a squeak and a moan then sank into a nearby chair.

"One or two at a time is one thing, Marius, but a roomful? I don't think I can do this," I said to my knees.

"You can and you will. Otherwise Eris will have a field day with your soul," he said, lifting me out of my seat. "There's food over there. Why don't you go stuff something in your face and try not to talk to anyone. I'll fetch the strongest liquor the bartender has and start a mainline into your blood. Sound good?"

I nodded furiously. "Whiskey. Rocks."

The creases around his eyes deepened as he gave me a wicked grin. "Well, then, maybe tonight won't be boring after all. I'll meet you over there." He motioned to the long buffet.

As I crossed the room without him, I regained some of my confidence. Maybe he was right. *No, scratch that. I refuse to live in a world where Marius is right about things.* However, I trusted his centuries of experience with the goddess. She picked me to do this job because I could. Taking Marius's advice, I picked up a small napkin and pondered the sushi and crudités.

"You can do this," I said aloud. "Get through tonight and you're free. Done. *Finito.*"

I nearly jumped out of my skin when someone spoke way too close to my ear. "Might want to be careful."

The man standing next to me wore a fashionable suit, his tie askew. His face was young and smooth as a baby's skin but marred with blotches. A Rorschach blot dark as obsidian here, a patch of alabaster there. The same discoloration showed on his hands and fingers.

Though his face appeared boyish, his short hair came in stark white. It had been meticulously combed to the side in an ultra-conservative style. He held my attention with wild, haunted eyes.

"You start talking to yourself and people will think you're crazy," he said.

I felt like I should know him. I squinted, rifling through memories to recall where we may have met. His name danced at the tip of my tongue but never made it into my mind.

"Crazy, I tell you," he muttered. Shifting from foot to foot, he reached a trembling hand out to the buffet, plucked up a single morsel of sushi, and popped it in his mouth. His head bobbed like a frantic bird's. "Believe me, I know they're all saying it. Why else do you think they stay clear?"

I glanced around and, sure enough, the crowd drifted in clouds of divinity far from me and my new friend.

"They stay away from us like we're made of wildfire. Afraid we'll bleed on them or infect them with the stink of madness. To them this is a crime scene. Nothing to see here," he said, voice rising. "Just a loon and a whore having a polite drink."

I bristled. "Did you call me a whore?"

"Did I say that?" he snapped as he whirled to face me. Desperation lapped at the edges of his expression like tiny waves on a sea of rage. A look of equal parts hunger and horror shot from his red-rimmed eyes, and I quivered. "I don't remember. Don't put words in my mouth!"

The man rocked on the balls of his feet, hands nervously touching his temples. Sanity eluded him as if he'd said, "No, thank you," when the waiter offered it to him. I felt uncomfortable, like standing too close to one of those homeless guys who rants about the end of the world. Something about him, though, tugged at not only my memory, but my sympathy.

"Who are you?" I asked.

"I am," he said. "I. Am. And isn't that enough? For you? For me? And what about you, eh? With your trinkets and baubles and painted face. Who are you?"

I stepped back to lessen the brute force of his question. He moved in closer, and I became dizzy.

"Who. Are. You?" he asked again, this time enunciating like the damned smoking caterpillar.

Had I missed the gala and fallen down the rabbit hole?

"C-C-Catherine," I stammered.

"Catherine? Lovely name. Once knew a woman called Catherine." He spoke quickly, the words bleeding out of him like water through a sieve.

"Spectacular singing voice. Good with kids. And then she died. That's it." He tossed another bite of sushi into his mouth. Before he could swallow he said, "But do you see what I mean?"

I dodged flecks of fish and rice.

After he'd gulped down the food, he continued, "Do you see how easy it is for you, you little fleshbag? You and your puny, insipid mind? I ask you a profound question like your *name* and you give it. Freely. Quickly. As if it were written in the stars and solid as a mountain. Easy peasy."

This guy—or whatever he was—had taken the A train from Psychoville. I looked around for Marius but couldn't find him in the cluster around the bar. The rest of the guests avoided this part of the room, so I couldn't attach myself to another conversation and politely leave. I began the calculations: *How close are his hands? How loudly can I scream if I need to? Can I duck away? If he follows me, where do I go?*

"Simple, stupid mortals," he sighed.

I rankled a bit for my race. Turning my own annoyance on him I said, "Dude, what is your problem?" I'd been fully prepared to defend humanity and give this nut job a piece of my simple, stupid mind, but another glimpse of that haunted face, and I was silenced.

"Stupid," he spat. "Don't know what's best for them. Can't even agree on black or white." His words were a blur of agitation and pain. When I looked at him I no longer saw a man but a series of fractures. Pity welled in me at the sight of such a splintered soul.

"Whore!" he shouted. His finger jabbed at the air between my eyes. "I see you. I see what you are, and I know by whose bidding you come. I see it all, like a kaleidoscope in the dark, twisting its shapes around. Shadows and mirrors. Trying to deceive. But I know." He tapped his temple. "I know you, C-C-Catherine, with your simple life and simple ways."

I turned to go. "I'm sorry to have bothered you," I said around a lump of sadness.

He took me by the arm and pulled me in close. Scalding heat flared over my brand, over my flesh where his fingers gripped me.

"What the hell?" I struggled against him, but his fingers were solid as stone.

His trembling breath blew softly on my cheek. "I know why you're here," he whispered. "I know what you've been sent to do. They won't let you, you know?"

I stopped squirming, curiosity getting the better of me. "What?"

"There are too many people who like things the way they are. You'll die before they let you finish the job."

The heat from his touch sizzled over my flesh. Twisting to get away only made the pain that much more intense. I tried to breathe, to speak with a strong voice, but all I had in me was a child's whimper. "I don't know what you're talking about."

"Of course not. It hasn't happened yet."

He licked at his pink-and-purple lips. Every muscle in my body shook like a leaf in the wind. Looking into his face with its confused skin and angry eyes, I quailed. My stomach in knots and my arm on fire…and yet I hurt for him. Inexplicably, I felt shame so viscerally that I wanted nothing more than to curl into a ball and beg for mercy.

"I'm sorry," I croaked.

"Alfie? Alfie, dear, are you all right?"

A woman in a blue gown appeared at his side, radiating compassion and the kind of patience you expect from hospice nurses. She said his name again and placed calm hands on his shoulders. At the sound of her voice, Alfie released me and stepped away. Instantly, my skin stopped boiling, but now I shivered with fear and at the sudden absence of his heat.

"Oh, hello, Mother," he said. Gone were the wild eyes and seething

34

anger. With a child's proud smile and a sweeping gesture toward me, he sang, "Have you met Catherine?"

"What a beautiful name," she said with a smile. The woman's brown eyes twinkled with fond memories. Her voice—sweet, dark, and thick as molasses—melted over me and soothed a bit of the ache in my soul. "I do hope he hasn't troubled you."

I started to lie then realized how ridiculous it would sound. "More than a little," I confessed.

Looking very much like a bored child, Alfie nibbled at his fingers. "Lovely. Lovely whore."

The woman in blue looked upon her son with love and sadness. "I am sorry, dear. He doesn't mean it." She looped her arm through Alfie's and began to steer him away. "Come on, Alfie, it's time to go."

"Yes, Mother, it is."

He took two steps then, in a blink, he was pressed against me. Again, his touch lit me on fire. Quaking, my legs buckled. I started to fall, but his strong hands held me fast.

"You are a pawn and a tool," he said. "But you're the right one for the job. For that, I am sorry." He took my face into both of his hands and brought his lips down. I thought he would kiss me, but instead he brushed his mouth over my forehead. "I love you."

Just when I thought I would collapse from the pain of his touch, from the terror in my belly, his hands dropped to his sides. Alfie breezed away, his mother following in his wake. A path cleared before them as other guests continued their calculated avoidance. Not to be ignored, the madman cackled as passed by, even stopping to snap his jaws and bark at one unlucky woman.

I stumbled, knees knocking together, and braced myself against the table. Cooling the burns from his fingers, tears streaked down my cheeks. I tried to collect myself, to control my breathing, but all I could do was shiver.

Marius's voice behind me, familiar and low, was comforting somehow. "It's a shame, isn't it?"

Nodding, I brought up a finger to dab at my eyes, careful not to smear my makeup. "He's so broken."

The satyr's face wrinkled in confusion or disgust. "I'm not talking about that nutter, I'm talking about *this*!" Spreading his hands he indicated the table. "It's disgraceful!"

Thanks to Alfie's conversational and emotional whiplash, I'd been spun a little too much to really grok what Marius was getting at. "What?"

"You would think that with all the water-into-wine types at this party someone would be able to put out a decent spread. Me? I once put together beef bourguignon for 150 people with little more than a jar of vinegar and a half-starved cow."

"Beef burgundy? For 150?"

"Of course. And then, they tried to flay me alive, the ungrateful bastards. Haven't been back to India since. Fuckers," he muttered into a glass of champagne.

In his other hand was a tumbler of whiskey. I snatched it and knocked it back. Blinking at the burn in my chest, I shook my head. "Marius, what are you talking about?"

"Bugger all, you are a lousy date!"

"This isn't a date," I contested. "This is a job. Nothing more."

"You could do worse than a date with me, Catherine."

I snorted. "Not by much."

"Do you honestly find me so repellent?" His face drawn in a mockery of disappointment, Marius stretched out his arms in a move that was equal parts pining for attention and putting himself on display. Once more, I humored the idea that for all of his personality flaws and inhuman traits, he sparked something in the deeper reaches of my interest. Maybe it was the sleek line of his shoulders in that suit. Or the silky thickness of his hair. I skimmed over our past, wondering if I'd ever seen it down rather than in a ponytail.

I shook my head and stopped pondering. This was *Marius*. I'd never seen beneath the glamour, but I knew it was there. I wouldn't deny that he was attractive, but I couldn't accept that what I saw was reality. Still…

"You're all right," I conceded, looking away and letting my eyes drift over the crowd.

"All right?" Dropping his arms, he chuffed indignantly. "Darling, I do believe I must fetch you a dictionary as your vocabulary is sorely lacking. I am better than all right. I am spectacular. I am an Adonis. Tantric sex in a suit, is what I am. And it wouldn't kill you to pay me a compliment. Here, allow me to demonstrate."

Marius gently parted me with my glass and put down with his drink. Then, he took my hands in both of his. Slowly, he spread my arms out so that his eyes could dance over me. My cheeks burned and my heart sped up as he looked. His gaze slid from my painted toes, up my bare legs, and lingered over the slight curve of my hips. When his tour reached my collarbones, his mouth formed the slightest of appreciative smiles. I could almost feel his eyes—like fingers—tracing up my hair and around, down my cheek. His stare settled on my eyes, and I held my breath.

"You are stunning, Catherine. You sparkle with the delicate fire of a star. A vision of grace and beauty that would make Aphrodite herself fume with envy."

Abashed and red-faced, I looked away. With a hooked finger he picked up my chin and drew my attention back to his too-sincere face.

"I am truly the luckiest of men to have the honor of escorting you tonight." He placed the faintest of kisses—little more than a breath and the brush of his mustache—on the back of my hand. "May I have the pleasure of sharing a dance with you?"

My stomach fluttered. I wasn't snowed by his pretty words, but the intensity of his stare gave me pause. *Could he mean it? Could I actually be entertaining the idea that Marius was anything other than a bother?*

I blew out a breath I hadn't realize I'd been holding. "Sure. Why not? Nothing better to do."

"That's the spirit," Marius said as he offered me his arm, a mercurial smile on his face.

As we made our way to the dance floor, the band started up a soft and airy tune. I put my hand in his, and we began to move with the music. Marius slid his hand up my bare back, his touch light and tantalizing. Doing my damnedest to ignore the electric chill brought on by his closeness, I peered around the room. While other guests mingled, some danced. With smiles vibrant and arms twining about one another, the creatures of myth enjoyed themselves.

I used to do that, I thought. *Seems like forever since then.*

I ached inside, jealous of anyone having a good time.

"Incredible," he said.

"What?"

"I've seduced queens with that move, and here you are plodding along in bored resignation."

"Putting your arm around me is considered a move? I must be out of practice."

He closed the distance between us, pressing the warmth of his whole body against mine. Once more, he traced a soft, delicate line up my spine. He cupped the base of my skull and twined his fingers in my hair. Marius's eyes held mine with a look full of silky intentions and dark promises. As more chills coursed through some of my naughtier regions, I drew in a sharp breath.

"Well," he purred, "perhaps there's hope for you yet."

I put some distance between us but kept dancing. "You're not my type."

"Keep on lying to yourself. I know your kind, Catherine, and by the end of the night I could have your knickers hanging from my rearview mirror if I wanted them."

I grunted in distaste, but I didn't grant him the honor of a response.

"All right then," Marius said, "what precisely is your type? Wait," he interjected before I could answer, "let me see if I can guess."

As we continued to dance, Marius passed a glance over the room, eyes flitting from person to person like a bee seeking the perfect flower.

"Ah. Probably something like him." Marius swung me around and with a tip of his chin indicated a man near the bar. "Tall blonde. Red suit."

The guy was slender to the point of being skeletal with a withered mop of dishwater hair. I wrinkled my nose. "No, thanks. Looks like a meth-head."

"Strike one," Marius muttered. "I'll take another swing, shall I?"

After twirling a circuit around the room, he swung me with the flourish of the music. With my back to his chest, he put his lips to my ear and said, "Third table from the left. Dreadlocks."

I had to give it to Marius—this one was more on the mark. Broad-shouldered with an eggshell-tan complexion, the man had dreads down to his ass. He was certainly pretty. But his suit… Gold lamé? I shivered.

"Eh. He's okay. His date's nice on the eyes, though."

Marius whipped his head to look at the woman on Dreadlocks's arm. All curves in her purple sheath gown, she was a vision of languorous delight.

The satyr passed me a sidelong, somewhat surprised glance. "Really?"

I shrugged. "I went to college."

With nothing more than a knowing smirk, he nodded as if storing that information for later. He lifted my hand and spun me once more. Face-to-face again, he said, "Strike two. I had better make this one count."

While Marius took one more survey, I let my eyes sweep over the milling crowd. I recognized more of the guests now. A few multi-billionaires pranced past with models on their arms. A few iconic musicians basked in the glow of admiration.

And then I saw a familiar soul. Her raven hair was pulled back into a sleek ponytail. The swath of midnight silk draped over her dancer's body complimented the soft ebony of her skin. Surrounded by other preternaturally beautiful members of the Fae hierarchy stood the one person in the world I hated more than Marius.

Dahlia.

CHAPTER FIVE
"Shallow Be Thy Game"

Her name blazed through my head in hot whispers and memories of anger and pain. As if I'd shouted for her, she looked up, her honey-colored eyes latching onto me immediately.

Using the satyr's height to hide, I cursed, "Oh, fuck me."

"Aha! I told you," he sang. "Very well. Shall we find a coat-check closet? Those are always fun."

I gripped his shoulder and tried to force him around, his back to the faeries. "Will you just shut up?" I hissed. "If we're lucky she'll stay over there."

"Who?"

The satyr peeled away from me to rubberneck. I saw Dahlia coming toward us in long, graceful strides.

"Oh, dammit," I moaned. "Just when I thought tonight might not suck."

"Well, hello," Marius said. "Who is this?"

With the click of a stiletto heel, Dahlia popped a hip out and crossed her arms over her chest. She looked exactly as she did when I'd met her most of a decade ago: haughty and mind-numbingly gorgeous. The only difference between that night and this one was the oak-leaf tattoo etched onto her neck: the mark branding her as a servant of Mab and Titania, the faery queens of the Winter and Summer courts.

Oh, how the mighty have fallen, I thought with a surge of glee.

"Cat," she said, "what a surprise."

I swallowed a lump of pride and bile. "Dahlia."

"Dahlia," Marius repeated. "A lovely name that wilts in comparison to its owner."

The faery rolled her eyes but otherwise ignored the satyr's advance. Marius made small talk with another guest on the dance floor, but I didn't take my eyes off of Dahlia.

"It's been a while," she said. "I was beginning to think you'd left the city."

"No such luck," I said, stepping away from Marius. "Slave to the queens, I see."

She arched a perfect brow. "I serve willingly."

"As willingly as I do, I'm sure."

At this, her expression darkened. I grinned. *Take that, bitch.*

Eyes narrowing, mouth pulling into a stern frown, she inched forward with preternatural grace. "I came over here to help you," she snarled.

I hugged myself to ward off furious shivers, but I hoped I looked like a confident, stone-faced badass. I laughed mirthlessly. "Why would I possibly need—or want—your help, faery?"

She glanced back over her shoulder to the Fae contingent, eyes lingering over a man with hair the color of spring grass. Her jaw flexed. Without looking to me, she said, "He has plans for you."

I couldn't fathom why at the time, but a familiar, cold dread flooded me. Hadn't we done this before?

The man with green hair let out a raucous laugh. His smile was broad to the point of caricature, a seam stretching across his rubbery, ageless face. Dimples stood out on his cheeks. He looked Fae: impossibly handsome, vibrant, and joyful. Something about him, however, set my teeth on edge.

"Who is he?"

"A servant," Dahlia said quietly, "but a god in his own right. Trickster and messenger."

"Puck?" I said. "*That* is Puck?"

Dahlia nodded. "But don't think he's all jokes and pranks. When the

Bard was writing plays it may have been so but even the gods evolve."

I gasped and brought a hand to my mouth in feigned shock. "Really? A faery being two-faced?"

She slithered forward, her face rigid, and placed her cheek next to mine. Her lips barely moved against my ear. I shivered and swallowed hard to shove away memories.

She is a viper, I warned myself. *Never forget how many times she has betrayed you.* I began counting backward over her sins. *That fiasco at the Bellagio. The Midsummer job. Chicago.*

"Do not cross him." Dahlia's voice cut through my thoughts. "Stay away from him at all costs. This is the only warning I can give you."

Stepping back a few paces, her eyes traced up Marius and meandered down the length of my dress. "You look…lovely."

I ignored her attempts at civility. She'd long ago lost that right with me. "Why would Puck have plans for me? I've never even seen him until tonight."

"You are relevant to his interests."

"That's sweet, I suppose, but I'm beholden to Eris, not to the Fae."

"Things change," she enunciated. "One flip of the cards and the world can tilt the other way."

My stomach fell. Dahlia's eyes sparked and crackled with electric intensity as if she could will her thoughts into my head. She didn't have to. I knew damn well what she meant.

Shame and fear began to boil at my center. "No," I said.

"What?" Marius asked, looking lost as he returned to the conversation. "No, what?"

"Not again," I snarled through my teeth.

Dahlia nodded somberly. "There is a game afoot, Cat."

"I love games," Marius said. "I'm particularly fond of 'Hide the—'"

I cut him off with a backhand to the gut. Shoving past him I got right up in Dahlia's face.

"Out with it, Faery. What the hell is going on?"

Her eyes floated around the room as if making sure we wouldn't be overheard. "The usual game," she muttered. "Same as always. Your mistress got in deep, apparently, and bet big." Dahlia's honey-colored eyes pierced me. "Very big."

Sick with fury and terror, my guts rolled and sloshed. Shaking my head I whispered, "No."

Dahlia nodded.

The usual game. A flip of the cards. Eris. She bet big. Piecing it together wasn't too difficult, but the reality was hard as hell to accept. Voice thick with nausea, I asked, "Eris wagered my soul in a game of poker?"

Dahlia dipped her chin.

Blood thundered in my ears like flowing magma. Any moment I might erupt. "How can I stop it?"

"You can't. The bet is made. It's just a matter of who has the winning hand."

Without another word, Dahlia spun on her spiked heel and sauntered to the tables of Fae lords.

"Incredible," Marius said, drawing out the word. "I haven't seen an ass that divine since—"

"Shut up," I barked. "Just shut up."

Hatred sizzled on the back of my tongue, acrid and bitter. I loathed Dahlia with the fire of a thousand constellations. And now? With this news? I was pissed at Marius for thinking her beautiful. Pissed at Eris for…well, where to start? Betting my soul? Sending me here? Any number of bullshit missions she'd sent me on in the name of paying off my debt to her?

More than anything, though, I was pissed at myself.

Did I actually think I could put on a nice dress and a little bit of makeup and be someone else? Did I think it changed the fact that I was stuck as a slave to a bitch goddess?

No. Nothing changed.

And that's the problem, I thought. *Nothing ever changes. Same shit. Different day.*

Livid, I rounded on Marius. "Call her!" I snapped. "Call Eris. I know you can."

Marius took a wary step from me. "Why should I bother her?"

"Just call her, dammit! This is important."

The satyr rolled his eyes and reached into the inner pocket of his jacket to withdraw his phone. With a few deft swipes he dialed the goddess.

"My Lady," he purred reverently into the phone. He didn't get a chance to say more. I snatched the cell from him and brought to my ear.

"What have you done?" I growled.

"Cat?" she asked. "Is that you?"

"What. Have. You. Done?"

Her laugh was a throaty glissando of *schadenfreud*. "Trouble at the party, dear?"

"What have you done with my soul?" I shouted. Red-eyed with rage, I didn't see the reaction in the room, but my skin prickled with gooseflesh as though every guest turned his or her attentions to me.

Marius took me by the shoulders and guided me off the dance floor to a quieter, more secluded area of the ballroom. In my ear, his voice murmured, "Why did you just bleed into a pool full of sharks?"

I shoved him away and found the first pocket of shadow I could along the outer edge of the ballroom. Over the phone, the goddess sighed.

"Cat, dear," Eris said, "you didn't think our arrangement would last forever, did you?"

"Fuck no! But I at least thought it would end with me getting what's mine!"

"And you may yet."

"How? You bet me in a poker game!"

"Listen closely, Cat, for this is all the aid I will give you. There are four others in the game. Each of them has a token. Procure these, bring them to me, and you may get what the freedom you desire."

"How am I supposed to—"

"Don't pretend to be inept, you silly girl. Your mind is keen, and I expect you to put it to use. Think. Follow your instincts, call in favors, break a few laws. You've done no less for me in the past. I don't care how you do it, but if you want your soul back you will get the tokens. And don't dally. *Tempus fugit.*"

"But who are the others? What are the tokens?"

She hung up. I spat an oath and stalked back to where Marius stood. As I thrust the phone back at him, he tossed me a carefree grin.

"Well, that didn't sound good," he observed flippantly.

I charged across the ballroom and elbowed my way to the bar.

"What are you doing?" Marius asked from behind.

"Getting drunk," I said.

Marius pushed past me and flattened his palms on the bar. "Whatever this woman wants, make it a double."

CHAPTER SIX
"Taste the Pain"

Never underestimate the short attention span of a satyr. I'd downed one already, but once he put the second Rusty Nail in my hand and parked me at a table, Marius abandoned me to go salivate on the enhancements of a showgirl. I didn't mind, really. While he cozied up to her breasts, I nursed my whiskey and Drambuie. Instead of calming down, though, I sank into a melancholic haze.

My soul was being used as a bet in a poker game. And now I had to find some stupid trinkets and take them to the goddess? Grinding my teeth, I played over all of the things Eris had said and questioned every syllable. Why send me here to this party? What was the point? Why get me all gussied up and send me on a pseudo date with Marius?

And then there was Dahlia. *He has plans for you*, she'd said. I know never to trust the Fae or take them at their word, but Dahlia's cryptic warning piqued my interest. Was Puck playing against Eris to win my soul? It seemed to be the case, but why? What could Puck possibly want with me? Knowing the Fae for the vicious, backstabbing pixies they were, I didn't think Puck's designs would be any prettier than Eris's.

Regardless of Dahlia's motives or a faerie's schemes, this latest "fuck you" from Eris served as yet another reminder that I didn't belong to myself. I couldn't live the way I wanted to. She had me trapped in a bell jar until she wanted to let me out to run on her leash. I took another drink, hoping to drown out the sound of my thoughts.

And now this…

I let my eyes drift and my mind wander. Before I knew it, my glass was empty.

"It's a shame to see a woman sitting by herself," a man said from behind me.

Before I even turned around, I'd already begun to wave him off. My hand fell to the table, though, when I got a look at him. He was Native American with deep laugh lines in his leathery skin and silver in braids hanging down past his ribs. His eyes twinkled in a friendly way, reminding me of a loyal dog.

And he radiated capital-P Power. My brand pulsed with a deep thrum that reminded me of low drums, thunderstorms, and desert rain.

The man placed a glass in front of me. I could smell whiskey and a sweet, citrus tang. He lifted his own tumbler to plump lips. "May I join you?" he rumbled after a drink.

I sipped from the new glass and let the cool booze slide through me. "Thank you," I said, gesturing for him to join me at the table. "You're welcome to sit, but I don't know that you'll want to. I'm not having a very good night."

He swallowed his whiskey. "For the drink, you are quite welcome, young lady." He sighed, and when he spoke again his deep voice reminded me of smooth, supple leather. "I see you wear Discord's brand. One rarely passes a good night in her company."

"Ain't that the truth."

"If you were with old man Coyote," he said, hooking a thumb at himself, "I assure you, you wouldn't be wasted here, sad and lonely."

I thought about the past, my empty present and dwindling future. "I'd be sad and lonely with anyone," I muttered.

We shared silence for a few moments. As he stretched out his legs, his weathered Levi's hitched up to reveal the pattern of his scuffed, brown, steel-tipped boots. Suit jacket, button-down shirt, and bolo tie heaved as he let out a long breath and relaxed into his chair. While the old man tapped out a rhythm on his glass with a large silver ring, I looked into the shapes of the ice in my drink. Glints of light twinkled from the melting cubes and created a prism in amber. Like finding pictures in the clouds, I named the ever-shifting forms. *A mouse. A dragon. An elephant wearing a space suit.*

When I downed the rest of my drink, Coyote smiled. "Not many women enjoy this particular cocktail," he said.

"Rusty Nails? They're my favorite."

"I'm fond of a Sloe Comfortable Screw, myself," he winked then looked around the room. "Where is your mistress?"

"She couldn't be here tonight. I'm here in her place."

The native's long face drooped, creases forming between his eyebrows. "What is your name?"

"Cat. Cat Sharp."

"Short for Catherine, I suppose?"

"Yes."

His laughter began in barks of disbelief, escalated into hearty guffaws, and ended in a lupine howl. "I can't believe it," he said. "My luck is good tonight."

"What are you talking about?"

Coyote reached into the pocket of his blue jeans and slapped a ruddy hand onto the table. He pulled it away to reveal a black poker chip with a golden apple at its center.

Through my whiskey haze, I began to remember what the spirit Coyote does in his pantheon. Like Eris, he creates some measure of havoc. The mischief playing at the lines of his mouth made me uncomfortable.

"What's this?" I asked.

"A promise."

"Of what?"

His parched lips peeled away from his teeth in a lecherous grin. "Your night is about to become considerably more pleasurable. You will be

49

coming home with me."

The Native arched his back and let out another howl, this one singing of victory. "Hot damn, I love redheads!" he said.

As I stared down at that damned golden apple, my blood began to burn with anger and embarrassment.

"What is it?" I growled.

Calm and cool, as if he were placating a child, Coyote took my hand and placed the chip in my palm. Curling my fingers over it and patting my fist, he said, "This is our agreement."

It took me longer than it should have to suss out, but understanding hit me between the eyes like a ton of bricks. A Trickster spirit with my mistress's symbol on a poker chip. *A token.*

I tried to keep my voice from shaking. Considering I'd had a few of cocktails, though, I don't think it worked. "Are you part of the game?"

Waving off my question, he reached into another pocket and handed me a slim, plastic card. "This is my room key. Tell me," he said leaning forward, "do you like it doggy style?"

I didn't answer the naked hunger in his eyes. I threw the key card in his face and scanned the room for Marius. He was over by the bar with yet another woman.

As I pushed up from the table a little too quickly, the room shifted in a kaleidoscope of divinity. Like a tender lover, the whiskey wrapped itself around me, encasing my mind in a gossamer sheet. The threads Marius used to stitch together his glamour sparkled in the air. His face seemed waxy, almost, glowing with ephemeral light. The longer I stared at him, though, little black holes began show. I could make out the slightest shadow of his horns, and they appeared jagged. Broken.

A waitress stood beside him, blushing as the air around her twisted like a mirage within the satyr's spell. I stalked toward him, picking up the last parts of a string of his lies.

"…think you'd be perfect for it. Shall we set up an audition tomorrow? My place? Dinner?"

"Marius," I said, punching him in the arm. "We're leaving."

He tried to wipe me off of his shoulder as if I were little more than lint. "I have no idea who you are," he snapped. Leaning over the woman's ample chest, he put on his best leer. "Now where were we?"

"Dammit, Marius, we're going." I grabbed him by the ponytail and dragged him after me toward the door. He spat protests at me the whole time. The other guests stared as we passed, but I didn't give a shit.

"You fucking harpy, let go!" He shoved me off. Looking around as if embarrassed, Marius began smoothing his hair, jacket, and tie. "What the hell is your problem?"

"We are leaving," I slurred. "I've had it."

"Are you drunk?"

"What was your first clue? Come on, Marius. Take me home."

"I thought you'd never ask."

I staggered toward the door. "Oh no. If you think this means you'll get me into bed, you're wrong. I don't sleep with you non-human types anymore."

He caught up with me a few steps away, past the centurion with his pike. "What has gotten into you?"

"Whiskey," I said, shrugging off his hand. "Lots of it."

"I can smell that, but what I mean is how do you expect the goddess will react if she finds you've left before finishing a job?"

I pawed at the air. "Fuck her."

Marius grabbed me by the upper arm and jerked me back. "You hold your tongue, mortal!"

"Or what? What are you going to do to me? Huh?"

It's probably not wise to pick a fight with a magical being. Especially when intoxicated. Oh well. I may be intelligent but wisdom has always been my dump stat.

"What do you think you could possibly do that is worse than anything already done to me by that bitch?" I spat.

Whatever he would have said went unspoken. I put too much effort behind trying to throw a punch, tripped, and crashed into him. The poker chip fell to the ground with a heavy, resonant sound. As Marius caught sight of the chip, all mirth drained from his face.

"Where did you get this?"

I blew a raspberry and started to stumble toward the valet. "That guy back there gave it to me. You won't believe what he said. Or maybe you would, you're both horny bastards. You probably hang out together."

A moment later, Marius was in front of me. He took my face in his hands and guided my gaze to his. "Catherine, answer me." The golden apple flashed in my eyes. "Where did you get this?"

"I told you. Coyote gave it to me."

"You are absolutely certain it was Coyote?"

"That's what he said," I sloshed with a shrug.

He pursed his lips and regarded me warily. As he shook his head, he gave the valet his claim ticket. When the guy had left, Marius turned back to me. Holding the poker chip between his thumb and forefinger, he asked "Do you know what this is?"

I pitched my voice low and added a little over-the-top gravitas. "It is the Mighty Poker Chip of Abundant Douchebaggery. He who holds it will inherit the powers of—"

"Shut up," he spat. "This is serious. This is one of Eris's personal markers."

"Okay, what's that supposed to mean?"

As the car pulled up, he went mute again. I melted into the passenger seat. When Marius had strapped himself into the car he leaned over to make sure he had my full attention.

"Catherine, if someone else has this chip it means the goddess has struck up a bargain with them. It means Eris may have sold you to Coyote."

Despite the fact that every line on his face was stony and sober, I giggled. "Boy, do you have some catching up to do."

CHAPTER SEVEN
"Storm in a Tea Cup"

Marius guided his car up the Strip, past the famous volcano at the Mirage, the sirens of Treasure Island. The lights of the casinos blurred around me, but I noticed nothing in particular. I spent the time rambling to Marius in a drunken slur of profanity and anger.

"She bet my soul in a fucking game of poker. Can you believe that shit?" I held up the poker chip. "This is all I am now! Little clay tokens that I have to track down if I ever want to be free."

"Did she happen to say from whom?" Marius asked.

"No," I sneered. "The bitch wouldn't tell me." He flinched at my disrespect toward Eris but didn't bother to reprimand me for it. "You wouldn't happen to know, would you?"

Without answering my question, he said, "Eris doesn't have to tell you anything, you know. You are her property."

"Bullshit," I said, my voice filling the car. "I am not something to be bartered!"

"Actually, you are. Eris has a mortgage on your soul. If she chooses, she can sell it to whomever she wants, and you have to go."

The taste of my own blood filled my mouth as I bit down on my lip. "No," I said. "Not this time. She said we'd be through after tonight."

"Funny how that's still true if someone else wins the game," Marius said as he made a left turn.

"I'm not laughing. Besides, she said if I get these stupid chips, I'll be free."

"Did she now? What else did the Lady of Strife and Discord tell you, hmm?"

I rolled my eyes. The whiskey haze was burning away beneath the heat of my anger. I stared out the window, watching the lights flicker by and trying to will my mind back into its drunken cocoon.

Marius called me out of it. "Do you know how many souls Eris currently owns?"

I shook my head.

"One. And that, my dear, would be you. Not many mortals actually wager with their souls these days."

He danced near an old wound. Through my teeth I said, "What's your point?"

"My point is that if you cared so much about who held the deed to your soul, you shouldn't have been playing with it in the first place."

I whipped my head around to glare at him. "What the hell do you know about it?" I snarled. "My debt with Eris was not my choice."

"That's what they all say." He smirked. "So tell me, then, how did you come to belong to our mistress?"

He'd asked *the* question, and I was drunk enough to give a half answer. "I fell in love with the wrong person."

"Love?!" Marius made a retching sound. "Oh, for fuck's sake, don't tell me it had to do with love!"

"You've never been in love?"

"Of course not! Why should I? It's a narcotic, love. A poison. Nothing more than a diversion from the real pleasures in life. You lot use love as some grand excuse to hide from your real desires. Forget religion. Love? Now that's the real opiate of the masses."

"Could you just stop being a dick for like five minutes? I've got a problem here."

Marius shifted in his seat. "Yes, it would seem you do. Eris won't be pleased that you've left the party."

"She bet my soul in a goddamn game of poker!"

"And Coyote may already have won. Better news, you just walked out on him. Not exactly the best way to greet your potential new boss."

"And there's the matter of these other tokens I have to find."

"And the other players," Marius added helpfully. "You don't have any idea who they are, do you?"

My forehead hit the window with a *thud*. I closed my eyes and moaned, "No." I was so out of my league. "I have no clue what I'm supposed to do."

The car purred along the asphalt making its way northwest toward my place.

When Marius spoke again, his voice was quiet. "Might I offer a suggestion?"

I flopped a hand in response. "If you insist."

"Hide," he said somberly. "Hide at a friend's house until it all blows over. See how things play out. Hope you don't get shipped off to Asgard. Or worse, Cleveland."

Hide? If that worked, I would never have answered my phone when the goddess called. "I don't much like that option."

"Cleveland is wretched, Catherine. Trust me."

"I meant hiding!"

"You must have friends. Someone willing to let you crash on a sofa for a few days."

That was part of the problem with my life, wasn't it? Ever since Eris took possession of my soul, I hadn't trusted anyone. Shit like that happens when your heart is broken and your whole world changes in the blink of an eye.

I supposed I could call Flynn but getting him involved in my drama was a last resort.

"Not exactly," I sighed to Marius. "I don't have many friends."

"What about me?"

I laughed until I snorted. "Is that what we are?"

"All right. If not a friend, how about a friendly guide? Does that sound more appropriate?"

My head rolled lazily on my neck, and I gave the satyr an incredulous look. "Huh?"

Marius gave me one of his cocksure grins. "You, my dear, happen to be on speaking terms with the personal assistant of a deity. I am rather well-connected, you know."

"You?" I asked, dumbfounded. "You're actually offering to help?"

"Nothing so sweet as that. No, I offer a business arrangement. An exchange of my skills and services for your payment."

"And just what sort of payment are you expecting for these skills?"

For a time he only had eyes for the road. The longer he waited to speak, the deeper the pit in my stomach became. I could imagine all the things a satyr would want, and I just didn't think I was that limber. Not to mention I didn't like the idea of yet another choice being taken away from me.

"If I help you," he said finally, "you owe me a date."

"A date? Didn't we just do that?"

"You said yourself that wasn't a date. I'm talking about you and me. Alone. Dinner. Perhaps more, but no less."

"Just a date?"

"Just a date."

I blinked in confusion. "You're serious? You'll help me, and all I have to do is go out with you? There's got to be a catch."

"No catch. Except for me, that is," he confirmed, a smile playing in his voice.

A date with Marius. Hell, hadn't I just proven that I could spend a night in his company without killing him? I didn't get why he would even want a date with me, but I wasn't about to bite the only hand that offered me his help.

"All right," I said. "It's a deal. You help me figure out who is in the game and where these tokens are, and I'll go out with you."

"Excellent," he sang. "Where shall we begin, then?"

"My apartment. I can't think in this dress."

His lopsided smirk made his eyes twinkle. "That's convenient. I can't think with you in that dress either."

***

The Mercedes pulled into the gravel lot of my apartment complex. As he put the car in park, he said, "This could work out to your advantage— this poker game. You might find a better employer than Eris."

I rifled through my bag, looking for my keys. "Well, it can't be all bad working for her. Pretty expensive car you've got here. She certainly pays you far better than she pays me."

"Not remotely," he chuffed.

I stopped and regarded him dubiously. "I've never seen you wear anything less than Armani. If she doesn't pay you, how can you afford it?"

"Let's just say I have other investments to meet my needs."

"Whatever, Mr. Cryptic," I slurred with a roll of my eyes.

Leading the way to my apartment, I didn't quite stagger but I wobbled in my stilettos. Whiskey sang to my brain, encouraging a blissful whimsy. I looked up to the sky and traced a line between stars.

My apartment complex isn't much more than twenty units stacked two-high in a few small letter-shaped structures that remind me of Tetris blocks. My place squats in the bend of a U facing the parking lot and a courtyard. If it can even be called that—the yard in question is a six-foot square of crabgrass. To get to my door, I had to cross this patch of earth and its garden of bottle caps, pull-tabs, and cigarette butts. I also had to pass my landlady's apartment.

"Miss Sharp, is that you?" she called from her window.

"Yes, Mrs. McIntyre."

"Oh, good. I need to talk to you."

I stopped and waited as she disengaged three locks and two chains. She shuffled out, looking very much like a tiny Fraggle with her fuzzy slippers and pink terrycloth robe. She hadn't bothered with her walker, but instead braced herself on the doorframe. Wisps of her thinning hair stuck out of her nightcap like tufts of cotton candy. She took one look at me and her eyes lit up like a Christmas tree.

She gasped, her toothless mouth falling open into an amused smile. "Dear, you look magnificent!"

"Thank you, Mrs. M," I said. "You needed to talk to me?"

"Yes," she said, drawing out the word with a bit of a phlegmy rumble. "You know, those water heaters in units six and seven are on the fritz again."

Mrs. M couldn't afford contractors to come out all the time or hire a regular maintenance staff. But she had a tenant with a knack for fixing all things mechanical.

I smiled, nodding to my landlady. "Of course. I'm on call this weekend, so I may not have a chance to get to them right away, but I'll definitely be able to knock those out by the end of the week."

"Oh, thank you, dear. You are a peach. How much do you think?"

I waved off the comment. "Mrs. M, don't worry about it."

"No, dear, I insist. Tell you what. I'll take fifty off your rent this month if you can get another six months out of those heaters."

"It's a deal," I said.

Her watery eyes focused on the night behind me. Immediately, her pale, paper-thin skin flushed pink, and her jaw fell open. She'd finally noticed Marius.

"Oh, Cathy, honey, why didn't you tell me you had a date? I'm so sorry. I won't keep you any longer."

I cringed at the shortened form of my name. "It's nothing," I said. I glanced over my shoulder at Marius, still looking handsome in his suit and golden tie. "Trust me."

He must have taken this as a challenge. Slinking up to me, he draped one arm around my shoulders. When he spoke, his voice was rich as chocolate and full of promises. "Come along, darling. Our evening is just beginning."

Mrs. McIntyre's eyes filled with memories of younger days, and she shooed me away. She padded back into her home and began doing up the locks.

The satyr gave me a grin and a waggle of his eyebrows. I rolled my eyes. "Good night, Mrs. McIntyre," I called as I lurched toward my door.

"Yes, good night, dear lady," Marius sang.

I shrugged out of his embrace and unlocked my apartment. Like the complex itself, my place wasn't much. I rented a few rooms of brick walls painted with an ever-yellowing eggshell gloss. The sandy carpet was worn in a few places but not stained. I tried to keep the place tidy, aside from the stack of dead laptops in the corner I sometimes use for spare parts.

Marius stood in my living room and turned in a circle, examining my over-stuffed bookshelves and secondhand furniture.

"This is the first time I've ever seen the inside of your home," he mused.

"It's not much, but it's mine," I said. My keys jangled as I tossed them onto the countertop that also served as my dining room table.

His gaze dropped to the floor where a mass of fur and muscle I call

Linux curled around his legs. The tuxedo tomcat turned hopeful eyes up to the satyr.

"You shed on my suit, and I will serve you with egg rolls," he said.

With a flash from his golden eyes, Linux turned up both tail and nose before strutting over to greet me properly as the personal deity of his food bowl. Purring, he rammed into me. On a normal day, his hello was almost enough to send me back against the door. In heels and slightly drunk, I was lucky I didn't break my neck.

I reached down to pet him and began working the straps on my shoes.

"It's a quaint little place," Marius said, adding, "Cathy."

I snarled. "Do not call me that."

Barefoot, I plodded into my bedroom to get out of the glitzy dress before Linux decided it would look better with his own personal accessories.

"Do you need any help in there?" Marius said loudly. "I'm quite good with zippers and underthings."

"No, thanks."

"You know you want me to come in there right this second and rip off your dress with my teeth."

A quick jolt of pleasure hit me in the pink parts as an image flashed across my mind. *Marius behind me, his hands gliding up my arms. Gently, he pushes my hair off of my neck and over one shoulder. I gasp as he places the lightest, most tantalizing of kisses on my throat. My head rocks back against him, inviting him to continue. His fingers slide beneath the straps of my dress and inch them down.*

With another gasp, I lurched forward, jostling the contents of my dresser. *What the hell?*

I was alone in my bedroom. I poked my head out to find Marius sitting on my couch with both arms sprawled over the back cushions. Linux stretched his tuxedo form at the satyr's feet, begging for a tummy rub.

"What was that?" I asked.

Marius's smile gleamed in his wicked eyes. "Something wrong?"

"You just...what the hell did you do?"

"Am I really the only satyr you've met, Catherine?"

"Marius," I growled in warning.

"It's a gift of my race: providing inspiration."

"So you put that in my mind?"

"Consider it a teaser," he said silkily. "The coming attractions, as it were."

"Stay out of my head," I warned.

Sliding the door shut, but not latching it, I stepped out of the sheath and rummaged in my drawers for a suitable change of clothes. As it was nighttime, my house, and I was more than buzzed, I opted for the blue plaid pajama pants and a black T-shirt printed with the power symbol. It even glowed in the dark.

"I think," Marius called from the living room, "you enjoyed that."

"Not interested, satyr. Your charms won't work on me."

"Oh, no? I believe they just did."

I winced at that particularly uncomfortable truth. Ignoring it, I asked, "How is it that I'm just now finding out about this little power of yours?"

"Professional courtesy," he said flatly. "I've got a block on you."

I may have snorted. "Right. A block. Good one."

"If I didn't, you'd be soaking your panties and flinging yourself at me. I wouldn't be able to go home because you'd be stalking me. So much would your need consume you that you'd spend every waking minute shagging me. This wouldn't be productive at all, would it? Then the goddess would get mad at me for interfering in her business and add more years to my debt. Not to mention the risk of dehydration from the hours and hours of athletic sex."

"The world may never know," I said as I plopped on the sofa beside him. "All right. You and I need to talk. Tell me what you know about Eris and this poker game."

"Who says I know anything?"

"You do." As I spouted off his earlier comments, I mocked his posh accent, "I am the personal assistant to a deity. I'm well-connected. Come on," I said in my own voice. "There's no way you didn't know about this."

"I do not sound like that."

I didn't respond with words. I gave him my most insistent, intense glare.

Relenting, he sighed. "The game was last night. Now, I'm not invited to the game, but this"—Marius took the poker chip out of his pocket and flipped it like a coin—"along with what you heard from the Faery, our mistress, and Coyote makes it damn obvious that you are in the pot."

"Who are the other players?"

"Well, the Lady is rather chaotic, so it's anyone's guess. But if your soul is in play that says it's likely to be one of her more exclusive games. And there are only five other beings that could possibly be at *that* table."

"Coyote and Puck," I offered. "Who else?"

"Maui, Anansi, and the bastard son of Asgard himself."

Anansi. Maui. I'd worked around Eris enough to recognize the names of her African and Hawaiian colleagues. Anansi, the Spider, came up on my radar often. Those emails from scammers posing as Nigerian princes or something? Yeah, that's the Spider's gig.

Maui I'd only heard rumors about, but if the lore holds true, he is the one you need to thank for those luscious islands. Myth says he cast his hook into the sea, snagged the islands, and pulled them to the surface behind him.

In the company of such avatars of mayhem, Asgard's son must be Loki. I didn't know much about the actual Norse god of mischief, but something told me he wouldn't be anything like the movie villain. The more I pondered it, I wasn't sure if that was a good thing or not.

Eris, Anansi, Maui, Puck, Coyote, and Loki. Tricksters and thieves, these six gods were among the most notorious deities in mythology. Architects of chaos and disorder, creators and destroyers, the tricksters are both revered and reviled. And they were poker buddies? I tried to fathom just how twisted a game among these bullshit artists would be.

Twisted enough that my soul was up for grabs to the winner.

I tried to imagine them all hunched around a green felt table. And there, in the center of the table with all the chips was my soul.

The idea filled my stomach with nausea and a fair amount of angst.

"Does this happen often? Betting with souls, I mean?"

Marius swung his head in a gesture of indecision. "Not precisely. Souls are a valuable commodity, but it's not as if there's a stock market with trading and such. No, souls are pulled out for big bets only. Or bluffs."

Great. She might be bluffing. If she loses, I still get screwed.

"So what does this mean?" I asked, plucking the black poker chip from Marius's hand. "Coyote had this. So, he won?"

"Not likely," Marius said. "He's a terrible player from what I hear."

"But, he had it. So…?"

Marius shrugged and tossed a stray lock of hair out of his face. "I've never been to one of her games, I'm afraid. I can't tell you the significance other than it is a token of promise. Sort of an I.O.U."

All the new information swirled around in my head. "Wait… You just mentioned five gods, but Eris said I had to get four tokens."

"Someone may not have come to the game," he offered. "I wasn't there."

"Great."

"Even if you knew for sure, getting the chips won't be easy," Marius added.

"No shit," I sneered. "Not that anything with Eris is ever easy, but what made you say that?"

Marius squirmed in his seat and loosened his tie. "You have to understand that you're not dealing with mortals, Catherine. These beings are ancient and take endless pleasure from causing strife. The only thing more enjoyable to them than wreaking havoc in human lives is fucking with one another."

I raked my hand through my hair. "So, in order to screw with Eris and make her life miserable, someone else might take a poke at me now that I'm on the table?"

He nodded.

"Shit," I hissed. "So where should we start? Anansi? Loki? How do I find these gods anyway?"

Marius didn't get the opportunity to answer. Something chose that exact moment to bust in my door.

CHAPTER EIGHT
"Slow Cheetah"

I screamed as the door exploded with a crack of splintering wood and popping metal. Standing in a cloud of mist was a bulky figure, its skin glistening gray and white. It had the basic shape of a man—head, arms, legs, and all in the appropriate places—yet the thing could never have passed for human. Its head resembled a shark, coming to an unnatural point, sloping off into his back without bothering with the formality of a neck. Twin glassy eyes stared out of its face, black and soulless like a doll's. And that mouth… Row upon row of jagged, razor-sharp teeth forced its jaws apart.

I scrambled backward to put as much distance between me and the thing as I could. As I skittered up and over the arm of the sofa, I fell to the floor with a painful *thud*. My heart raced, and I gulped in panicked breaths.

Instinct took over. I hopped up, grabbed Marius by the arm and yanked him toward my bedroom. I slammed the door behind us, locked it, and started using anything I could find as a barricade. A chair. A dead server I was hoping to Frankenstein someday.

"Help me. Get the other side," I said, pulling at the dresser. When no help came, I looked up to see Marius jiggling the lock on my window. "What are you doing? Help me or it will get both of us!"

"Not if I get out of here. Then it will just get you."

"You can't leave me here," I pleaded.

"Oh no? Watch." Marius pulled back his fist and punched through the glass.

The creature began to beat against the bedroom door. Hinges rattling and wood trembling, I got the impression it used its whole body as a battering ram.

Think, Cat!

66

While I continued to shove at the dresser, Marius knocked loose teeth of glass out of the window and started to maneuver his body into the hole. The door shook with another cacophonous impact. I jerked in shock and tried to jimmy the dresser out of its rut in the carpet.

"We had a deal!" I called to Marius.

He stopped, one leg dangling out into the Vegas night. His eyes swam out of focus as he thought about it.

"I can't go on a date with you if I'm dead," I pointed out.

"Bugger all," he hissed.

Marius pulled his leg back in the room. As he took the few strides to my side, he muttered darkly to himself. "Of all the damnable agreements I could make. Supposed to be a simple night at Caesars and now I find myself—"

"Just shut up, and help me get this in front of the goddamn door," I snapped.

And then, with a noise like a gunshot, the door burst open and Jaws reached in with clawed hands. No. Not claws. Teeth. Serrated teeth jutted out of its fingers where its nails should have been.

"What the shit is that?" I called, my voice pitched high.

I snatched up the nearest weapon I could find: a defunct laptop. I hauled off and swung the computer at the thing's deformed arm. There was no satisfying crunch of bone. I'd hardly met any hard resistance at all. The creature's arm had a bulk to it, sure, but it was like a slab of thick meat. Or cartilage.

"That's messed up," I said to Marius.

The shark's head thrashed back and forth as it pushed through the few things I'd used to make my ineffective barrier. I swatted at it again, using the computer as both shield and bludgeon. At my side, Marius stretched out his hands, palms up and fingers splayed. He began chanting. I have no idea what language it was. Possibly Greek. Maybe Latin. Or maybe he just made it all up.

"What are you going to do, seduce it to death?"

Then the air around Jaws rippled as magic congealed. Whatever he said, I could see the effects of the satyr's spell. The earth beneath me trembled, and the carpet split apart. Vines sprang up from the soil and twined their way around the shark's ankles.

Shocked and awestruck, I whipped my head to look at Marius. His face contorted with strain, his eyes taking on a verdant glow. His glamour began to fail, and I could see his horns—real and whole—sticking out of his forehead. Wisps of black hair had come free of his ponytail.

The vines, thick and ropy, coiled up to the shark's knees. Slowly, they tugged at it, sucking it into the ground. The thing roared as it struggled. Gill slits in its chest flapped with a sickly, wet sound in perfect time of my racing pulse.

Marius snarled something guttural, curling his right hand into a fist and yanking at the air. With a fierce snap, Jaws lurched forward. Marius drew a sword from the ether. Its long, curved blade gleamed like righteous fire. The sword sliced through the air so quickly I heard it whistle just before it sank into the hide of the shark. I let out an embarrassingly girly squeal and brought the laptop up to block out the gore. Squelching noises of cartilage bursting and muscle ripping replaced the soundtrack of the creature's struggle. Instead of an alien roar, the shark hissed as it died.

Shuddering, I dared to look up at the satyr. A layer of red stained his blade. Marius stared coldly. His eyes still glowed with ephemeral light. Marius—the pompous ass I'd known for years—wasn't there anymore. A horned warrior stood in my room in his stead. A fine layer of sweat glistened over his flesh as he let out a heaving breath. This Marius was no fool or personal assistant. This Marius commanded respect.

My muscles quivered, and my stomach and chest tightened at the primal power radiating from him. For a split-second I even considered that a date with him might not be such a bad idea after all.

"Wow," I said, reeling my jaw up off the floor.

As his eyes returned to their normal leafy green, some of the ruddy gaiety flooded back into his flesh. His horns faded away, too.

Marius's voice was even, as if he did this every day. "See something you like, Catherine?"

Despite myself, I smiled. "Maybe."

Then I made the mistake of looking down. The shark's corpse oozed blood onto my carpet. Its black eyes rolled back, exposing milky white and the crimson of burst capillaries. Using the creature's body, Marius wiped his blade clean then sheathed it into thin air. With a convulsive jerk, I dropped the laptop, ran to my bathroom, and promptly threw up.

"Oh, yes," Marius said, "you're a marvelous date."

Shaking with adrenaline, I wiped up my face, and sluiced off the make-up. After brushing my teeth, I combed my hair then put it up in a knot on top of my head. I was as put-together as I would get, all things considered.

Back in my bedroom, Marius stood over the corpse. I willed myself not to look, but every couple of seconds my eyes would dart to the creature with a sick fascination and curiosity.

"So," I said staring at Marius like my sanity depended on it. "You ruined my carpet with that trick of yours. What the hell was that?"

Marius hunched over the shark—and I found something else in the room to look at. I presume he was searching the corpse, but I couldn't stand to watch.

"A bit of earth magic," he said quietly.

"Is that a satyr thing or just something you picked up along the way?"

"Most of us have a connection to elemental magics. Earth, wind, water," he answered. "Not all of my kind make use of those gifts or strengthen them."

"Look at you. A jackass of all trades. Who'd a thunk?"

"Being a Renaissance man has served me well. And if I'm not mistaken, it just saved your life."

"Yeah, yeah. What is this thing anyway?"

"I'm not sure," Marius mused. "Someone might have conjured a golem. There are some demons that can take forms similar to this, but I don't think our friend here is from the Pit."

"Why is it here?"

"Remember what I said about being a target for someone wanting to take a bite out of Eris?"

I slumped. "I thought they'd just try to mess with me, not try to fucking kill me!"

"Gods are funny like that."

"Well, they can go fu—"

From the next room, a watery screech pierced the air. I peeked into my living room to see another shark taking ungainly steps over the rubble its predecessor had made.

"It has a friend!" I shouted.

"Right. Back to my plan, then."

Without further ado, Marius and I climbed out of my bedroom window and ran for his car. I may have short legs, but I'm fast. I darted around the building, behind Mrs. McIntyre's apartment, and cut to the left. Another twenty yards or so and we'd be climbing into Marius's silver Mercedes.

"Oh, shit," I hissed breathlessly.

Two sharks and three porcine creatures flanked the Mercedes, eyes shining with malice. The pig-men, like the sharks, resembled animals wearing human costumes. Their noses squashed against their faces, and the pigs' pink skin—bristling with wiry hairs—glistened like fresh sunburn. Two tusk-like teeth curled up from each creature's lower jaws. With hungry snorts, the pigs charged forward.

I ducked beneath a pair of, well, I suppose they were hands. Not five fingers but two thick digits and a thumb. These strange things flailed at me, swiping at my shoulders.

Glancing around for Marius, I saw that once more he brandished a sword. With a flourish, he cut sidelong into one of the pigs and whirled to face off with another shark. Just then, a slab of pork hit me in the chest. I fell to the ground, the gravel slicing the soles of my bare feet.

The hog that hit me hadn't intended to. A few feet away from me, it lay on the ground, holding one cloven-hand to its head. Blood flowed into its eyes from a gash on its forehead.

I turned around to see who else could have joined the fight. No magic ally appeared. On the ground, though, I saw a hammer.

"Yes!" I breathed. Crawling across the ground, I grabbed my new weapon and held it so I could sweep the prongs at whatever came toward me next.

"Catherine!" Marius called. "I said I'd help you, not die for you."

He'd killed one more of the creatures, and another mutant lay on the ground, cradling the stump of its arm. The pig near me was too concerned with his seeping head for the moment, but three other creatures engaged Marius. Crowding around him, they backed him up against a parked SUV. Soon, he would have little room to maneuver and the three assailants would pounce, ripping the satyr apart.

I pushed to my feet and took a running jump at the nearest monster. Flying down, I drove the hammer into the thing's shoulder. Hot, salty blood splashed on my face, clothes, and hands. With the hammer still deep in its flesh, the shark spun to swat at me. As I still held the tool, the force of the creature's movement dragged me along the gravel. My feet screamed with the fresh abrasions, and my shoulders jerked. When I had better leverage, I yanked my weapon out of the shark's body and prepared another swing.

The shark swiped at me with those abominable hands. The teeth-claws whistled as they cut through the air. I sucked in my stomach just enough to avoid being torn open. Bringing the hammer down in a feeble arc, I tried to parry the thing's strike. The shark responded with by backhanding me across the face.

Trembling with anger and terror, I rocked back from the blow.

"Oh, hell no," I said.

As the shark charged me for another strike, I lashed out with the prongs of the hammer, advanced, then kicked it where a man would have very tender bits. The shark, it turns out, didn't have those parts, but my kick had enough force behind it to send the thing staggering back. Right into one of the pigs sparring with Marius.

The shark turned to see what new threat might be lurking behind, and I used the distraction to land a mortal blow. I raised the hammer with both hands and lunged forward. The prongs landed in the beast's skull with a sickening crunch. I rode the shark to the ground as it crumpled.

At this point, the world began to jerk and skip like an old film projector. Sounds modulated and images flickered past in a formless haze. I remember the horrifying, wet slapping as I tried to get the hammer out of the shark's body, its flesh ripping in chunks. Fresh gore spurting onto me. The *snicker-snack* of Marius's sword slicing, followed quickly by a squeal of agony. The fetid scent of rotten seaweed and copper. An arm on the ground.

I crouched next to the car as two injured Bacon Brothers scrambled toward the Mercedes, dazed and howling in pain. Marius yelled for me again.

"Get in the car!"

I fumbled with the latch and hopped into the passenger seat. Before I could even shut the door, the satyr revved the engine, backed out of the space, and peeled away into the night.

We'd driven for a minute or two without further attack when I realized I was repeating the words, "Oh my God." My whole body trembled. Try as I might, I couldn't make it stop.

"Where are we going?" Marius asked.

If the quaking in my limbs didn't quit, I might shake myself to pieces. Couldn't he see that? I tried to form words, but I'd had enough. I guess some would call it shock. All I know is that my systems were shutting down. I'd reached my breaking point and needed to reboot.

"Eris," I said. "Find her."

"Without the chips?"

"Fuck the chips! Things are trying to kill me!"

He didn't argue. While he pulled out his phone and started dialing, I leaned my head back against the seat and closed my eyes. Teeth flashed there in bloody jaws. *No*, I thought, snapping my eyes open. *I don't want to see that.* My head rolled to the side and I stared out the window. The reflections of Marius and me superimposed over the shops and buildings we passed. It gave everything the quality of a dream: nothing was real, just wraiths floating past in a moment.

"That's strange," Marius said. "She's not answering."

His reflection hit redial and waited.

I tried not to think of my dirty clothes, soggy from some freakish creature's blood.

"The hell?" he said. "Says her number has been disconnected."

As the world sped by, I went numb. I'd processed all I would for the night.

"Are you listening to me?"

I made a noncommittal sound, but otherwise remained motionless.

"Catherine, until I can get Eris on the line, you need to think of someplace we can go."

"Why me?" I asked. I may have been responding to him, or I may have been asking someone else for a grander answer.

Maybe I should've taken Marius's earlier advice and hidden from this bullshit. How often had I wished that I could just run away from Eris and this weird other life where gods and satyrs and Fae existed? Often enough.

I sighed. I gave Marius a set of cross streets.

In the window, I saw his face wrinkle. "There's nothing there," he said. "Just a derelict warehouse and some abandoned buildings where kids go to drop ecstasy and get arrested."

"Trust me," I said.

He went silent and I settled into the rhythm of the car. The soft, steady hum of the tires gliding over the asphalt, the light *tick tick* of the turn signal. The Mercedes spun a subtle symphony, and the perfect cadence of engine and forward motion lulled me into a gentle, black sleep.

CHAPTER NINE
"Factory of Faith"

I woke up as Marius cut the engine. My lips were dry, and a headache percolated behind my bleary eyes. Bringing my vision back into focus, I took a peek around. We were in a shitty part of town far northeast of the Strip. Tourists didn't come out this way unless they were fans of a particular crime drama. They'd filmed an episode or two out here. Good atmosphere in a creepy-body-dumping sort of way.

The place was mostly abandoned, just like Marius had said. A disintegrating furniture warehouse sat next to a rundown shopping center. Weeds grew through the crumbling sidewalks, and lizards shared meals with spiders. A few homeless kids squatted in one of the buildings, but mostly the area maintained the parched, desolate look of a post-apocalyptic wasteland.

"Lovely vacation spot you've picked," Marius said. "Do you have a time share?"

I got out of the car and padded carefully in the loose dirt, muscle memory kicking in and guiding me to the correct loading dock off the back of the warehouse. Marius followed, muttering his disapproval the whole time.

"…and the dirt is going to make my car dustier than Eris's tits."

As we reached the door, I turned to him. "Give me your coat."

"What is this, the high school prom? You can't be cold. Why on earth do you need my coat?"

Too tired to argue, my voice came out quiet. "I'm covered in shark-man blood, and I'd rather not advertise it to everyone here."

"Everyone? Who, the rocks?"

Closing my eyes, I rubbed at my temples. "Marius, give me the goddamn coat."

"Fine," he said. As he slid out of it, I took a good look at him. His shoes lacked their high shine, but other than that, Marius's clothes showed no sign of our earlier troubles. No blood, no rips, no dust. He could've waltzed right back into the gala and no one would be any the wiser that less than an hour ago he sliced up a—

Nausea wrenched at my guts as I thought of the creatures. I had to shove those memories away, push the bile back down.

Keep moving forward, Cat, I said to myself.

"How is it that I'm a mess and you look perfect?" I grumbled thickly.

"You think I look perfect?" he asked with his lopsided grin. "Considering that mere hours ago I garnered a meager 'all right', I'm touched."

"Don't let it go to your head."

As Marius passed me the jacket, he explained. "Glamours are all part of the service. Magic allows me to conceal my finer qualities for you simple-minded humans, but it also means I can make my clothes look fabulous. Far better than dry cleaning, if you ask me."

"Didn't realize your glamour was that extensive. Thought it just took care of your horns and legs."

He shrugged. "What can I say? I'm a man of many surprises."

I took his jacket and pulled it on, covering my gore-soaked pajamas. Then I turned my attention to the door. The slab of corrugated metal worked on an electric motor like a standard garage door. If I were a few inches taller, I might have been able to peek into the two grimy windows. Gangs and taggers had sprayed the place with graffiti for years. On this door, someone had painted, "YmFy."

Most people assumed it was a typical tag, indiscernible jargon from the subculture of graffiti artists. Well, those people had the right idea. They just didn't understand which subculture they were actually dealing with.

"I still don't see anyone here," Marius said, peering in. "Just a dirty, dusty garage."

"Don't trust your eyes," I said.

I held up a hand and pressed it against the glass. Immediately, the pane gave off an acid-green glow. Like something out of Star Trek, a digitized keypad appeared beneath my fingers. I tapped in my password, and with a groan, the garage door began to rise.

Music flooded the night, a throbbing bass beat with electronic melodies cascading over it. As shafts of light shifted in blues and greens, shadows writhed on the floor. Marius watched the dancers grind against one another then passed me a questioning look.

"What? You think you're the only one who knows a bit about glamours?"

The door shut behind us as we ventured into the press of bodies. Designer colognes blended with the primal scents of sweat and musk. The crowd boiled with the music, dancing in a chaotic choreography. Moving through the throng, my muscles relaxed, and I took a deep breath. The forbidden radiance and communal ecstasy of this place was balm for a weary soul.

YmFy. My home away from home.

The place served the hacker and technomancer crowd. Occasionally, I'd seen vanilla mortals like me or other magical beings like Marius, but that was rare. The bar maintained a steady stream of loyal clients without advertising itself.

Marius stared at the mixed factions on the dance floor. Barely legals in cyberpunk latex and LED clothes gyrated against one another. Lurkers in black trench coats clung to the walls. Jeans and T-shirts, low profile or high maintenance; YmFy hosted all types.

"Excellent," Marius said. "You've decided to jump into a scene out of the Matrix in your hour of peril. Shall we go sing our sorrows to the bartender and wait for Morpheus?"

"This isn't the kind of place where everyone knows your name," I called, standing on tiptoe to reach Marius's ear. "Come on." I tugged at the satyr's arm and guided him toward the white-and-green light pulsing from the acrylic bar. In orange and blue, I could make out *YmFy* being spelled in light over the bodies on the dance floor. My feet were tight, swollen, and ached in a million places. My steps were slow and careful, but each one set my soles on fire.

"What the bloody hell is a Yim Fee?" Marius asked.

I shook my head. There would be time to answer him. But right then I had to get the hell out of the crowd. And before I could do that, I had to find Flynn.

Sliding onto one of the egg-shaped barstools, I swept my gaze down the row of bartenders. Flynn glanced up from the drink he poured. When he caught sight of me, he grinned and nodded once in a way that said he'd be right over.

"What are we doing here?" Marius yelled over the driving bass.

I held up a finger. "Wait a minute."

Good to his unspoken word, Flynn glided over to us an instant later. "Cat," he said, his voice carrying over the din. "I didn't think you'd make it tonight. Want the usual?"

"No, thanks," I said. "I need to use the bolt hole."

His cheerful face fell with concern, and he leaned across the bar. "Are you all right?"

I wanted to say yes, to assure him all was good with the world, but how could it be? Flashes of hot blood spurting beneath a hammer, of my hands coming down to split the sandpapery, gray hide. All this and more rushed through my mind.

My chin quivered as I tried to hold myself together. I shook my head.

Flynn jerked his chin. "Come on back."

Leading Marius around the other patrons, I met up with Flynn next to a flat, black wall. He bristled at the sight of my companion. "Cat, who is this?"

"It's okay," I said. "This is Marius."

"The satyr? You brought him here? No, Cat. I don't like this."

"He's helping me out," I said. "Please. We need a few minutes."

As if trying to read him, Flynn's eyes passed over Marius for an ungodly long minute before the mage finally nodded with approval. Well, maybe not approval, but at least begrudging tolerance.

Flynn passed a pale hand over the wall and with that same toxic-green glow another keypad appeared. He punched in his code, and the wall slid away. Darkness concealed the room from the rest of the bar.

My friend bowed gallantly. "Ladies first."

I tried to smile but couldn't hold back the grimace as I passed Flynn and entered his sanctuary. When we were all inside, Flynn closed the door behind us, and the sounds of the club dimmed to little more than a background hum with a beat. Soft at first, so as not to blind us, the lights came up. He thinks of everything. It's one of the reasons I like him so much.

The bolt hole—this little secret behind the wall of YmFy—was a rectangular room running maybe a quarter of the length of the warehouse. With little else but a few black leather love seats, it acted as a salon or waiting room. A visible door led to a bathroom, and a few hidden exits connect to the more enjoyable areas of Flynn's playhouse. While I knew my way around, I never assumed I'd seen every part of his complex.

With the lights up to full power, Flynn finally got a good look at me.

"Jesus, Cat! What happened to you?"

I looked down. The coat did nothing to hide the gore on my pants, and my bare feet were dirty and covered in abrasions.

"I've got a problem," I said weakly.

He pawed at his ginger mop then dragged a hand down his face, still staring at my stained pajamas. "I'm guessing that's not your blood."

I shook my head and clenched my jaw against the scream threatening to consume me. Flynn nodded and took me into his arms. I sagged, limp as a doll, and the tears began to flow. As I sobbed into his chest, his large hands stroked my shoulders and held me close.

"Shh," he said, rocking me gently. "We'll fix it. Whatever it is, we'll figure it out." He took my face in his hands and made sure I could see his smile. "Right? It's what we do."

He winked, brushing my hair back and wiping a few tears from my cheeks. "You need the bag?"

I nodded.

"Okay," he said. "Tell you what. Go on into the bathroom there and type in your code to give me access. I'll run down to the locker room and pick up your things, okay?" After I'd agreed, he went on, "Then I want you to take a long, hot shower. I'll drop the bag in there so you can get into some clean clothes. When you're done, come out here, and we'll talk. All right?"

I clutched at his hand, still holding my chin, and gave my best attempt at a grateful smile. "Thank you, Flynn," I said.

"Any time," he said. With one last pat on the cheek he sent me to my tasks.

As I padded into the bathroom, Marius cleared his throat.

"Need any help in there?" he asked.

I was too tired to roll my eyes. I shut the door behind me and palmed another keypad into existence. After I'd granted Flynn access to my personal storage locker, I glanced up at the mirror.

Bad idea.

Quickly, I turned away from the lady with the haunted eyes and red crust drying all over her. Shivering, I stuffed my hands into the pockets of Marius's jacket. My fingers curled around something small, round, and flat.

The poker chip.

Smooth clay, it was like all the others you'll find in this town. Almost. I sighed, worrying at the golden apple at its center with my thumb. And I had to collect three more when gods were trying to kill me?

Weary, I shook my head.

I carefully put Marius's coat on a hook then slipped out of my dirty clothes. I wadded them up into a ball and stuffed them in the bin. Maybe I'd burn them later. I would never wear them again, that's for sure. Some stains can't be washed away.

Cranking the hot water and letting the steam fill the room, I stepped into the shower. There, finally alone, I came face to face with horrible reality.

I killed it.

The words echoed in my head as if bouncing off the shower walls. I cried. I'd never killed someone. I mean, I'd stepped on bugs and swatted my fair share of spiders, but never willingly *killed*, never purposely ended a life in such a brutal way. Not like this.

With shaking hands I took the bar of soap and scrubbed at myself, hoping this suffocating guilt would slough off with dead skin. *It was a monster,* part of me said, trying to rationalize what I'd done. *It wasn't human.* This thought, however, brought with it no more comfort than the idea that I'd used the hammer in self-defense.

I wept for something that had seeped away with the shark's life: a purity within me, an innocence. I mean, I'm no saint, that's for sure, but people tend to go through life reminding themselves, "Well at least I'm not a cold-blooded killer or anything."

I couldn't think that about myself anymore.

And if this pillar of my being had fallen, what would come next?

While scalding spray pounded on my back, the water sluiced away my pain, panic, and terrible memories. I sank to the tile floor and huddled my knees to my chest. For a long time I sat, bawling, letting myself fall to pieces and flow down the drain.

I'd fix me later.

Right?

***

True to his word, Flynn had silently placed my bag on the floor inside the bathroom along with a fluffy white towel and a steaming mug. I caught the scent of sugar and cinnamon. Bless him—Flynn had prepared a chai latte. As the spiced tea warmed my insides, I could almost hear Flynn telling me everything would be all right.

After I'd dressed in simple jeans and a T-shirt, I pulled on a pair of Chucks, and brushed my wet hair. I shouldered the bag and stepped back into the outer room of the secret chamber.

Marius paced back and forth like a caged lion. He'd smoothed his hair into its ponytail once more, and at some point he'd rolled up the sleeves of his black shirt. His golden-apple brand, a twin to my own, peeked out from beneath the cuff on his left arm.

"There you are," he said impatiently.

I draped his suit coat over the back of a sofa and settled my bag on the ground. I found comfort in order and tidy courtesy.

"Did you get in touch with Eris?" I asked.

"No, dammit. I keep calling, but every time it's different."

"What do you mean?"

"Well, one minute the recording tells me the line's been disconnected, the next, this bint's voice tells me all circuits are full. A few times I even got a busy signal. Seriously? A busy signal? I haven't heard one of those since before MTV stopped playing music."

I drew in a breath, adding this information to what little I already had, and sank into the folds of the couch.

"Care to enlighten me as to what we're doing here?" he asked.

"Remember that job in Belize a few years ago?" When he nodded, I said, "Well, I figured it wouldn't be a bad idea for me to have a bug-out plan. Flynn offered to help. He gave me a place to stash my GTFO bag."

"GTFO?"

"Yeah. You know how some people have a suitcase in the trunk or something for emergencies? That's what this is," I said patting the duffel. "It's got my passport, phone charger, clothes, toiletries—all the necessities in the unfortunate event I need to *Get The Fuck Out*."

He nodded. "Fortune favors the prepared."

"Something like that."

The door slid open as Flynn returned. He took a seat in one of the black leather armchairs and propped one leg over the side. More often than not, my bartender friend dressed in the style of the bar: edgy, dark, and somewhat enigmatic. Sometimes he poured himself into vinyl or some other tight-and-shiny clothing. Since the music out in the club had faded and tonight's last call had come and gone, Flynn lounged in his favorite torn jeans and a vintage tee. Tattoos showed over his lanky arms in the shapes of mechanical veins and pathways like those on a motherboard. Here and there, his pale flesh glistened with metallic studs. Tonight he'd spiked his red hair up into a fauxhawk.

"Hiding in a wall with the bartender," Marius mused. "You surprise me, Catherine. By the by, are you going to tell me what the hell a Yim Fee is?"

"Y-M-F-Y. It's computer code," Flynn explained. "Base64, specifically."

"That's great, but does it actually mean anything?"

With a smile my friend said, "Means 'bar.'"

"Delightful." Marius sneered. "He thinks he's clever."

Flynn ignored Marius and fixed me with a level stare. "So, what happened?"

"Eris bet my soul in a poker game," I said bluntly.

He drew in a breath, those ancient eyes hardening with anger. "Well, fuck."

I took off into a cold report of my night, starting with our arrival at the gala and ending with our appearance at YmFy.

When I finished, Flynn heaved a sigh. He pawed through his spikes and gave me a wary smile. "Everything old is new again, eh?"

I hung my head. "Complete with a visit from Dahlia."

"Joy. You okay?"

I repressed the urge to scream, *No, I am not okay!* and opted for, "I will be."

Flynn steepled his fingers, deep in thought. His gaze kept darting to Marius. The satyr was a fly buzzing too near. As if he couldn't stand the constant annoyance of his presence, Flynn stood and stalked right up to Marius's side. I hadn't noticed it earlier, but Flynn towered over him.

"What's your angle on this, satyr?"

Marius took a step away from the looming technomancer. "What are you talking about?"

"Why are you here?"

"Eris bade me to escort Catherine to the gala. I do as I am told."

"And he said he'd help me figure out what was going on with the poker game," I added.

Flynn snorted derisively. "I'm sure that help comes with a price. What's in it for you?"

Marius leered. "An evening with the pleasure of Catherine's company."

Like lightning, Flynn's fist blurred through the air. Equally fast, Marius's forearm came up to block the punch. As he twisted Flynn's wrist with his left hand, Marius's right attempted to jab my friend in the ribs. Flynn slid, his torso shifting out of the satyr's reach. But the bartender's arms were longer and impossibly fast—faster than Marius could dodge. Flynn's hand shot out and gripped the satyr's throat.

I darted across the room to tug at Flynn's arm. His flesh no longer felt pliant and smooth, like a normal arm. Rather it seemed I fought against steel.

"What the hell are you doing?" I asked.

Marius choked, hands scraping at the one pinning him to the wall while his feet kicked uselessly at the floor. Like glowing blood, orange light pulsed through the mage's tattoos.

"Stop!" I yelled. "Flynn, let him go!"

He shot a glare to me, eyes emitting the same citrine light. "Why?"

"He saved my life."

As I looked to Marius, the light coursing through Flynn traced lines up the veins in the satyr's purple face. I saw his horns splitting through the glamour again. While he gripped at Flynn's clenched fist with one hand, Marius worked the other as if groping in the air. What if he pulled the sword again? I couldn't stand to see Flynn impaled on the blade.

"Flynn, please," I said.

Without ceremony, he let go. Marius fell to the floor, gasping. The glow left their bodies. Brooding, Flynn straightened himself and stepped back.

"You are corrupted," he spat at Marius.

The satyr didn't answer but warily eyed Flynn.

I gulped. I'd never seen Flynn go über-protective of me, or anyone. I appreciated the sentiment, but the quick escalation left me guarded. And since when could he make his limbs light up and turn hard as marble?

"Flynn," I said quietly. "Do you want us to leave?"

"No," he grumbled. "Just…something's not right with him, Cat."

"I'm right here," Marius complained. "You don't have to talk of me as if I'm not."

Flynn stared a hateful challenge to the satyr. "Did I hurt its feelings?"

"Just who the bloody hell do you think you are?"

Still fuming, Flynn turned his blazing gaze to me. "Did he make you a promise, Cat? Like a real, binding contract, or did he just nod or something?"

"Christ, Flynn," I said with a roll of my eyes. "We made the deal. He offered. I accepted the terms."

The mage chewed on this info and ground his teeth. Something about Marius rubbed him the wrong way, and I didn't think it was the satyr's affiliation with Eris or the shit I'd been through at her whim. No, Flynn had called him corrupted. There was something deeper going on that made him think Marius was playing false. But what?

Flynn jabbed a finger at Marius. "So help me, satyr, if you break your word or if any harm comes to Cat, you will beg me for a swift death."

Venom flashed in Marius's eyes. As he picked himself up off the floor, he kept his stare locked with Flynn's.

"Catherine's bargain is with *me*. I will honor my word so long as she keeps hers. I've done nothing to her—or to you—to make you believe I'm anything less than sincere."

Flynn snorted. "You're a satyr. That's hardly the most honorable race in existence."

"Furthermore," Marius said loudly, ignoring the slight on his species, "I've already risked my neck for her by fighting land-walking sharks and a side of bacon. That should earn some trust, I think."

"You work for Discord," Flynn retorted. "I can't trust a damn thing you say."

"In case you didn't notice, Eris isn't exactly forthcoming with me these days." He waved his phone in the air.

I said the first thing that came to mind. "Maybe she sold you, too."

Marius scoffed, but I caught a glimpse of his fear before he recovered. "She would do no such thing. As a personal assistant I'm invaluable."

"And I'm sure you're an amusing little puppet," Flynn added.

"Excuse me, did I shag your mother and forget to invite you or something?"

"She bet with my soul," I said, "why not yours?"

"Well, for one thing, she doesn't have my soul. I owe her a debt. There is a subtle, but important difference. For another, I still have this." The satyr lifted his sleeve and presented his brand. "If she'd traded me off, surely I'd have been claimed by now."

Flynn and I both looked to my wrist. My own brand remained, clear as ever. This gave the mage pause. Pensive, he returned to his seat. Marius braced himself against the back of the sofa.

"So, since you still wear your brands," Flynn said, eyes tracking to the ceiling, "we can assume you are both still Eris's property." When I snarled a protest, Flynn held up a hand. "Cat, you know I don't think of you as cattle, but they do. And, like it or not, she has a rightful claim to your soul."

Mollified, I flopped into a chair and studied my hands in my lap.

"What exactly did Dahlia say to you?" Flynn asked.

Without looking up I told him. "She said Puck had plans for me. Made it sound like he's angling to get me on his roster." I shuddered. I'd had enough bad news come from being around Fae. I didn't need to work for them.

With a wave of his hand, Flynn produced a rectangle of light. Translucent images began to flow over it as if someone were channel surfing on a TV. While most of it flashed by too quickly for me to read, a technomage like Flynn would have no trouble absorbing the information.

"Dahlia has never exactly been trustworthy," he remarked, his tone dark yet casual.

"That's true," I admitted. "But it's what I've got to go on at the moment."

He kept his attention on the makeshift monitor, surfing through terabytes of code. Then large words blazed that Flynn had been granted access. On his ethereal screen, green numbers flashed. Squinting, I realized he'd pulled up someone's bank records.

I whistled. "A lot of zeroes," I said.

"And it's in the red," Flynn said. Turning to Marius, he said, "Your boss is damn near destitute."

Marius said nothing.

I, on the other hand, couldn't hold my tongue. I'd been chased by sharks, bet in a poker game, pissed off by Fae, and creeped on by a god. My tolerance for the random and absurd had been blown away.

I pinched the bridge of my nose. "Wait. You're telling me gods use regular bank accounts? Like normal people?"

Flynn nodded as if I'd asked if the sky was blue. "Yeah. This world is based on money. Gods want power. If you can adapt to the corporate climate, you have a better chance of survival. You can't buy governments with religion anymore."

Well, you learn something new every day. "You know, you'd think that after working for a deity for years, I'd be used to feeling insignificant and tiny. Does the sting ever go away?" I asked Marius.

He lifted his chin, haughty. "I wouldn't know."

I turned back to Flynn. "So she's going broke. What does that mean?"

"It means she's desperate. And that makes her all the more dangerous."

CHAPTER TEN
"Show Me Your Soul"

Sitting on Flynn's sofa, I tried to puzzle out the goddess's plan. Her bank accounts showed a significant debt, and she'd been in a high-stakes card game with other gods. She'd bartered with my soul, but why? To sweeten the pot? To try to bluff her way into a big score? Then, for her own twisted reasons she ordered me to attend a swanky party with Marius. And now this quest for a handful of poker chips. What the hell was she playing at?

I felt so small. Powerless. And it made me angry.

"I thought this would be it, you know?" My laugh had no humor to it. Tears scalded my cheeks and stung in my eyes. My voice shook with the swell of emotions. "When she said that after this job I'd be done, I actually believed her. How stupid is that?"

The technomage sat beside me and wrapped me in his long arms. "Cat, you're a brilliant woman. Having hope doesn't make you stupid."

Clearing his throat, Marius weighed in. "Besides, if Eris disappears and can't finish the game, no one can claim you. So, you'd effectively be free."

"What makes you think she's disappeared?" Flynn asked. "Maybe she put you into the pot and cut you off, like Cat said."

Marius waved the comment away with a bored flick of his wrist.

"But, what about the other gods?" I asked. "Won't they be pissed? I've already got someone sending fucking sharks after me."

Flynn leaned back, one arm still wrapped around my shoulder. "I think it's safe to say Maui sent your guests. The specific animals fit with his mythology."

Holding my head in my hands, I groaned. "What does he want though?"

Marius clapped his hands. "See! This is the question! I mean, it's obvious what Coyote wants from you—even if you are a bookish prude—but I can't understand what's so special about your soul that all of these gods are willing to take it, let alone fight for it tooth and claw."

I glared at him. "Thanks ever so much."

"It's not an insult but a fair question. What makes your soul such a handsome prize?"

"Belief is currency," Flynn said. He added a piercing glare of condescension for Marius. "Surely you know that."

I waved. "I don't."

Flynn sighed, gesturing with his hands as he sought the right words to explain. "A person's soul represents their purest beliefs. Therefore, in a market based on such things, souls are as good as blue-chip stocks. Plus, it doesn't suck to have a talented technomancer beholden to you."

I narrowed my eyes at him. "Flynn, don't start with that again. Please."

"Cat," he said down his nose. "For years I've respected your desire to keep it private, but look at who you're talking to. You don't have to hide from me. Besides, it's not like you're keeping some big secret. I've known since we met."

"I'm not keeping anything from you." I got to my feet, annoyed. "Flynn, I've watched you play with tech for how long? Believe me, if I was one of the cool kids with magic powers I would've told you."

"And yet you haven't."

"Dude, if I was a technomancer do you think I'd be working in my shit job?"

"Or be such a lousy date?" Marius added.

"Shut up," Flynn and I barked in unison.

"I'm just me," I said sadly. "Since coming to Vegas and learning about the *other* world, I've been scared out of my mind. Magic, mythical creatures, gods? I don't understand those things. They're bigger than me and have brought me nothing but bullshit. Watching you, though? That's the only time I see magic as being good. I've been idolizing you like some geeky freshman."

"Cat," he began, but I cut him off.

"I wasn't born under the right sign or with the correct birthmark, okay? No blind oracle visited my crib or some arcane shit like that. I'm just a kid from suburbia with normal folks and an aptitude for all things tech. That's it."

Flynn unfolded from the couch and took slow steps toward me, all the while fixing me with a stern stare.

"You're either lying to me or you are completely oblivious."

"I'm not lying!"

His eyes lost focus. Flynn seemed to be looking past me. "It's there. Power, light, connection. It courses through you at a trillion cycles per second."

"I. Am not. A mage!" I hissed.

He took my hand, his grip inhumanly strong. Once again the tattoos on his arms flashed to life, but this time, another glow appeared. The veins in my own hand flickered at first, like a short circuit. Then a white light mapped out the capillaries and blood vessels up to my shirtsleeves.

Magic boiling the air, the world shimmered and pulsed. Colors, pathways, filaments tying every atom to one another. As if for the first time, I *saw* Flynn.

Orange beams raced through him, pumping where blood ought to be. Glinting over his flesh, I finally understood what I'd long mistaken for piercings were cybernetic implants. Machines. I could see them working to power his muscles, his nerves. I could read all of the lines of him, all of the glyphs and spells he'd woven together to create a functional body.

I'd never known, never even guessed. Flynn was more than just a technomage—a being in constant communion with machines and electronics. His true nature pulsed before me in a beautiful dance of humanity and machine. A digital angel, a hybrid of flesh and information, of meme and genome.

Slack-jawed, I stared at him.

"Oh," I whispered. "Oh, Flynn."

He may as well have been naked before me, and I saw it play out over the synapses that made his thoughts. In baring himself this way, he'd given me the greatest secret—the greatest gift—he possessed.

Flynn regarded me with glowing amber eyes. "Even now, when I've shown you all I am, you deny it? You hide yourself from me?"

My own white light arced across my shoulders and flowed down my other arm. As if downloading a feed from Flynn's eyes, I could see myself, haloed and shining. Flesh glimmered with signals to and from my brain, to my other organs. My heart beat like a piston, and every other cell in my body responded. Everything in perfect order.

"You won't let me in," he said, face wrinkling with disappointment.

Again, through his vision, I saw myself, luminous save for a thick black band around my neck. Like a dam, this dark collar blocked the flow of power. I *needed* that dancing energy. I could taste it on my tongue. I craved more of it. I ached for it as if devouring it would make me whole.

I reached for my throat, fingers finding nothing but my rapid pulse beneath the moist flesh. "What is it?" I asked, breathless.

In a bird-like movement, Flynn's head cocked to the side. "Not yours?"

Words failed me. Constant messages flooded my senses. I reeled beneath the pressure, unable to form whole sentences. "Not welcome," I sputtered.

"It's a binding," Flynn said. His voice came out oddly modulated like a techno-pop tune. "Magical obstruction restraining your abilities. Dampening your energy."

It was as if the black band became sentient and understood I wanted it gone. As soon as I processed the thought of removing it, the thing seemed to tighten around my throat. I gasped for air, fingers scrambling at my skin seeking the physical choker.

"Want it off."

Sweat beaded my brow as I pooled as much of the delicious current as I could, shaping it into a ball of white-hot emotion.

"Want..." I said. "Want...to be..."

Swelling with my will, the ball of power surged, and as it did the pressure behind the binding grew. Tiny hairline fractures began to appear in the dark collar. Flynn's energy swarmed me, forcing its way through the cracks to widen the gaps I'd created.

"Say it," he urged. "Say it and make it so."

"I want to be free!"

My hands clasped over something solid and cold around my throat. With a guttural yell, I ripped off the collar. Blinding light and a rush of power filled my entire body with warmth, ecstasy, and contentment. I felt whole. Sated. I closed my eyes and let the bliss wash over me.

As boiling energies calmed, the lights pumping through each of us dimmed. Drowsy, I looked at Flynn. I sensed the current there, beneath his flesh, as a steady hum of life, magic, and thought in perfect sync. He still held both of my hands in his.

"I didn't know, Cat," he said softly. "All this time I thought you'd built up a firewall to shield yourself. And the binding...I thought you knew." His eyes glistened with pity and contrition. "I'm sorry."

"What just happened?" Marius asked.

"I wish I knew," I murmured.

Gently stroking my face, Flynn answered for me. "Someone bound her powers, stunted her growth. We broke the binding."

Still reeling and overwhelmed from the truths I'd seen, I whispered, "Thank you."

I never believed myself to be anything more than a vanilla mortal who'd gotten her heart caught in a particularly vicious meat grinder.

Apparently, I was wrong.

This geeky kid had graduated, and a new world opened before me.

"I've had powers this whole time?"

"Looks like," Flynn said with a wry smile.

"How'd that happen?"

"Some are born to greatness," he sighed, gesturing to himself "Others…"

His voice trailed off as he eyed Marius.

"Well, then there are just others. But you, Cat! This is amazing!" Flynn's face spread into a wide grin. "I have so much to show you."

"Oh, for fuck's sake, would you two get a room?" Marius chided. "We have work to do."

I whipped around to smack him with some snarky retort, but I tripped over my own feet. My head spun, and my stomach rolled. Limbs flabby, I melted into the couch again. Across the room, the bastard satyr snickered. Flynn, though, put the chai in my hand and guided it up to my lips.

"It happens," he said quietly. "Lesson number one, grasshopper: you can't get something for nothing. Technomancy can knock your body down a few notches. Get some rest or something to eat and you should be okay soon."

I sipped the hot tea and took deep breaths. "I've never seen you fall all over yourself like you've just run a marathon."

"You're new to it," he said, smoothing my hair back from my face.

"Like anything else, practice builds up stamina. These are senses and abilities that have always been in you. Like your body was built to walk upright, it just took your muscles a bit to learn the steps. You'll catch up."

"If I'm going to need a nap after rebooting a computer, I think I'll pass on the super powers."

Flynn smirked. "Little stuff like that shouldn't be too taxing. Turning on a light, unlocking a door, starting a car—all easy tricks. We'll play, though. You'll be opening an interface with your mind in no time."

"Right now turning on a light with my hand seems like a Herculean task. I can't even imagine how I would do it with my mind."

He rolled his eyes at me. "Come on. Let's try something simple."

"Now?"

"No time like the present."

Marius barked out a laugh. "She can't even stand, let alone work magic."

I glared at him, and Flynn gave me a knowing look. "Fine. Where do I start?" I asked.

Giddy, Flynn flew out of his seat and bounced across the room to Marius. "Excuse me. Need to borrow this." In a blur of tattoos, Flynn swiped Marius's cell phone out of the satyr's pocket.

"Now wait just a minute," Marius protested.

Flynn plopped next to me again and took my hand in his, laying the phone across my palm. "Turn it on."

"How?"

Flynn beamed. "You'll know."

"That's not very helpful."

"Shut up and try it, Cat!"

I looked at the dark screen and black plastic in front of me. At first it was nothing more than a commonplace object. Dead as a stone. After a moment, though, a picture began to form in my mind. A tiny spark of life bloomed into being, and with a snap of static I could see the nervous system of this inert object. The battery glowed like liquid moonlight and the circuitry reminded me of dim stars.

I gasped.

Flynn's voice, low and comforting, came from a distance. "Good. Now what are you going to do?"

"Make constellations," I whispered. I didn't even understand what I meant until the glittering points of light spread out feathery tendrils to one another. Shapes formed: a microprocessor, a memory card, speakers, a microphone. A blueprint of sorts lay in my palm, empty of color.

Paint inside the lines, I thought. Using awareness as a brush, I dipped into the pool of lithium power and traced through the schematic. In my hand, the flat screen pulsed, and the phone powered up with a merry chime.

I drew in a deep, refreshing breath.

"I told you," Flynn whispered.

"Holy shit," I said.

I tossed the phone to Marius who then inspected it.

"You didn't change the language or erase my numbers, did you?"

"No," I growled. "I didn't mess with your precious black book."

Flynn smiled. "I did."

"You cheeky bastard!"

While Marius clicked through his phone looking for errors, Flynn asked, "How do you feel? Worse? Better?"

I took a moment to check in with my body and mind. Though I should have been gummy-eyed and falling down with exhaustion, I felt clear and clean. I wouldn't be leaping tall buildings in a single bound or anything, but I was alert and awake enough that I could go for a few more hours.

"A little better," I said. "Oddly enough."

"Like I said, little stuff like this shouldn't be any more exhausting than clicking a mouse. Harder things, though, like interfaces and tapping into power supplies, that stuff can knock the wind out of you for a while."

"This is wild."

Flynn nodded and smiled. "Do you need to crash here tonight?"

I wanted to stay with Flynn and discover this unearthed facet of myself. My excitement for all I could learn and be, though, took a backseat to my anger that someone had kept it all from me. It wasn't hard to guess who'd worked that bit of magical fuckery.

There would be time for learning later. My soul was up for grabs to the god with the best hand, and no one was going to hold me back again.

"Later," I said. "Right now, I have a goddess to find."

CHAPTER ELEVEN
"One Hot Minute"

Back in the car with Marius behind the wheel, I should have been exhausted. Instead, my mind raced, trying to put together everything I'd learned tonight.

I am a technomage, I thought gleefully. I traced back over memories of times I'd fixed something that should've been irreparable. How many times had I resurrected old clocks or computers? How often had I walked into a job and known immediately what was wrong with the system and precisely how to fix it? I understood now, that was part of my gift.

And someone had tried to keep that from me.

Someone bound her powers, stunted her growth, Flynn had said. It was just one more way Eris could lord her power over me in our already lopsided relationship. Add it to the list of things I'd bitch about when I finally got in the same room with her. My fury ebbed, giving way to the childlike elation that came with these new sensations.

Las Vegas looked as she had a few hours ago. She wore the dark night around her glittering form like a silken robe. However, if I focused—shifted my awareness as if trying to look through a reflection—I could see tiny strands of energy connecting the city. I saw the electricity coursing through it like a river. Even the Mercedes itself sang to me as Marius sped back toward the Strip. I watched the way currents flowed into the radio. Streams of light flowing like water from one mechanism to the next.

What if I just…pinched it here?

Like a kid trying to levitate like a Jedi, I focused my mind on the current of sound coming from the car. I stretched out my new sense and interrupted the flow as if I put my hand under the stream from a running faucet. I did this over and over then turned my attention to other little tasks, like playing with the windshield wipers. When Marius glared at me, I stopped and snickered. Then I locked and unlocked the doors in perfect rhythm.

"So," Marius said, "does this mean you get to go to Hogwarts next year?"

"I'm not sure what it means. I'll deal with it after I figure this mess out."

Marius nodded and kept his attention on the road. Tonight had changed some of my opinions about him. He'd saved my life—that was worth something. He even didn't fuss too much as I explored my newfound power. I looked at Marius and saw someone new, as I had after the shark attack. Someone worth further inspection.

"Thank you, by the way" I said. "For saving me back at the apartment."

"*Pfft.* Nothing more than enlightened self-interest on my part."

"Will you shut up for two seconds? I'm trying to pay you a compliment here. Seriously, Marius, if you hadn't thrown me the hammer when you did, I'd probably be dead right now."

"Hammer?"

"The hammer I used to—" A flash of gory memory warded off additional comment. "The hammer. It fell down next to me and gave me a way to defend myself. You threw it to me."

"I did nothing of the sort. For one, I was a bit occupied with Porky to bother with you. For another, hammers are for working stiffs and are, therefore, most definitely not my style."

If he hadn't passed me the tool, who had? I was about to ask him, but he kept prattling on.

"You also may have noticed I prefer my saber, and you'd better believe I wouldn't have thrown *that* to you."

Ah yes, the sword he pulled from thin air. "Where did you get that thing anyway?"

"Hephaestus made it for me."

I gaped at the satyr. "Heph—*the* Hephaestus?"

"The very same. God of the forge, blacksmith of Olympus himself. Heph has a bit of a problem with the ladies, you see. Well, one night, I took him out and got him laid. Triplets, too," he said, eyes glazing over with memories. Soon, though, his expression grew grim. A frown of frustration pulled his mouth. Was that sad nostalgia?

"Damn, that was a good night," he breathed. "Fantastic wine."

The moment of frailty passed. Marius's casual, aloof mask realigned over his features. There was a finality to his silence.

"So, you're saying you took him out and helped him get some action, and he was so grateful he made you a sword?"

Marius flashed a cheeky grin. "I'm a spectacular wingman. I could probably work the miracle of getting a woman to notice your friend back there." The humor faded from his grin, leaving behind stony malice. He rubbed at the pinkish lines on his neck, reminders of Flynn's grip.

"I think Flynn can do well enough for himself," I said.

"Really?" he asked. Marius turned the Mercedes south onto the Strip. "Have you shagged him then?"

"Flynn? No way!"

"Why the bloody hell not? He's protective enough of you. You'd think he'd peed on you and marked you as his territory."

"Ew," I said, shaking off the mental image. "Look, Flynn is a friend. He and I don't think of each other like that."

"Well, whatever it was you two were doing there, it seemed to be quite intimate. Breathing all heavy, incapable of forming complete sentences. I thought he'd need a cigarette afterward."

Marius shifted in his seat, and his chest puffed out ever so slightly.

Was he…? No way.

"Are you *jealous*, Marius?"

"Of him?" He chuffed out a caustic laugh. "Why should I be?" There was bitterness in his stare as he peered out into the night.

Jealous or not, he had a point. What *had* we been doing? I mean, Flynn and I had touched each other before. Friendly hugs, a back rub or two, the absent contact of nudging or accidentally bumping into one another. What made this time different?

He wanted it to be different, I thought. He'd wanted me to see, to understand. His intent transformed a simple touch into so much more. My thoughts spun over the revelation that I'd been bound by someone, that choice taken from me.

Speaking of…

"Hey, how did you get into hock with Eris?" I asked Marius.

Taking his eyes off the road, he glanced at me with genuine surprise. "You honestly want to know?"

I nodded.

Marius seemed to think about it, and once again, I could almost see past the illusion he clung to. Fissures in the satyr's façade began to open. Finally, when he decided he could let me in, he blew out a puff of air. "I'm cursed."

"Cursed?" I asked. Immediately, a swarm of cartoons and fairy tales buzzed through my brain. Instead of sleeping princesses or dancing beasts, I imagined Marius in those roles. "Like *cursed* cursed?"

Marius nodded. "Zeus laid a punishment on me. Eris promised to lift it."

I tried to hide my shock. I may have been naive about the gods, but Marius would've known better. Wouldn't he?

"How long have you worked for her?" I asked.

Marius silenced me with a level stare. I chewed on this new information for a while. As we closed in on the Strip, the buildings became brighter and my enhanced senses flared. Distracted by the brilliance of such familiar things, I zoned out and our conversation fell into a lull. Soon, though, my curiosity got the better of me. "What did you do?"

"Hmm?"

"To piss off Zeus. What did you do?"

"Oh, that." He eased to a stop, the traffic light painting his face red. "A tryst with a particularly delectable nymph near Athens. Fantastic legs."

I blinked in confusion. "Isn't that what satyrs do?"

"Often," he said. "And with great gusto. However, it seems this nymph was one of the god's personal favorites. Zeus shares about as well as a hungry bear. The rest is history."

"So you're screwed because of who you screwed?" I asked. "That's rich. So, what's the curse? How did he exact his vengeance upon thee?"

Marius's face grew grim and cold. "Nothing of interest to someone like you. Besides, at least I have impeccable taste and control my impulses enough not to go blathering on about love."

I sighed, letting my head fall back on the seat. "Are we there yet?"

"Almost," he said. "I don't see what you hope to accomplish by going to Eris's office. It's not as if she lives there."

Chewing my lip, I watched the casino loom into view, its lights a beacon for the world to see. "It's a place to start."

Marius swept the Mercedes down a soft slope leading into the parking garage below the hotel. He flashed a pass to a weary security guard and pulled into a side lot reserved for executives.

As we made our way to the elevator, our steps echoed in the low-ceilinged garage. Marius still wore his suit slacks and black shirt. He'd taken off his tie and opened the first couple of buttons. With his sleeves rolled up and his typical indifferent gait, he looked like it was perfectly normal to be going to the office at zero dark thirty.

On the elevator, he sagged against the back railing. Pinching the bridge of his nose, his face puckered for a second then split into a leonine yawn. "I'll be glad when this is over. I could use a few hours of sleep and a massage from Swedish triplets."

"Past your bedtime, Marius?"

"Lousy date. You've kept me up and running about all night, and what do I get for my troubles? Attacked by some deity's minions and throttled by a geek with a god complex. You could at least have had the courtesy to invite me to watch you slink out of your dress." He closed his eyes and tilted his head back against the wall. "I bet you won't so much as offer me breakfast."

In the years we'd worked together, I had rarely spent this much time with him at one sitting. Now, in light of all we'd been through, I was seeing more than a snarky goat. I saw something human about him. God help me, I'd started to like the bastard. In spite of myself, I smiled. I may have even giggled.

"What's so funny?" he asked.

I shook my head. "It's nothing."

"Nothing, she says. I'm beginning to think that a date is precisely what you need."

"Oh, really? That's the magic that will fix all my woes?"

Marius eyed me up and down. "It's a place to start. You need a sleepless night…and not one where you're running from gods and monsters. You, Catherine Sharp," he said, taking the few steps toward me, "need a *real* date."

I laughed uncomfortably and tried to slide past him, to put some space between our bodies. He edged forward. With an arm on each side of my body, he wedged me against the wall.

"You need someone to seduce you within an inch of your small and sorry life. A night with good wine and the promise of soft kisses. Perhaps," he said, his breath tracing warm lines over my cheeks, "a dance beneath the moonlight."

His fingertips glided over my arm. My head swam with his closeness. The heat of his body so near to mine called to my blood, and my skin flushed. The scent of him—a clean, spicy cologne and natural musk—set my senses swirling. My breaths came in shaky, shallow draughts.

His eyes held mine captive. "Spend the hours until dawn touching and in a tangle of pleasure and silk sheets," he purred.

Marius gently lifted my chin, and my stomach knotted with anticipation. This wasn't some illusion as it had been in my apartment. This was real. Nerves standing at attention, heart pounding in my chest, I waited, breathless.

His voice was little more than a whisper. "Yes, I think that is exactly what you need."

Marius tilted his head. As if it were the most natural conclusion, I closed my eyes, ready to welcome his mouth over mine.

With a polite *ding*, the elevator came to a stop at the penthouse. Marius pushed away, leaving me waiting and wanting. Confused, I stared after him as he strutted down the hall.

Looking over his shoulder, he called out, "Are you coming?"

No, I thought, *you just left*. I mentally smacked myself for even humoring the idea. In an instant the heat of desire shifted into a swell of embarrassment and unfulfilled resentment.

I shoved away from the wall and stalked after him. "That was a dirty trick."

Marius's swagger went all the way to his wicked grin, but he said nothing.

I followed him down the familiar hallway. I knew this place, but at this obscene hour, it looked different. Quiet and abandoned, it reminded me of an amusement park after-hours. The door to the goddess's office was closed as always. Marius tapped the wall, and a panel slid aside to reveal a touchpad similar to the one at YmFy. The satyr's fingers twitched over the keys as he pecked out his password. A red light blinked and a buzzer sounded. Marius frowned.

"Odd," he said.

"What is it?"

Marius poked at the keypad again with the same result. "My code isn't working." Reaching into his pocket, Marius pulled out a small gold card and slid it into the slot to the side of the keypad.

Red light.

Buzzer.

"Bloody hell," he said. "The security codes have been changed. I can't get in. I don't suppose you could make yourself useful and talk to the computer?"

I shouldered him aside and looked at the keys, intent on hacking my way through the system with variant code. However, the moment I stepped up to the wall, all ideas of hacking fell to the side. My vision shifted so I could see the other version of the world, the one made of filament and light. Like red-hot wire, lines streaked through the walls, around the windows and doors. Capillaries from the touchpad traced to cameras, through shared arteries into the beating heart of the security system in a server room many floors below.

I saw the entire network.

Like electric fire, the keypad itself seemed to swirl with red, orange, and white. Strands tangled in a snarl of flashing luminescence. Without thinking about how or why, I put one hand on the touchpad. While the screen flickered, the lines that should have gone into the keys, transferred into my other hand, held flat against the wall. Now that I had a hold of all of those threads, I could sort them.

Red with red. Orange with orange. Like untying knots in a bundle of string. I don't know how I understood what I needed to do—I just *knew*. Beneath my fingertips, chaos became order.

The lock opened with a resonant *clack*, and Marius eyed me. I couldn't tell if he was scared or impressed. I realized I wouldn't have minded if both were true.

He reached out and turned the knob. The door graciously gave way.

As he took long strides into the office, he said, "Helpful trick, that."

I lifted my hands from the wall, releasing the energy I held, and disengaged from the building's systems. As I did, I sagged. My limbs felt like limp noodles. I wasn't tired per se, but working with these new skills left me deflated. I staggered in behind Marius.

"I didn't know you could sing," he said.

"Huh?"

"And so eloquent, too," he muttered. "When you were doing the thing with the wall?" He sighed. "You were singing. It sounded surprisingly lovely."

I rolled a shoulder. I'd been told before that I hum while I work, but I've never noticed it. "Thanks," I murmured, joining him at the goddess's desk.

A simple piece of paper lay there with a few words written in a flowing hand:

Gather my trophies. Claim your reward.

Taking the letter from the desk, I turned it over, reading it again and again. "This is it?" I asked. "This is all the help we're going to get?"

"I don't know what you expected," Marius droned. "A treasure map?"

"More than this," I said, tossing the note back to the desk. I dragged my hands through my hair. Between Marius's con job in the elevator, the magic with the security system, and an utter lack of direction with Eris's little scavenger hunt, I didn't know if I was frisky or exhausted. Frustrated. That was a damn certainty.

I glowered at Marius for the little stunt in the elevator. Here I was, seconds away from letting him kiss me into oblivion and not so much as a single hair seemed to be on edge for him. Did he feel nothing? Was it just a game? *Curse him!*

That's when the idea hit me…

This curse of his. What was it? How would I get revenge on a satyr? I began listing little occurrences—his body against mine as we danced, in the elevator—and putting puzzle pieces together. He talked a good game, but when we'd been dancing together I hadn't felt the slightest nudge of actual arousal. What if that was it? What if that was how Zeus had cursed him?

Testing a theory, I grabbed Marius by his shoulders, pulled him to face me.

"Hey," I said. I took a deep breath, snatched fistfuls of his shirt and yanked him to me. As I pressed my lips to his, Marius made a muffled noise that sounded something like *merp!* His body went rigid against mine, but I was pretty sure it was out of surprise rather than excitement.

He pushed away and gaped at me. "What are you doing?"

I almost had it figured out. I just needed one more piece. "What? Suddenly you disapprove?"

For a moment, I'd done the impossible. I'd rendered the satyr speechless. Disbelief sparkled in his eyes, but his lips hitched into a lopsided grin. Letting out a breath he'd been holding, he chuffed, "You're just trying to get back at me, Catherine."

Okay, if I was going to confirm my suspicion, I had to pull out all the stops and make a particularly large bluff of my own. I closed the distance between us and slowly slid my hands up his chest. Marius took a couple of quick steps back but found himself pinned between Eris's desk and my insistent body.

I rocked my hips against him. "Am I?"

The satyr bit his lower lip. "You're not serious."

"You're sure about that?" I waited for the more intriguing parts of his body to respond to me, but they didn't. Sliding my hips against his, I leaned in, lips taunting the threat of a kiss. Still, nothing beneath the belt so much as trembled. When he turned his head away from me I took his earlobe into my teeth and gave a gentle but hungry tug.

He hissed as if I'd burned him and shoved me away with both hands. "Enough!"

He stalked away to the other side of the room, and I gawked. Holy shit.

"That's it, isn't it?" I asked. "That's how Zeus cursed you."

The glare he tossed me couldn't have been darker if I'd forced him to eat bile and cancerous pus. Rather than answer, he clenched his jaw.

"You're...you're impotent," I said softly.

Marius's eyes flashed with ferocity. "Impotent? You think a god with infinite imagination would stop at merely rendering a satyr impotent?"

I swallowed a lump of shame. Had I really needed to know this? Had it been worth putting him through this humiliation?

He sighed with resignation. "I feel no pleasure," he said, voice quiet but hard.

"None?"

"Oh, sure, I can get a good laugh out of watching you make an idiot of yourself, but that hardly counts for much, does it?"

"None?" I asked again, this time amazed. "So, you can't have sex?"

"Certainly not for lack of desire," he snapped. "And, if you must know, it doesn't stop there. That lovely sense of intoxication you were floating on earlier in the evening? Restricted. The feeling you get after a damn good meal? Off limits. I can't so much as enjoy a cool breeze on a hot day. Which, by the way, makes summers here murder."

I took a moment to wrap my head around that concept. No pleasure? From what I'd learned, pleasure flowed through a satyr's veins like lifeblood. Sex, drugs, and rock 'n' roll were the appetizers on this creature's menu. To not feel any of it? To take no joy whatsoever from life?

And worse, Eris chained him to Las Vegas! Pleasure hawks itself on every street corner, and when one well runs dry there's always another show or club.

Now, after all this time of working with Marius, I understood the hold Eris had over him. I longed for my freedom, and I'd been in service to the goddess for less than a decade. The promise of being able to feel fulfilled once again? She may as well lock up his soul, too.

For the first time, I felt well and truly sorry for Marius.

"How long has it been?" I asked.

His stare darkened. "Does it matter?"

"I suppose not." I pondered his situation a bit more. "Okay, so if you can't follow through, why act the playboy? Why the thing in the elevator and the head game back at my apartment?"

"It's hardly public knowledge that I can't—." Frustrated, he dragged his hands over his goatee. "Look, I have a reputation to maintain. A little bit of magic, a kiss or two, a little over and under, and I can make anyone believe that I'm the best shag they'll ever have. If Eris decides to lift my curse tomorrow, I'm already set up for business. No one need know anything to the contrary."

My stomach twisted at the thought of this sad imitation of joy his life had become.

Then, I blurted, "You mean you can't even rub one out? No wonder you're such a snarky bastard."

"Oh, do shut up!"

"Sorry, Marius. I wasn't trying to get a rise out of you." That time I snickered.

He raised his brow then grinned mirthlessly. "I'm so glad she wagered your soul in the game. Having to deal with you now that you know would be insufferable."

Shit. I'd gotten so swept up in deciphering Marius, that I'd almost forgotten my larger problem.

I glanced around the office. "There's got to be something here that can tell us where to find the other gods."

"What? You think the Lady keeps a Rolodex with the addresses of her poker buddies?" He snorted and let out a wheeze of laughter. "I thought you were supposed to be intelligent."

I turned away from Marius and stopped short. My breath caught in my chest as I gazed out the window at the panoramic view of Las Vegas. A shadow passed over the city, a black hole floating over the dazzling splendor.

At first, I thought an airplane was coming in low on its descent into McCarran Airport. That idea evaporated when the shadow banked sharply and came about. A massive bird, black as tar, spread its wings and glided north toward Eris's penthouse windows.

Toward me.

Cold dread slipped down my spine and into my already weak knees. Without taking my eyes off of the inky shape, I backed away from the windows and reached out for Marius's arm.

"Come on," I said. "We need to get out of here."

"What is it?"

"There's something out there."

He followed my gaze and looked out onto Sin City. "I don't see anything."

The colossal bird swooped up, exposing its full form to us. For a terrifying instant the lights of Vegas were blotted out by the body of the creature, easily ten feet tall. With its wings stretched wide, scaly feet tucked in against its body, the thing climbed into the night. I may have imagined it, but I thought I heard the sound of groaning metal as it landed on the roof above us.

Marius's stare locked onto the ceiling and the color drained from his face. "Scratch that. Let's make ourselves scarce."

Without another word, we bolted out of the office and down the hall. Marius reached the elevator first and punched the call button. Once we were inside and on our way back down to the garage, I looked to Marius.

"What was that thing?"

"I have a few ideas, and none of them are good."

"Care to elaborate?"

Eyes tracking along the ceiling, Marius answered, "Perhaps it could wait until I don't run the risk of conjuring it by speaking its name."

We'd traveled a few floors when the elevator lurched to a stop. The doors opened, but no one was there.

"Hello?" Marius called into the dim hallway.

Answered by a flicker in the overhead light, Marius pushed a button and the doors closed. The car, however, didn't resume its descent. Clicking and creaking, the elevator settled in the shaft, immobile.

"I don't like this," he said, jabbing at the button to get us to the garage.

"Let me take a look," I said.

I stepped to him and began to open my senses to the control panel when the air cracked. A flash, a small *fzzt* sound, and the compartment plunged into darkness. Without power traveling to the car, the elevator became null to my new senses. A dark void surrounded me. Trembling, I suppressed the urge to shift my back to the wall.

"I need to look at the control panel. Do you have a lighter or something?"

I could feel Marius turning around beside me. He whispered something, and a small, sphere of light appeared over his palm.

"Excellent," he muttered.

The amber ball floated into the air, passed over his shoulder, and stopped over the dual rows of buttons. It hovered there, flickering like a candle.

"Helpful trick, that," I murmured, echoing Marius's earlier comment.

He gestured to the control panel. "There you are—a little bit of my magic to help you do yours." The satyr tried to hide his fear, but the arrogance had fled his voice, leaving it thin and dry. His words spilled out, "Now, if you'd be so kind as to hum a few bars and get us out of this elevator, I would really appreciate it."

I put a hand to the wall and searched the control panel, but all I could think about was my desire to get away from the huge bird.

That's when the thing's long beak slashed through the roof like a knife forged in Hell.

CHAPTER TWELVE
"Higher Ground"

I flattened myself against the wall with a shriek of pure terror. The creature's beak, as long as my arm and whip thin, tapered to a gleaming point. As it retracted through the roof I couldn't imagine how either of us would survive an encounter with that wicked edge. In the wan light of Marius's sphere, I could make out the seam in the ceiling. As obsidian claws curled around the warped metal, I caught the flash of a single, red eye.

"Pan's balls!" Marius shouted as he fell back across the compartment. The satyr came up in a low crouch and drew his saber with his right hand.

Seeing the razor-sharp blade of the sword threw my mind into a torrent of commands. The memories of the shark coming to the same end made my stomach churn and my legs wobble, but it also encouraged me. While something in the back of my mind quailed and screamed, the rest of me focused and searched for a weapon. Something told me no hammers would fall from the sky this time.

With a trembling hand I yanked open the maintenance hatch in the control panel. Shadows fell over the twisting cables and circuits, making it seem as though the maintenance box was full of writhing snakes. I needed the little ball to drop so I could see properly.

"Lower," I hissed. To my surprise, the orb pulsed once and floated down in compliance. "Um, thanks." With enough light, I set to work, trying to get the elevator to talk to the power grid. After, we could chat about getting us to the garage.

The metal ceiling squealed again as the creature's claws peeled it back. Marius grunted and his blade slashed at empty air. Each time one of his cuts came close to the mark, the bird let out a series of piercing complaints. However, the satyr didn't score any direct hits.

The power began to flow through the control panel with the sluggish rhythm of an old music box as I coaxed it. The cables sucked up the current irrigating the parched circuit board, but the energy quickly ebbed away. I tried again, forcing my will into the dead connections. Once more, the jerking rhythm started but ground quickly to a halt.

I kicked the wall and growled, "Work, goddammit!"

The lights above had been trashed by the bird, but all of the lights in the button panel flared to life. Percussive maintenance for the win!

Energy hummed through the car, and above us the bird shrieked again.

"Garage!" I yelled at the elevator.

The brakes released and it shuddered. Marius stumbled, the sword cutting wide and slashing the bird's cheek. Dripping black ichor into the car, the bird let out a hideous wail. Thunderously loud, the beat of its wings filled the air and metal tore again.

The car picked up speed.

"Slow down," I insisted. "Slow. Down!"

With a plaintive whine, the power drained from circuits beneath my fingers. I slouched against the wall. In an instant, Marius stood behind me.

"What's happening?"

"We're falling!" I yelled.

"Anything you can do to stop it?"

"No, the board is fried."

Over our heads the bird let out a rasping caw as it thrust its beak down. One of the thick cables snapped, and the sides of the compartment began to rattle. Just before the flickering orb of light petered out, Marius set his face to stony concentration.

I strained to see, but darkness had fallen over the elevator.

Above, the bird continued to stab at us and tear the ceiling with its ferocious talons. It let out a guttural purr like some gigantic pigeon. Its wings flapped with the sound of snapping flags in a windstorm.

Marius was close enough for me to reach out and touch, but I couldn't see him. His voice, though, joined the din of sounds pressing on my ears. As he chanted, murmuring again in some arcane language, my stomach quivered. Energy swarmed the compartment as Marius called up his own brand of power.

The elevator doors began to shake. Air whistled and whipped around the hole in the ceiling. A feather brushed against my face, and I screamed. Sinking to the floor, I huddled myself into a protective ball, all the while fighting away the mental image of the beak spearing through my spine.

With a cacophonous lurch, the car came to a stop. All at once, the bird squawked, Marius growled in pain, and he hit the floor. Groping blindly, I found the seam in the smooth metal and forced my fingers between the doors.

"Catherine!" Marius called. "Open the goddamn door!"

No sooner had he said it than light from the parking garage began to stream into the shredded car. Still in a crouch, I moved forward, but the satyr's strong hands pushed at my bottom, and I fell to the concrete. The two of us tumbled out of the elevator. I felt a hollow pop and a warm, wet feeling as my knee exploded with pain. My palms scraped along the concrete, and I tasted blood. Chancing a glance back, I saw why I'd fallen. The car had stopped on a cushion of air a few feet off the ground.

Standing up, Marius tossed his mane and let out a snarl. The car smashed down. Like a limp shadow, the bird fell from the ceiling and collapsed in a heap of feathers. I didn't wait to figure out if it was dead.

Pushing myself to my feet, I put too much weight on my knee and stumbled into Marius. He hissed in pain.

"Shit," I said. "You're bleeding."

"Bugger! This is one of my best shirts," he snapped, holding the soaked fabric to a gash on his biceps. "What about you? Did it nip you?"

I shook my head. "Just a little wobbly."

"Can you run?"

"I can make it to the car."

"Come on then." Marius grabbed my wrist, and I took off at a pained trot toward the silver Mercedes.

Behind us, the bird let out a peal of anger. I shouldn't have looked but I did.

Framed in the bulging doors of the ruined elevator, the creature hunched over, its sharp beak scraping the ground. Turning its head, it flashed one red eye at us and rasped again.

"Bugger!" Marius cursed.

We ran. The Mercedes—blessedly close thanks to the executive parking—gleamed like a mirage. Marius let go of me, and we flanked the car. The moment I touched the car, the locks popped open.

"You're handy, you know?" Marius said as he slid behind the wheel.

With a screech of tires, we hauled ass out of the parking garage, the bird taking flight in our wake. Even at this obscene hour, people were still on the Strip. Drunk—or wishing to the gods that they were—revelers milled about on the street in a distracted haze. That is, until a car trailing a gigantic fucking bird came careening toward them.

Marius dodged a few scattering pedestrians and got us back onto the Strip. We didn't make it far when the oversized crow slammed into the trunk, and we spun out of control. Tires screeching on the pavement, we ended up on the opposite side of the median. A tour bus, its horn blaring, swerved into the next lane and barreled down the Strip. We'd been caught in a skid. As he tried to right the car, Marius took out a bank of newspaper machines, finally coming to a stop just shy of the Mirage's famous waterfall.

While some bystanders cheered or gathered close to gawk, most fled.

Marius fought with the key, grinding the engine, but I knew the Mercedes wouldn't start. She needed a mechanic, not a magician.

"We have to run," I said, my voice as loose and shaky as my limbs.

Marius peered out the back window. I watched the rearview and saw the bird, dazed and wounded, pick itself up in an ungainly way.

He glanced at my knee. "Can you make it?"

"Do I have a choice?"

"Fair enough." He pushed out of the car. I grabbed my bag, hitched it over my shoulders, and started down the Strip.

I hadn't made it more than a handful of steps when Marius grabbed at me by the shoulders. "Wait!"

Ahead of us, right where I would have run, three people stood bathed in the streetlight. All of them were lithe and ethereally beautiful, like elves or angels. The oak leaves tattooed on their flesh gave them away as servants of the Fae. Out of a swath of shadows, Dahlia stalked forward, heels clicking on the pavement. She'd traded her evening gown for red leather.

"Cat," she said, "I tried to warn you. You should've run far away from here. Now, I have no choice but to do as my master bids."

Behind her the waterfall surged with energy, and the liquid began to course like blood, crimson and thick.

"Oh? Puck is pulling your strings now rather than the queens? Wow. That's a demotion, isn't it?"

She ignored my slight. "You need to come with us. The Fae request your services."

When I spoke, my voice quivered with fear and rage. "If I refuse?"

Her lips peeled back into a leer. "You will offend us."

"Like I've never done that," I scoffed. "Sorry, I'm not available."

Dahlia's eyes went cold. "Suit yourself." She called an order to the faery on her left, a blond man in artfully shredded clothes. "Kill the satyr."

The faery had taken two steps when the devil bird plunged its beak into his chest. A screech of panic filled the air as the few witnesses left on the street took off at a run. As the blond twitched and gurgled, the bird sank its talons into his abdomen and used its victim's body as leverage while it feasted on the faery's still-beating heart.

I could only watch in stunned horror. Even Dahlia seemed surprised, her icy mask cracking at the seams. Further, her eyes widened as fire scorched the air with a resonant roar. The Mirage's waterfall had transformed itself into an erupting volcano.

The dancing flames reached sinuously up into the night sky like the fluid arms of a dancer. Then, two of those blazing arms dipped down and pushed on the lip of the volcano. A figure rose into the night. The body of a woman made entirely of fire emerged, her flaming hair whipping in a dangerous wind. Her eyes, black as obsidian, focused on us as she lifted a hand.

Dahlia's mouth fell open. "The goddess stirs. Flee!"

As the faeries turned their backs on her, the volcano goddess—Pele—cast a burst of fire into the night that swallowed the one being mangled by the bird. With an indignant squawk, the bird flapped into the air and swooped to land dutifully on Pele's shoulder.

"That means us, too," Marius said. His arms flew around me, and he shoved me into a run. The faeries turned right and fled across the street while Marius and I pounded forward, away from the demon birds and volcanic sirens. Hot pain flared in my injured knee, and my breath came in gulps of burning acid. With his longer legs and super-human constitution, Marius pulled ahead of me.

I mustered the breath to call his name.

"Almost there," he shouted over his shoulder.

I started to ask what he considered to be *there*, but the slaps of my shoes changed to hollow *thunk*s as I left the concrete pavement and began running across the wooden gangplank leading up to the Treasure Island hotel. To my right, the Strip. To my left, a world sculpted to look like a seaside mission town. Two pirate ships made port in the manmade lagoon, casting shadows in the purple and blue floodlights.

Doubling over, holding the stitch in my side, I gasped for air. Every needle-sharp breath I heaved tore at my side. My knee throbbed. I wheezed as I tried to catch the satyr's attention. "Marius…"

Of course, he was barely winded. He stopped, turned, and plodded to where I leaned on the bridge. His eyes darted around, seeking out throats. "Are you all right?"

If I'd had the breath to spare I would have tossed him a snotty retort. I settled for an annoyed glare. His skin shone with a layer of sweat, and he'd lost his gold ribbon somewhere, leaving his hair free to fall around his face in a tousled, ebony mane.

I caught sight of his bloodied arm. "You?"

"Oh, this?" he asked, examining the wound. "Stings like a bitch, but the real travesty is that it ruined one of my best shirts."

I pushed out a weak laugh. "Your horns are showing."

"It happens from time to time. Not unlike tonight, those times often involve a lot of sweat and screaming. Maybe you'll see them again under better circumstances."

Rolling my eyes, I said, "Just give me a second, okay?"

Craning his neck to look back the way we came, Marius said, "I think our feathered friend has gone along with the goddess. I don't see them following us." He looked across the Strip. "They may have chased off the faeries for us."

"Or they led you right where I needed you to be."

Marius whirled around at the voice and pulled his sword from the ether at his side, ready for whatever came next. Blocking our way off the bridge stood a stocky man with a broad chest. The stranger's glossy black hair hung in a sheet down his back. Caramel skin and eyes the color of Kona coffee, he wore baggy cargo shorts, flip-flops, and a garish red aloha shirt. Around his neck was a fishhook carved of bleached bone.

As if I needed the confirmation, a warm trade wind seemed to blow over the surface of my apple brand. My voice was small as I spoke. "Maui?"

CHAPTER THIRTEEN
"If You Have to Ask"

As Maui nodded my body wanted nothing more than to collapse there, maybe melt through the wooden planks and into the lagoon below. But one should have a bit more spine when meeting a deity. I stretched to my full height and winced as my knee protested.

"You can lose the sword, man," Maui said to my companion. "I'm not here for a fight."

The two eyed one another—Marius wary, the god confident. Finally, Marius brought his sword hand to his left side, and the blade disappeared. His fingers twitched in the air as if he waited for an excuse to draw it again.

"Catherine Sharp, I presume?"

I nodded. "That's me."

The god grinned, the sun in his smile. "You surprised me, little *wahine*. Not many mortals survive an encounter with the *wakwak*."

"A what-what?"

"The bird. I'd been impressed you escaped the *kupua* at your home, but this?" He let out a resonant belly laugh. "You are damn lucky or blessed. Either way, I dig you. Eris has offered a choice prize indeed."

My eyes widened, and my knuckles popped as I tightened my fists. So this bastard *was* responsible for trashing my home. I bared my teeth. "You sent those monsters to my apartment? The shark things."

"*Kupua*. Yeah. On loan from a few of my friends."

"You destroyed my home!" I snarled. Fueled by my temper, I lunged forward but Marius caught my arm.

Maui didn't budge. "I'm sorry about that. My people will get to repairing it right away."

I snorted. "What, a gang of Hawaiian carpenters is just going to show up at my apartment and get to work? Right."

"*Menehune!*" Maui sang. He gave a whistle strong enough to summon a cab in New York City during rush hour. Seconds later, the grass at the end of the bridge rustled. Footsteps echoed over the wooden planks, and tiny shadows raced to meet the god.

Little people, pygmies, whatever name you give them, they were tiny versions of humans. With bronzed skin and dark hair, like the god himself, they wore black beads around their necks and leaves about their waists. Their hands and feet were chubby, like those of toddlers. Padding barefoot to Maui's side, the little folk—the *menehune*—stared at me and the satyr, obviously curious.

Maui squatted before the tallest of them—who was less than a yard high—and began to speak in the fluid vowels and glottal stops of his native language. He wagged a finger in gentle warning then flashed a radiant smile. The pygmy raised a fist and shouted some enthusiastic response. As he darted into the night, some of his kin followed.

The god stood. "They are excellent craftsmen. You'll see. Tomorrow morning your place will be good as new. Better even."

Marius stood straighter and glared down at the islander. "Do they sew?" he asked, holding out his torn sleeve.

I swatted him in the ribs.

"If Eris knew your true value," Maui said to me, "I doubt she would have so carelessly tossed you into our bet."

Now, I knew not to expect a straight answer from one of the gods of mayhem, but I was just tired enough to give it a shot. "What do you all want from me?"

Sirens began to wail as the police made their way to Marius's wrecked car. I looked over my shoulder to make sure none of them were headed our way. Breathalyzers work and I would've passed any test, but if I told a cop we'd been running away from a huge flesh-eating bird when we'd crashed on the Vegas Strip and fled the scene because faeries were chasing us? Yeah, that was a surefire way to get chucked into the drunk tank.

Marius licked his lips and shifted his stance, preparing to run.

Maui smiled. "The answer to this question is complex. Perhaps we could discuss this inside and away from those mundane lawmen?"

As the god extended a hand toward me, I jerked away.

"Catherine Sharp," the god said, "I'm not going to hurt you. Please, be my guest here. Take a room and rest. It is the least I can do."

"Do I have your word?" I asked.

Maui nodded. "You will be under my protection as long as you are within the hotel. I swear it."

Sagging with exhaustion, I reluctantly placed my hand in Maui's. Damn, did I look pale against his suntan.

"Come," he said with an easy grin, "let's talk story. Then you and your friend here can get some shut eye."

As the sirens drew closer and people flocked to gawk at the mysterious wreck in front of the Mirage, Maui led me into the hotel. Shuffling to downplay my bad knee, I didn't move quickly, but the god was kind enough to hold pace with me. Marius, on the other hand, was wound so tight I thought he might shoot around the lobby like a pinball. When we reached the elevator bank, I twitched as anxiety flooded my stomach.

"This one is safe," Maui said with a knowing wink.

"What, did you have the crow from hell on a remote control or something?"

He smiled. "Now that's an idea…"

Safe or not, I huddled in the corner. Marius took a place on the opposite side. While his body appeared loose and relaxed, his eyes darted between Maui and the doors. When the compartment opened again near the top floor, I got out as fast as my injured leg would allow. After a short walk down the hall, Maui stopped in front of a pair of doors and motioned to the key-reader near the knob.

"Would you please?" he asked.

I snorted. After all this shit he wanted me to pop a lock? Maybe I should quit my job and start a magic show like Penn and Teller. Placing my palm on the knob, I gently asked the machine to flip the lock. With a soft beep and the flash of a green light, it disengaged, and I opened the door. Cool, rich air-conditioning spilled out over me, and I swear the fluffy mattress and clean sheets sang to me, begging me to join them.

Maui spread his lips in a satisfied smile. "You've got a subtle touch." He gestured for me to enter. "*Wahine*, your room."

I stepped into the huge entryway and flipped the light switch. The room was a study in cool sophistication and subliminal seduction. To my right, a long, red sectional couch sidled up beside a sleek, black coffee table. To the left, the king-sized bed sat dressed in ivory sheets with a thread-count higher than Flynn's IQ. Red throw pillows decorated the bed simply, but with the bedside lamps angled like spotlights, it was obvious this room was for more than just sleeping.

Doors to the left of the bed led into a massive bathroom and vanity area. Silver fixtures and track lights accented the furniture. A small round table and chair set had been placed at the center of the floor-to-ceiling windows to maximize the epic view. Everything came in complimentary shades of crimson, ebony, and white.

With memories of the gigantic bird swooping over the city, I let my bag fall to the ground and immediately moved to close the curtains.

Bye-bye pirate ships moored in the lagoon. I refuse to see you in my nightmares.

For a brief moment, I entertained the notion that if it meant I got access to this room on a regular basis, working for Maui might not be such a bad proposition. Then I remembered this would not be worth my soul no matter how deep the hot tub.

By the time I finished surveying the suite, Maui and Marius stood in the room. Marius appraised the space, eyes lingering over the pristine bed. I couldn't tell if the longing there was for sleep or the sport the mattress offered.

Limping across the room, I flopped onto the sofa. It wasn't too comfortable, but it sure as hell beat standing on my aching feet. I folded my hands in my lap and regarded the god with tactful respect.

"I believe you said you'd tell me what you want from me."

Sitting on the corner of the bed, Maui flipped his sheet of hair over his shoulder. "You don't waste time, do you?" he asked with a chuckle.

"I don't know how much time I have," I said bluntly.

The god nodded, a sad smile playing at his lips. "Fair enough, *wahine*. If I can, I will answer. But beware of what you ask."

Wow, I thought. *A god just offered to answer any question I asked. Yeah, no pressure.*

"What's your beef with me?"

He raised an eyebrow as if I'd just asked him the airspeed velocity of an unladen *wakwak*.

"You've tried to kill me twice tonight, and now you're putting me up in a posh room? It doesn't jive."

"I mean no harm, *wahine*."

"My front door and his arm call bullshit," I said, hooking a thumb toward Marius.

"And my car," the satyr added.

"So again, I'm left wondering: what's the deal, Maui?"

The god grinned. "I like you."

I let out a frustrated snarl and tossed a throw pillow at him. He batted it away with a hearty laugh. "I had to make sure you were a worthy bet," he explained. "There was even a party specifically for the purpose of checking you out, but I'm told you left the ball early, Cinderella."

I chewed my lip. "Wait. The gala was for me?"

"Well, it wasn't exactly common knowledge, but yes. Those of us in the game wanted to see you and the rest of the guests just wanted to have a good time."

I blinked. "Wow. I guess I shouldn't have ducked out when I did. Who'd a thunk that little old me and my soul would be so interesting."

"What about mine?" Marius asked. "Did she add me?"

Maui looked sidelong at the satyr. "Who are you again?"

I couldn't help but snicker. Marius spat an oath, gave an "I'm done with you" wave, and stalked off to the bathroom. A few seconds later, the water began to run in the shower. With him gone, I felt awkwardly exposed. And exhausted. The hours and exertions catching up to me, my head began to fill with a cottony haze. I grasped for a coherent thought.

"Am I the only soul up for grabs?"

"Yes. But this is not what you really want to know." He tilted his head down, his silky hair falling in front of his face like a luxurious curtain. Studying me as if I were a student trying to pull one over on the professor, he said, "Ask your questions, Catherine Sharp."

I swallowed a lump of worry. "Tell me about the game."

As he stood up and crossed to join me on the couch, Maui pulled a small black poker chip out of his pocket and began rolling it over his knuckles, the apple glittering in the diffused light of the room. The next of the tokens I was supposed to collect for Eris. I tensed, hands clenching the cushion.

"Anansi folded early. Coward," he spat. "Eris, Loki, Coyote, Puck, and I kept up the game. At the turn—the fourth card—your mistress bet it all. To sweeten her offer, she added this." The golden apple on the chip gave a particularly sinister wink. "She told us it was the debt of a human soul, one with a mild gift of technomancy. None of us is stupid, so naturally we all suspected Eris was lying. The dealer called a break in the game so we could all check out the bet."

I jabbed a finger at my own chest. "Me."

"You," Maui confirmed.

"And to that end you decided to send sharks, pigs, and giant birds to try to kill me?" I asked, disgusted.

He pawed at the air carelessly. "The *kupua* are what they are. I do not tell the shark to hunt, but if I let him swim free, he might kill a fish. Like I said, I'm sorry about your apartment. I didn't want to hurt you, but if you didn't survive then I would know you were not right for my needs."

I let out a skeptical laugh. "Yeah, Coyote gave me a good idea of his needs. What are yours?"

Maui stood and began to pace the room. The poker chip flashed over his fist. For a while he seemed deep in thought but finally he spoke. "Have you ever been to my home, *wahine?*"

Like many people, I'd always wanted to visit Hawaii. I'd planned little trips in my head and dreamed up exotic vacations, but those ideas always dangled in the nebulous world of Someday. In answer to Maui's question, I shook my head.

He sighed dreamily. "It is truly paradise. My island is, of course, the best. The sun rising over Haleakala Crater is a divine sight. The lush green mountains, soft beaches, the smell of plumeria blossoms mingling with the salt of the ocean. We gods have played there for lifetimes, and we fostered the land since it was little more than molten lava hardening in the sea. When I am not there, my heart aches to return.

"But," he went on, "this ache is nothing compared to the anger I feel when I see what has become of my people."

"I don't understand," I said, genuinely curious.

"Coyote has said much the same of this place. You look outside and you see these decadent buildings, these palaces for the wealthy to come and take what they will. It's the same on my island. Tourists come to spend nights in luxury while my people, the natives of the land, are left to scrape together what life they can in their tin sheds. Our traditions are seen as quaint exhibits at museums. Soon, it will all be legend, and there will be no one left to sing our songs."

"If no one sings," I mused, "no one believes?" Flynn's words echoed in my head. *Belief is currency.* "And you'll die," I whispered. He whipped his head toward me as if I'd smacked him. "If people stop believing in you, you'll die. Right?"

Somber, he bobbed his head in assent. "Something like that. And this is where I have need of someone like you, *wahine*." Maui returned to the couch. "I have plans to take back the islands for the Hawaiians, to set things right."

"How?"

"That," he said with a smirk, "is for me to know, Catherine Sharp. Perhaps one day you will know, too, but as long as you wear the brand of another, I won't tell. I will say that being so remote, out in the middle of the Pacific, we need those with the gift to speak with machines and computers."

"Like me."

"Like you," he said, tapping my nose with a single finger.

I swayed in my seat, bone weary.

Maui got to his feet and made his way to the door. "And now, *wahine*, I think you should rest. You are my guest here and have my protection. Stay as long as you need. Eat. Drink. Enjoy your lover."

I looked to the bathroom. Steam crawled up from the door as Marius continued his shower. Neither of us would be enjoying much of anything for a while, let alone one another.

"He's not my lover."

"No?" Maui eyed the bathroom door. "Good. You can do better. Aim for the sun." He winked. "Oh, and this belongs to you. Tell Eris I am in."

The poker chip flipped across the room, and I caught it with both hands. I could only stare at Maui.

"I hope I'll see you soon, *wahine.*"

The god left the room, the door locking behind him.

I shuffled the few steps to the bed, pulled back the covers, and climbed into the soft bliss it offered. Before my head hit the pillow, I passed into oblivion.

CHAPTER FOURTEEN
"Torture Me"

Cannon fire jolted me out of my dark, dreamless cocoon. With my heart beating as fast as a jackrabbit on cocaine, I sat bolt upright, eyes skittering around the unfamiliar room. I started to remember I was in a hotel right about the time people far below started cheering.

My brain put things together in simple ideas. *Hotel. Show outside. Not being attacked by angry deities or mutant, flesh-eating beasties.*

The fluttering in my chest began to subside, and I took in my first gulp of air.

"Good morning," Marius sang cheerfully.

He'd opened the curtains, and the sun spilled in to fill the room. At the small table by the windows, he sat wearing a pair of black pajama pants and a smile.

"Did you sleep well?" he asked.

While I tried to remember how to form complete sentences, I pawed at my gummy eyes. Dry and caustic, my mouth felt about as hospitable as the desert outside.

"I suppose," I muttered, smoothing back my hair. "What time is it?"

Marius retrieved a carafe of orange juice from a bucket of ice and poured some into a small glass. "Almost three in the afternoon."

"Shit! So late?"

"You were dead to the world. Care for some breakfast?"

Next to the satyr, a cart practically sagged with a collection of covered dishes. On the table were a bowl of fresh fruit and a steaming pot of coffee. My nose finally woke up and caught the scent of a hazelnut blend, hot buttery pancakes, and bacon. My stomach growled, ravenous, and I threw back the blanket to hop out of bed. I gasped and whipped the covers back

131

over my bare legs.

"Marius, where are my pants?"

His grin widened. "Wouldn't you like to know?"

"Yes," I said, "I would like to know. And while you're at it you can tell me why you took them off to begin with."

Reclining in his chair and putting his bare feet up on the table, Marius sipped black elixir from a mug, mischief dancing in his eyes.

"They're on the sofa," he said simply.

Sure enough, my jeans were draped over an arm of the red couch. I couldn't just lean out of the bed and snag them. I would have to get up and walk in full view of the satyr in nothing more than a T-shirt and panties.

As if he'd read my mind he said, "You have no need to be modest, I've seen your underthings. I must say, I was pleasantly surprised. I didn't figure you for a pink-and-lacy type. But really, Hello Kitty?" He clucked his tongue. "Poor choice there."

My face burned with embarrassment. I mustered what little dignity I could and steeled myself for the humiliating walk across the room. As soon as I stood up, my left knee buckled under me. I stumbled and dropped back down to the mattress, hissing with pain. Marius left his seat by the window and flitted off to the bathroom. A moment later he returned with a plastic bag full of ice.

"And that," he said, "is precisely why I relieved you of your trousers. Come on," he ordered as he offered me his arm. "Sit here and get yourself a proper meal."

Marius helped me up and supported me as I shuffle-limped over to the table. Pants could wait, I realized. For one, due to his impairment, it wasn't as if he could throw me against the wall and ravage me. Furthermore, he'd seen me half naked and was now helping me around the room. My humiliation was complete.

With my good leg, I hooked my foot around the adjacent chair and pulled it a little closer. Bad knee propped up and the ice pack on top, I turned my attention to a more pressing need.

"Bacon." I pointed to the covered dishes. "Now."

"My, but you are a delight in the morning!"

He selected a couple of the dishes from the cart and set them on the table before us. As he removed the covers, steam and decadent aromas flew into the air. A short stack dripped with butter and maple syrup next to three strips of crispy bacon, a heap of scrambled eggs, and a few sausage links. I slid a plate toward me and set to stuffing my face. It wasn't ladylike in the slightest, and I didn't give a damn.

"So," I said around my meat candy, "you stripped my pants to play doctor?"

"Well, when I got into bed last night, your knee was giving off more heat than Hades's scrotum. Impossible to get comfortable next to that. I stripped off your jeans—slowly, of course—slapped some ice on you, and finally managed to get a few hours of uninterrupted sleep." He brought his mug to his face then stopped to add, "You've got fantastic legs, by the way."

I blushed and filled the awkward silence with more food. After I'd appeased my grumbling belly, I asked, "We shared the bed?"

"Of course! Did you think I'd trade a king-sized mattress and Egyptian cotton for that rock of ages they call a sofa? I may not be able to enjoy the bed like you, but I certainly don't need to make things worse for myself." He downed the rest of his java. "And another thing," he said, his empty cup clattering against the table. "You snore."

"There's the selfish bastard I know and despise," I said. "You were being so nice I was starting to worry."

Marius blinked. "Incredible," he said, "I save you from freakish monsters, faeries, and a swollen knee and *I'm* selfish?"

"You were saving your own ass."

"I—well, all right, that's true, but I helped you, too. And see? I ordered breakfast like a good date should. What did you do besides drool on your pillow? Hmm?"

I pondered my bacon, pushing aside all thoughts of the night before. As I lifted my eyes, I noticed the wound on Marius's left arm. The *wakwak*'s beak had torn a six-inch slash along his biceps. Around the cut itself, the flesh puckered in angry reds and sickly purples.

"Are you okay?" I asked.

"Hmm?" When he followed my eyes to the scabbing wound, he said casually, "It's healing along. Another day or two and you won't even know it was there."

I let my eyes drift over his body. Marius wasn't ridiculously buff or anything, but with toned arms, nice abs, and a defined, firm chest, he pulled off the shirtless look. A bit of black hair curled at his sternum, and his olive complexion was set off well with the black silk of his pajama bottoms. He hadn't bothered with a ponytail. Ogling him, I realized I could come up with a few fantasies of my own, no satyr magic required.

My face wrinkled in confusion. "Where did you get those pants?" I asked.

"Did you expect I'd sleep in the suit? No, thank you. But in deference to your prudish sensibilities, I glamoured myself a pair of trousers. See? I'm not completely self-centered."

"Magic pants?"

"Without them I'm starkers. Shall I show you?"

"No, I think I prefer the pants."

"Suit yourself."

For a bit we each tucked into our food. Pancakes crumbled at the ruthless whims of our forks. The plates were nearly clean when Marius dabbed at his mouth with a napkin.

"So, while I was showering last night, did Maui have anything interesting to say?"

Savoring the last of my breakfast, I replayed my conversation with the god in my head. "Apparently, no one trusts Eris. Go fucking figure. He wanted to make sure I'm a worthy bet."

"And yours is the only soul in the pot, yes?"

I nodded. "You're safe."

"Excellent. Anything else?"

"Only that Anansi folded early. Oh, and Maui gave me his chip."

The satyr picked a link of sausage off of my plate. "That's good news. You can get the two remaining chips without any problem."

"Yeah, easy." I snorted. "Just get something from Puck and Loki. Dahlia came to collect last night, and I haven't the faintest idea what Loki's doing."

"Ah, don't worry about him. Loki is lazy. Probably doesn't care one way or the other. Knowing him, he will just wait to see what everyone else does in the meantime."

I shrugged. I'd never dealt with Loki or his Norse companions, so I'd have to defer to the satyr's judgment on this one. But the Fae I knew. Thinking of Dahlia, I pushed my eggs around on the plate, no longer in the mood to eat.

"What about the Fae?" I asked. "Last night it didn't seem like they wanted to get together for a bit of milk and honey."

"About that," he said clearing his throat. "Unless my ears deceived me, I believe I heard Dahlia order her friends to kill me last night."

"Don't flatter yourself, Marius. Dahlia says the same thing about almost everyone she meets."

"That hardly makes me feel any better, now does it? No, Catherine, I think it's best if you go play with them by yourself."

My stomach flopped and twisted at the idea of facing the Fae alone. I also didn't like that I wanted to keep Marius around. Suppressing a shudder I put down my fork. "Look, you promised to help me get to the bottom of this."

"Yes, and I helped you right to the bottom of an elevator shaft and up to this lovely suite."

"This isn't finished," I snapped.

"As far as I can tell, my part of it is. Maui answered all of your questions, and now it's merely a matter of you getting these little trinkets from a couple of gods and taking them to Eris." A smug smile fluttered at the edges of his mustache, but he otherwise appeared sincere. "My work here is done."

I gaped at him, speechless. I couldn't avoid it, no matter how much I wanted to. He'd followed our deal to the letter. What burned, though, was that I'd never make it through to the end of this mess without assistance. I knew it, and against all things sane and holy, Marius was right.

I dropped my eyes to the table then spoke, my voice small. "I need your help."

"I'm sorry, what was that?" He put a hand to his ear. "I couldn't quite hear."

"I need your help," I snarled.

Casually stalling to let me simmer in my own anger, Marius hummed to himself and poured another cup of coffee. With a carefree smirk, he added a bit of cream and stirred it around. Over the brim of his mug he gave me a twinkling, mischievous look. "I do believe you said you need me."

Exasperated, I rolled my eyes and flung my napkin down on the table. "Yes, Marius, I need you."

Smiling smugly, he plucked up another bit of sausage. "Could you say it again?" he asked around the bite of pork. "And this time could you slow it down and make it a bit more breathy? Maybe add a pout."

"For fuck's sake, Marius!"

"Now hold on there," he said holding up a hand. "I'll help. Just stop being such a bitter harpy, all right? Of course, there is the matter of payment to discuss."

"I've already said I'll go on a date with you," I said through my teeth. "What the hell do you want now?"

For an answer, he popped his eyebrows.

"No," I said. "I'm not sleeping with you."

"I don't recall asking you to." He shook his head. "No, Catherine, when we have our date, I swear on my honor that I will not use magic to seduce you. You and you alone will decide where you sleep. Assuming you choose to sleep at all."

My cheeks flared as I remembered the encounter in the elevator. My skin rippled with chills at the memory of his lips so close to mine. With a throb of desire, other parts of my body began to respond to the idea, but I didn't give a good goddamn what those regions had to say. They make bad decisions.

The quirk of his smile told me he'd noticed. I suppose it would be ridiculous to try to hide such a thing as arousal from a satyr.

"What do you want?" I asked, my voice barely a breath.

His eyes locked onto mine. For the first time I noticed they were a dull green, like worn money or the underside of a leaf. Riveted, I leaned forward, waiting to hear his terms.

"What are you prepared to offer?"

"If it's money you're after, I am sorry to disappoint you."

Marius waved off the idea. "I put in a call or two to some of my contacts this morning while you were snoring like a lumberjack. I know where you need to go to find Puck, and I have an in with Asgard. That kind of information—particularly for someone in your position—is worth more than money."

"I don't know what it is you expect me to give you, Marius. I don't have anything."

"Are you so certain of that?" He took another drink without breaking eye contact. "Mage?"

A shiver coursed through me. *Get used to the title*, I thought. *This is the new normal.*

I gave a feeble laugh. "What? You want tech support?"

Marius sighed and put down his mug. As he stood, the silk of his magic pants flowed and rippled with suggestive shapes. "Well, Catherine, it looks like you and I have nothing further to discuss."

Shit. "Wait, where are you going?"

"I'll call you next week." He padded toward the door. "You can let me know how this all turned out over dinner. I'm thinking Thursday night."

Mentally I scrambled for something—anything—I could use to barter for Marius's further aid. Goddamn, satyr. No wonder Zeus cursed him.

Oh…now there was an idea.

Marius's hand was on the doorknob when I blurted out, "I'll fix you."

He stopped, his body stock-still. With a glance over his shoulder, face sober, he asked, "What did you just say?"

"Your curse. I'll lift it."

Calm as the eye of a storm, he didn't move. I could see the gears turning in his head. "How?"

Okay, there was that. I had no clue how I could accomplish it, but if I could rewire computer systems and dead servers, couldn't I fix a broken satyr? I'd figure that part out later. Right now, I needed him to not walk out that door.

"It's what I do," I said with my most confident smile. "I fix things." I remembered how Marius had appeared at times to be made up of cracks and fissures, so I added, "I can see how the curse looks on you. With enough time, I think I can break it."

"You think?"

I nodded.

Marius walked away from the door, fingers stroking his goatee. "You think…" He sat at the table again, regarding me with a hard, calculating stare. "I *know* that I have something of value to you. You *think* you can free me of this curse. That is hardly a balanced bargain. Can you or can't you, Catherine?"

"I can," I said, my throat tight around the lie. I clenched my fists, willing him to ignore my treachery. *Just say you'll stay.*

Marius licked his lips and curled his fingers over the table. His tone was both eager and hesitant. "I help you through the end of the game and you will cure me of this?"

"Yes," I said. "Before our date," I added, hoping to appeal to his need.

"Promise it, Catherine. Swear it."

"I swear."

"Then on my own honor, I swear to do my part."

As we shook hands, I tried to keep my sigh from sounding too much like relief.

"Pleasure doing business with you," he said brightly.

Taking the ice pack off my knee, I tossed it into his lap. "How would you know?"

Marius yelped at the lump of ice on his junk. I sniggered as I limped to the sofa.

"Hey!" he said, throwing the ice pack. "You may call them magic pants but that doesn't mean they keep my bits from shrinking in the cold."

I grabbed my bag and mustered as much swagger as my knee would allow. As I closed the door to the bathroom, I heard him yell, "Don't think I won't get you for this!"

The sound of hot water drowned out his protests as I filled the gargantuan whirlpool. I needed to find Puck, the Faery trickster, and convince him to give me the poker chip before he decided to end me. I also had to steer clear of Dahlia if I didn't want to kill *her*. After that was the simple task of finding a god who took care to ensure he wasn't found.

Great.

***

After a good soak, my knee loosened to the point that I could walk without gimping around. I put on fresh clothes, washed my face, brushed my teeth, and by the end of it all, I felt human again.

I rummaged through my pack and found a few of Flynn's inventions. He'd given me his own version of a stun gun the size of a Chapstick tube, and a few other goodies that would ensure I got out of any jam. I pocketed them. The last thing I wanted was to get mobbed by more Fae or whatever Loki might send my way—Valkyrie?—and have to flail about with the backpack to defend myself. Then I tucked the two poker chips—Maui's and Coyote's—into my hip pocket and stepped back out into the hotel room.

Marius wasn't there. For a split-second I panicked that the satyr had gone back on his promise to help me. Then I remembered that as much as I needed him, he needed me. Both of us craved our freedom, and we couldn't get it alone. Rather than worry, I slipped into one of the chairs and gazed out the window at my city.

Like a watercolor painting, the hues of dusk bled across the sky. Daylight still had an hour or so left on its shift, but already the neon of the Strip began to glow, letting my imagination run with wonderings of what horrors Loki and Puck would concoct. Would they test me as Maui had? Would they try to just take me out of the game? I shook my head, warding away these dark thoughts. If I dwelled on all the horrible things standing between me and my freedom, I'd never step out into the world again.

The temptation to hide was strong. Maui offered his protection and hospitality for as long as I needed? Fine, I'd hole up here, swim in the big bed, eat room service, and wait for the cards to drop and show me my fate. But I didn't really like the sound of that last part. After being a pawn for so long, it was time to make my own destiny. So, I had to hit the streets, find the gods, and get those damn poker chips.

The lock clicked, and Marius stepped in through the French doors. He still hadn't bothered to tie his hair back, and his glossy locks fell free past his shoulders in lazy waves. Beneath a long leather jacket, he wore a plain white T-shirt and faded blue jeans with cleverly placed tears. I could've gotten a pair like them at a thrift store for five bucks, and I'll bet he paid more than two hundred for them at some designer store.

The satyr spread his arms, putting himself on display. "What do you think? I popped down to a few of the shops and picked up some things. I figure this little task of yours could prove dangerous, so I wanted something more substantial than a glamour. And," he said, dipping a hand into his jacket pocket, "I bought something for you."

He handed me a ball of fabric. Stretching it out, I saw it was little more than a black cocktail napkin with an elastic string. The front of the thong was bedazzled with rhinestones that spelled out *Pirate Booty*.

"You can wear them on our date," he said proudly.

Shoving the panties back in his jacket pocket I let out a frustrated sigh.

"No, thanks."

"Ingrate. Don't women like it when men buy them clothing?"

"That's not clothing! You could use those as an eye patch!"

Bouncing on the balls of his feet, he leered down at me. "Only after you wear them."

With a growl I slapped the satyr in the arm.

"Gah! Devil woman! Did you have to hit me there?"

"Oops, did I get you on the bad arm? I'm sorry," I lied.

I shouldered my pack and headed toward the door. I cast a longing gaze back at the sanctuary the room offered.

Here goes nothing.

I opened the door and set out to get the last pieces of the puzzle that would change my life. For better or worse.

CHAPTER FIFTEEN
"Walkabout"

The sun dipped behind Treasure Island, casting the lagoon and its ships in cool shadow as I left the hotel, Marius on my heels. Crowds gathered on the street, waiting for the staged battle between tempting sirens and swarthy pirates. Up and down the Strip, people traipsed the sidewalks. It smelled of chlorine and a million bodies. Colognes and perfumes, sweat, hotel shampoo, and beer all mingled in a cloud over the foot traffic.

As I joined the river of humanity coasting down Las Vegas Boulevard, Marius grabbed my hand. I jumped. "Hey, what's this about?"

"Just trying to blend in with the crowd. Are you aware that there are some people who come here not on missions from gods but to actually enjoy themselves?"

"The hell you say," I said, deadpan.

"It's true. You might want to give it a go sometime."

We didn't talk for a bit then. Marius's hand around mine was a solid comfort—I wasn't alone. I let my thumb glide over the softness of his. It had been so long since I'd walked hand-in-hand with someone. So long since I'd just touched somebody else. And here, in the span of a day I'd danced with Marius, planted a kiss on him, and now this.

Thinking about it made my chest ache with a familiar, bitter loneliness.

Distracting myself from my thoughts and woes, I listened to the sounds of the Strip. Applause cut through the cacophony, and a small pocket of tourists snapped pictures of a street performer. The man wore luminous white clothes and make-up. Standing perfectly still, he imitated a statue as people cast coins into his hat. At some unseen signal, he slowly shifted into another pose.

"That takes discipline," I said.

Marius let out an annoyed breath. "I hate those people. Creepy buggers the lot of them if you ask me. They're worse than mimes."

"Why?"

"Never trust something that refuses to speak," Marius said, his voice dark.

"I take it you're not a fan of Blue Man Group."

"Don't get me started."

His grip tightened on my hand, and I found myself squeezing back. My stomach flopped at all the stupid things that could mean. Liking Marius, agreeing to go on a date with him was one thing. Falling for his charms and breaking my hard-and-fast rule to not date another non-human? That was something else. Still…I couldn't deny that I enjoyed the feeling of Marius's hand clasped around mine.

"So where are we headed?" I asked.

"I have a line on where to find Puck," Marius answered. He tugged at my hand and bobbed his head toward the Forum Shops, the mall at Caesars Palace. "I've got a contact who says he can point us in the right direction. We're meeting him here."

The Forum Shops presented a monument to the gods of Commerce and Ostentatious Decorating. Circular with high, golden ceilings and column-lined walls, the building evoked classic Greco-Roman architecture. Flanked by two enormous caryatids—columns carved into the shapes of women—the famous spiral escalators formed a moving double helix reaching up into the vastness of the space. Shoppers worshipped at any number of altars here to the high priests of Gucci, Fendi, and Christian Dior.

The real attention grabber in this joint was the fountain. Not quite as big as the one over at the Bellagio, the Forum's display was made in the gods' images. At the center sat Caesar on his throne, raising a cup to his lips. At the cardinal points around him, four other characters—two women and two men—paid homage to the emperor. Every half hour or so, the statues came to life as part of a watery spectacle.

As Marius and I walked around the perimeter of the Forum, new sounds accosted me. Over and under the constant susurration of water came the chatter of a million voices bouncing from floor to ceiling and back again. More than that, though, I could hear the whirring of the cash registers, the throb of the nightclub's speakers, and the gears spinning beneath the fountain's quintet. The ether teemed with signals clicking to and from cell phones. Being a technomage apparently had its downsides.

"Well," I said, standing on my toes to be closer to Marius's ear. "Any bright ideas?"

"He said he would be here," Marius muttered to himself.

"Who?"

"It's better if you don't know his name."

I rolled my eyes. "Fantastic."

We walked around the ring of shops on the first floor, passing the fountain's version of Bacchus.

"Looks nothing like him," Marius said with a sour grimace.

"Come on," I said tugging at his hand. "Let's look on the other side."

He gave a slight salute to the Roman god of revelry, and followed along. Sure, I was trying to guide him closer to the chocolate shop, but he didn't have to know that. We spent a half hour or so riding the escalators, meandering around the mall, but Marius's mystery man never appeared.

Back on the ground level, Marius came to a halt at the base of the fountain. I stepped in front of him and turned in a circle to take one last look around.

"Anything?" I asked.

"Dirty, lazy bastard," Marius said, jabbing at his phone and swiping through screens. "If he blows me off…"

Out of the corner of my eye, I caught a hint of movement within the fountain. The taller of the two female statues tilted her head and reached out a hand. At first, I thought the show was starting, but as the figure pulled up her skirt and placed a sandaled foot into the water, I knew this was no performance.

Next, Caesar rose from his throne and threw his cup to the side. Tourists began clapping and snapping pictures or taking video with their phones. The female statue waded through the fountain toward us, her hands out before her like a marble zombie. I grabbed Marius by the lapels and pulled him away from the fountain.

"When the mood takes you, you don't kid around, do you?" he said, oblivious.

"Shut up," I said. "Look!"

I turned his jaw to the side, forcing him to share the horror of what I saw. Caesar and his mistress ambled slowly, their carved features twisting with anger, sightless eyes pinned on us.

"This," he said, "is precisely why I hate those blasted street performers."

My brand began to sting as if I'd rubbed poison ivy over my skin. With that extra sense I developed from my time spent as Eris's puppet, I knew I'd found the Fae. Or—more accurately—they'd found us.

"Fae," I said.

Marius sneered at me over his shoulder. "You think?"

Caesar drew closer and more tourists gathered around for the "show." Smaller statues stepped off their plinths and lumbered to block the main doors.

"Well? Here they are," Marius said, inching back into the crowd. "Do your thing."

I shot him a panicked look. "What thing?"

"I thought you had some plan!"

146

"Me? I'm not a planner! You were the one with a reason to be here!"

"That was before statues started coming to life."

Shit. Okay, Cat. Think. This could get messy very quickly in such a public place.

I didn't want to have to fight statues or Fae, so I swallowed hard and composed myself. Perhaps diplomacy would work here.

"I need to see Puck," I said to the stone lady.

As she hitched a leg up over the lip of the fountain, water sluiced over her and pooled on the marble floor. Instantly her eyes began to glow with icy malice. "Warned you," the statue said, her words gravelly and hoarse. "Should have listened."

Her pale arm arced through the air toward my head. I ducked out of the way and heard screams from the onlookers. When I glanced up, I saw why. Marius, his blade naked and horns protruding in nubs from his forehead, had engaged the Caesar.

So much for diplomacy.

The shrieks of the bystanders spread like a flame, twisting up the spiral escalators and into the stores. As if someone had dropped a stone into the pond of humanity, the crowds rippled outward, away from the fountain and its animated warriors.

Still, some people thought this was all part of the show—maybe a flash mob or an artistic performance. They gathered in closer, phones and cameras out to capture it all. Others, though, noticed that the exits were blocked by all the living art and began a mad dash for the escalators.

They're going to get themselves killed.

Fumbling in my pocket, I pulled out one of Flynn's inventions; a small, black cylinder no larger than a tube of lipstick. I pressed the orange button on the end and the thing expanded into a thin plastic rod about eight inches long. My instincts screamed, and I ducked just as the female statue lunged at me. She took a swipe, and I dodged the grip of her cold fingers. While

Marius held his own against the emperor, I huddled into a crouch and moved around the back of the fountain.

A high-pitched whine came from the stick in my hand. A tiny display on its slick surface slowly filled with tiny green bars, indicating that it was charging.

It wasn't ready yet. I needed to buy some time.

How the hell do you distract a statue?

More screams echoed from above, these tinged with absolute terror. Dust rained down and masonry began to crumble as one of the large caryatids unshouldered her burden and stepped out of the wall. The floor beside me split as a pair of titanic feet landed a few yards away. The caryatid lifted her head and locked her eyes on me. Like the other statues, her eyes glowed ephemerally blue.

"Fuck," I shouted.

This was not going as I'd hoped. I wanted to find the Fae and get to Puck. I wanted the chip. I did not, however, feel like being pummeled by a giant figurine.

From the other direction, the fountain goddess came barreling at me, those well-sculpted arms stretched out before her. I decided a hug from her would be a bad idea, so once again, I dodged. But this time, her hand got around the shoulder strap of my pack. Once she closed her fingers around it, she wouldn't let go. The statue yanked me backward and held me up like a prize fish on a hook. I squirmed there, feet flailing above the ground as the caryatid took ponderous steps toward us, her hands preparing to scoop me up.

Throwing my arms in the air, I slipped out of my backpack and fell to the floor, rolling to the side. As my knee protested, I gave a pained yelp.

Tough shit, I thought. *Pain is temporary. Death*, I added, *is permanent.*

Fueled with adrenaline, I ran away from the fountain and toward the escalators. As my arms pumped, I chanced a glance at my ace in the hole. It gained more than half its charge, but still, the electro-magnetic pulse wasn't ready.

Behind me, I heard a monstrous screech. Whirling around, I saw Marius's god-forged blade strike the head of the Caesar. The blue light in its eyes began to flicker and turn into a thick smoke as the statue wailed with pain.

Steel. The Fae are allergic to metal!

I broke off at a run, once more aiming for those spiral escalators. The first one I came to was, of course, going down. Fuck it all—I had to get upstairs for my idea to work. I pushed through the people cowering on the escalator, swimming upstream as fast as I could while shouting to people to throw anything metal they could find at the figures.

I reached the next floor and kept running all the way to the top level. People flocked into shops like rats fleeing a sinking ship. Store clerks closed their doors, all the while pressing against the glass windows to watch the horror outside. Below, the Caesar became rigid and motionless, rooted to the ground outside his fountain. More blue steam erupted from his maiden as Marius speared her through the forehead. I took a moment to appreciate Hephaestus's handiwork: that was one kick-ass sword.

"Marius!" I called. "Get up here!"

He found me with his eyes then gave a roll of his shoulders. He followed my path up the escalator, long legs taking two steps at a time. As I checked the charge of my toy, it shot from ninety-nine percent to full.

"Yes!" I hissed.

On the lowest level, the massive caryatid turned in a circle and trained her eyes on me, there at the center of the forum.

"Sister," she said, her voice horribly low and unnatural.

The masonry cracked above me as stone tore from stone. The other caryatid came to life one massive inch at a time.

By then, Marius was at my side. "I really fucking hate caryatids!" Just as they did when he fought off Maui's *kupua*, Marius's eyes took on a greener hue, dazzlingly bright. He stretched out a hand, palm down, fingers splayed like claws, and with a wrenching motion, he flung his hand up and water shot up from the fountain below. The mighty plume stretched to the ceiling and showered the caryatid on the ground. With his other hand, he punched at the air and called out a word of power. The colossal woman burst apart, her remains raining down to the floor in glittering motes of powder. For an instant, I saw the hovering image of the blue eyes before that too was carried off by Marius's spell.

Behind me, though, her sister gained momentum.

No time.

Holding the stick out in front of me, I looked Marius in the eye. "Grab on."

"Why? What is it?"

"Trust me!"

The satyr shot out his hand and gripped the device. As the statue behind us swept an enormous hand toward our backs, I thumbed the button. With the smell of ozone and a bass thrum of power, an orange wave of light rippled out in a ring, spreading over every last living thing in the Forum. In an instant, every man, woman, and child lit up like a Christmas tree. Whole nervous systems gleamed, spidery filaments dangling from luminous brains. Bodies collapsed to the floors in immobile heaps.

Marius and I were rocked forward by the impact of the caryatid. He held his ground, but I went tumbling over the railing, a terrified yell catching in my throat as the wind was knocked out of me.

"Catherine!" he yelled.

My tiny boom stick fell from my fingers and crashed to the wet floor in an explosion of plastic and circuits.

With a painful snap of my shoulder, I jerked to a stop. Shooting a surprised look upward, I saw Marius's face contorted with exertion. His hand locked around mine with incredible strength. Hanging there, thrilled to be alive, I realized I was dangling nearly thirty feet in the air with little more than the satyr's goodwill keeping me from plunging into the now-empty fountain. It reminded me of the last time someone had me dangling high above terra firma. The night I'd met Eris. I'd ended up learning I had a soul, and nearly dying out of stubbornness. I sincerely hoped this time would be less painful.

I watched over Marius's shoulder as the Faery enchantment over the caryatid failed. Sapped of the magic giving it life, the statue froze in place, stooped over and poised to grab Marius.

I swung my free hand around to grip his wrist. "A little help here!"

The satyr took my arms and heaved me up as if I weighed little more than a sack of groceries. I got a leg over the railing and shimmied across, crashing to the floor ungracefully. Marius stumbled and slid onto his ass. He came to a stop with his back against the statue's open hand. As the power ebbed from his eyes, his horns retreated beneath his glamour.

"You," he said breathlessly, "are going to wear that thong."

At the moment, I didn't care what parts of my body hurt. I didn't care if I was panting, sweating, and terrified. I didn't even care that I was covered in the dust of the destroyed caryatid. I simply reveled that I was not a broken pile of Cat on the floor of the Forum Shops.

"Yeah," I nodded. "I'll wear the thong."

As I stood, my legs wobbled coltishly but held my weight. I straightened up and looked around the Forum. In the shop windows, people had fallen in masses like cordwood. Still, others sprawled on the floor. There were even arms and torsos draped over the sides of the twining escalators.

Walking down the stairs and dodging bodies, Marius asked, "Am I wrong, or did you just kill everyone in the building?"

"They're not dead, just rebooting."

He thought about it for a minute then said, "You're going to have to explain that one to me, I'm afraid."

"The plastic rod I had you grab onto? It's one of Flynn's inventions. Are you familiar with the concept of an EMP?"

He nodded, kicking at the Caesar's shins as we passed him on the ground floor. "Electromagnetic pulse," he said. "Burst of energy that takes out any electrical current nearby, yes?"

"That's the idea. Well, the body has its own electrical current constantly running through it, too, but an EMP won't target that kind of power." With my toe, I kicked one of the pieces of my shattered weapon. "In short, this one does. It causes a split-second hiccup in the body's current and triggers sleep in anyone within a few hundred feet."

"Clever," he said. "But why didn't it work on us?"

"Direct contact with the device shields you from its effects. Since we were both touching it when it went off, it masked our signals."

He bobbed his head toward the caryatid. "And the statues?"

"They were being controlled by Fae. Fae, while not human, still have bodies that run on electrical stimulus. So, when they went down to the pulse, so did their spells. What about you? What was the thing you did with the water?"

"Old World trick," he said. "Some magic can be undone with running water."

"And pulverizing it?"

He bobbed his head from side to side. "Letting go of some repressed anger?"

I reached into the fist of the fountain goddess and pulled out the nylon strap to my backpack. After a quick check of my pockets to make sure my stun gun hadn't fallen out, I hitched up my bag.

"So," I said, "do you want to stay here and wait for the faeries to come get us?"

Warily, he eyed the statues. "Will they come back to life?"

"I don't know. Possibly."

"Then, with all due respect, I'd like to get the fuck out of here. I told you I hate statues, especially the ones that move."

"Why?" I asked as we made our way to the door.

"Remember how I said I got caught with one of Zeus's favorites?"

I nodded.

"Well, it was in his temple. The caryatids ratted me out, the jealous bitches." His face hardened. "After Zeus was done with me, he let his informants play a bit."

The past played over his face as rage, and Marius pushed out into the night. I shuddered. I didn't want to think about what they'd done to him. Quietly, I followed him on the path to the Strip.

I didn't see any bodies out here, so I assumed the pulse had restricted itself to the inside of the Forum Shops. I made a mental note to thank Flynn…and to beg for another one of his pulse sticks. That thing came in handy. I also made a promise not to let the next one fall thirty feet to its demise.

"I suppose this is one way to find your contact," I said cheerfully. "We could just go look over all the bodies until you recognize him."

"I see you have a date, Cat," a voice said.

Dahlia's slick, dark form materialized in front of us. The oily folds of black leather enhanced every curve of her lean body. The old anger boiled in my stomach to the point I thought I might be able to breathe fire.

Great. Not the person I was hoping to find. However, if she could get me to Puck, maybe I could put my loathing aside for a few minutes.

I looked the bitch squarely in the face and said, "Take me to Puck."

She drew in a breath, eyes widening. Her lips tightened, and her skin lost some of its deep color. "Why?"

"He has something I need. Take me to him."

She searched my face for trickery. When she found none, she closed the distance between us. A breeze tossed her hair, and I caught her scent— jasmine and honeysuckle, as always. Her voice was a frightened whisper. "Do you have any idea what he has become? He could kill you."

"He won't. Not yet."

"He will torture you, Cat, until you are begging for death."

I straightened myself and pulled on a mantle of authority. I was Eris's emissary, dammit. A mage in my own right. That commanded some respect.

"A third time I ask you, faery. Take. Me. To. Puck."

Dahlia's smooth cheeks flexed as she clenched her jaw. "As you wish."

The leaf brand on her neck shimmered. Gold and green light swirled around the three of us like a winding cocoon. In ever-faster revolutions the light flared to a blinding white, and I closed my eyes. For a time all I knew was darkness.

CHAPTER SIXTEEN
"Hard To Concentrate"

The toes of my shoes barely touched the ground as I dangled. My arms were stretched over my head, bound at the wrists around a cold cylinder. My hands ached and muscles complained from the suspension. I couldn't see for the velvet darkness all around. Along with the pain at my wrists and shoulders, I felt moist air over my skin. The temperature teetered on the edge between comfortably brisk and wintry. Soon, the cold would lose its novelty and I'd be shivering. My nose wrinkled at the dank smells of mold, mildew, and earth.

"Marius?" I asked, voice echoing strangely.

Silence yawned in response.

"Dahlia?"

Nothing.

The terrible quiet pressed at me, and I trembled. Though I was alone in the darkness, I felt horribly exposed. Predators lurked a breath beyond those shadows, teeth aching to tear me apart. Sweat trickled down my forehead despite the ambient chill, and my stomach quivered as my primal instincts flared to get the hell out of here. My shoes scraping against the floor, I shimmied and struggled with my bindings. I groped to see with my fingers what held me prisoner. A bracelet of steel around each wrist linked together by a few rings of metal. Handcuffs.

I jerked and squirmed, trying to slide my hands through the cuffs, but it was no use. I was stuck. My shoulders burned and my breaths came in shallow, panicked draughts. With the sandy scratch of a match striking and the hiss of the flame, darkness parted to reveal a face mere inches from mine. I saw the strobe-flash of wild eyes and pointed features, but it's difficult to say which parts of the face were real and which had been sketched by shadow and a terrified imagination.

Behind me, someone chuckled. I froze, feeling as if ice had been poured into my spine. Gulping down a lump of fear, I closed my eyes and counted out twenty even breaths.

As calmly as I could, I spoke into the darkness. "Where am I?"

Mocking laughter echoed off of the walls, a tittering, high-pitched giggle that wormed its way under my skin and sent me straight back over the edge of terror.

"Where am I?" I bellowed.

Angry and beyond terrified, I closed my eyes and let out a roar. Something electric snapped in the air, a presence that I sensed with my blood. Power. There was a power outlet or something nearby. Something I could tap into as a technomage. Focusing, I reached out with my magic and groped for the source. As if I'd used sonar, a picture formed in my head of a cold bulb. Dormant. Off.

I poured all of my fear and rage into one word: *On.*

Directly overhead, a light bulb flared to life, burning my eyes and painting this odd place with fire.

Holy shit. It worked.

The wan light wasn't much, but some of my fear ebbed away at the idea that I could control something even if I was dangling. Again.

The shadows receded in every direction, but anything more than five feet away was bathed in nightmarish murk. In the gloaming I made out stone walls and a packed dirt floor. I thought a rickety wooden staircase stood in one corner. It appeared I'd been strung up in a basement. For the life of me, I couldn't say how I'd gotten there.

Though I still felt as if hungry monsters lurked just beyond the circle of light, I saw no evidence of the person who'd laughed or the haunted eyes I'd seen briefly in the match glow. A few feet in front of me was the slack face of my companion.

"Marius?" I whispered.

He didn't answer.

At first, I thought his hair hung across his face, but looking closely, it was blood oozing down from a gash at his temple. Another cut formed a crust over his swollen right eye.

"Marius!" I barked. "Wake up!"

Panic churned in my stomach, sending the acrid taste of bile to my mouth. Did he look pale? Were his lips blue? I couldn't even tell if he was breathing. Shit! I'd gotten him into this. I'd promised to help him, not get him killed by fucking faeries.

Hooking my foot around one of his legs and using the bar above as leverage, I shimmied closer. My lip quivered as I said his name. "Marius?"

I felt his response as a gentle rhythm against my stomach. He was breathing.

Relieved, I let my head fall forward and my body sag. His forehead on mine burned fever hot.

"Marius," I said wearily. "Please wake up."

In the wan light, I saw his eyes flutter open. It took him a few moments to focus, but he lifted his head and looked at me with confusion.

"Cat?" he asked. His voice, weak and thin, lacked his signature bravado. His brow furrowed. "You're bleeding," he said.

This was news to me. I had a dull headache, but I ignored it. "So are you," I said.

"Bugger," he whispered.

I swallowed hard, willing my hands to stop shaking. To get my mind off the horrific things the Fae could have done to us—or what they planned to do—I focused on Marius.

"Do you remember what happened?"

He shook his head sleepily. "Not really. Last I recall you told the faery to take you to Puck."

"I don't know where we are and I don't remember what happened," I said, giving over to the shivers. "And my goddamn shoulders are killing me. I hate dangling!"

"Look," he said as he emerged from his daze. "I don't suppose you've got a hair pin or something we can use to pick the locks on these handcuffs?"

Then I remembered what I'd done with the car locks, with the hotel room door, and with the bulb above us. Those were all electronic, sure, but I'd seen Flynn work his trade on simpler machines, too. Machines of all kinds, even the most primitive. I could turn on cell phones and rewire security systems in Eris's office. Surely, I didn't need a bobby pin to pop the lock.

"Hang on," I said, eager to prove myself. "I've got an idea."

"Not much else for me to do but hang on, is there?"

Believe it or not, the tinge of his snark gave me hope. I smiled. I could do this. We'd get out of here.

I shuffled myself forward, groping for a grip on his handcuffs. As I did our bodies came together.

"I've almost got it," I said, rocking into him.

My fingertips grazed the steel of his shackles, but couldn't get a hold. I needed to be closer. Wrapping my legs around his waist, I swung myself forward. Cheek to cheek, I fumbled for the keyhole on his cuffs.

The soft curls of his mustache and goatee tickled my face. Then came the sensation of his dry, cracked lips along my jaw line. My pulse hammered against his mouth as he traced temptation down my throat. Marius laid another whisper-light kiss on my neck, and my body responded. Nerves I'd thought long dead perked up and swelled with life. My skin prickled with desire, and the small hairs on my arms stood on end as if reaching for him with aching need.

Breath staggered out of me, and I glanced away from the cuffs. "We…we need to get out of here," I said weakly, my words trembling.

Marius ignored me, his attention devoted to the hollow of my throat.

"Marius…" It was a plea, but for what? His focus? For him to stop? To continue?

I swallowed hard, steeling myself against the intoxicating moment. I closed my eyes, and there was only his touch. Like tunnel vision for the senses, the world distilled into just the feeling of his body near mine. The cloying scent of cologne and blood mixed with the indescribable aroma of pheromones.

His kisses began a slow ascent back up, and then he stopped. He tilted his head as he had in the elevator, and this time I moved to meet him. As our lips almost touched, I pulled away.

Don't kiss him. Kissing him changes everything.

Dammit all! Hadn't I already sacrificed so much? Hadn't I always given other people what they needed? Wasn't it time for me to have something I wanted? I compiled a list of all the chances I'd let fly by as Eris sent me hither, thither, and yon for her stupid tasks I'd been a puppet on strings for so long.

This, though? This I had control over. No goddess to order me around. No friends to sway my decision. Just me.

From beneath his long lashes, Marius's green eyes burned with a question. I tightened my legs around his waist and pressed my lips to his in a smoldering kiss. Rather than quench, it ignited a fervid desire. Bolts of pleasure shot through me as he returned the kiss with a guttural noise, equal parts moan and growl. Marius rocked his pelvis into mine, and I felt his whole body stiffen.

Overwhelmed by a surge of need, I clutched at his bonds. It had been too long since someone had gotten to know my body, and I ached to be touched. I pooled all of my longing, all of my desire, and used my will to break the lock. His arms fell to his sides, and he let out another growl. Gripping my ass in both hands, Marius yanked me forward in rhythm with another thrust of his hips.

My head fell back as I gasped. Marius's hands moved up under my shirt, and each nerve, every cell of skin he touched, responded with a flare of heat and an extra beat of my heart. He gave a teasing flick of his thumbs over my breasts then pawed down my ribs. Arching my back, I bucked against his body. With a flood of hot breath and the tickle of his soft beard, he buried his face in the bend of my neck, teeth nipping. Clawing at the pipe over my head, I hissed at the sweet snap of pain and pleasure.

My fingers fell over the handcuffs, the lock popped free, and I wrapped my arms around him. Even though the pipe no longer supported my weight, Marius's strength proved to be up to the task. With one hand cupping my ass and the other pressing against my back, Marius took quick steps until I found myself up against a wall.

I set my feet on the floor as he whipped off his leather coat. Greedily, I pulled at his T-shirt and helped him get rid of it. As my hands traced over his firm chest, fingertips curling in the soft hair there, the satyr loomed over me, blotting out the weak light from the lamp. I stood on tiptoe to taste his lips while his fingers danced at my belt loops. He pulled my hips against his, and I raked my nails over his shoulders.

His name escaped on my breath.

"Will you?" he asked.

Grinding against him, colors flashed in my vision. I wanted him, craved him. His hands tugged at the pockets of my jeans, pulling them down a fraction of an inch. Whatever he asked of me, I would do.

"Yes," I whispered.

"You will? Do you swear it?"

His fingers slipped into my pockets and rooted around, taunting me, urging me toward recklessness.

"Yes," I moaned. I lurched forward to taste his full lips again, but he drew away, keeping his mouth a promise away from mine.

I opened my eyes, disoriented, and a golden apple flashed. Marius's stare was cold, now, laced not with desire but with malice. He held a poker chip between us.

"You'll give your soul to me then?" he asked. "To have as my own?"

"What?"

Pinning me against the wall with the promise of pleasure, Marius rocked forward. Nuzzling my neck, he said, "Swear that you're mine, Cat, and I'll give you everything you need."

His lips hovered a scant breath away from mine. Though my body still vibrated with yearning and my being cried out for him to fill me, to make me whole, I shook my head.

"No," I muttered.

Marius's hands gave me every reason to change my mind as they moved down to my hips. As his fingers slid up my thighs he said, "I don't think you mean it."

Loud and clear my voice rang out. "No!"

Shuddering, I felt the tattoos of his kisses still fresh and hot. I squirmed away from him and staggered a few steps down the wall. The light from the overhead lamp pooled around the satyr, making him look all the more dangerous and attractive.

He flipped the poker chip like a coin. "I wonder," he mused, voice even and cool, "if I collect all these tokens myself, does it mean I would hold the deed on your soul?"

An old wound on my heart burst open. As the heat of embarrassment blazed in my face, my mouth tingled with the taste of battery acid.

I'd gone and done it again.

"Then again," he continued, "I don't know that it would do me much good."

He flicked the chip, and it hit me in the chest. I didn't move for it. I stared at Marius in horrified disbelief.

Stupid! I screamed at myself. *So damn stupid!*

"Go on," he barked. "Take it. It's worthless, after all. Who would want anything to do with a scrawny, weak, little thing like you?"

Tears rolled down my face as each of his words stung me like the lash of a whip. How often had I asked myself the same thing? *Who would want me?*

"Used goods," he sniped. "Victim to the charms of love and look what it got you: it made you a slave."

Marius took slow, confident steps toward me. Shivering, I moved away from the wall. As I backed into the lamplight, my knees gave way, and I fell to the floor.

He circled me, his expression dripping with derision and cruelty. "Nothing but a slave. Worthless! Empty!"

The words bit into me, drawing fresh tears that fell like hot blood.

He squatted and took my chin in his hand, forcing me to look into his glacial eyes. Flashing his lopsided grin, he said, "You gave yourself up, and now you're just being passed around. You're like the nub of a joint at the end of a good night. There's nothing left of you anymore. Nothing worth taking. Well…" He laughed. He traced a single finger down my throat into the valley between my breasts. "Almost nothing."

Vines shot up out of the ground, and I screamed as they twined around my ankles, my neck, and my wrists. As the tendrils yanked me to the floor, Marius's eyes once again took on the verdant glow signifying he'd used his power. Horns curled out of his skull, longer now and hooking back like those of a ram. As if finally able to stretch after a long time spent in a cramped space, Marius's eyes rolled in satisfaction, and his mouth dropped open with a sigh.

I kicked, trying to skitter away on my back, but the vines held me pinned to the dirt. With the slow, lean stretch of a cat, Marius crawled to where I struggled.

"Waste not," he said.

CHAPTER SEVENTEEN
"Breaking the Girl"

The more I pulled and strained against the living ropes, the tighter they wound about me. Coarse thorns sank into my flesh with a searing pain. Flashing a malevolent smile, Marius lowered his face over mine. My stomach knotted, and my pulse raced. As his breath splashed over my cheeks, I turned my head.

What happened? How had I gone from taking what I wanted to being taken against my will? How had I lost control?

"Marius," I said, pleading.

"Good," he purred, "you're going to be saying my name a lot tonight."

"Please, Marius, don't do this."

"No? Mere moments ago you ached for a kiss, and now you don't want me? Not even in the slightest?"

"No," I said through my teeth.

"Your mouth says no, but when I do this"—His hand tantalized me, and my back arched to meet his touch—"your body says yes. Which is it, Cat?"

Blood flowed as the thorns cut deeper into my arms.

"Well? Which is it?"

I tried. I wanted so much to explain.

I don't want it this way, weak and out of control. I want to be my own person! The words caught in my throat with a sob. I no longer begged for his body but his pity. *Please. I didn't mean it. It was a mistake. I didn't know what it meant.*

In my mind, a more cynical, dark voice responded. *This is what you get.*

I knew that voice. So many nights, I'd tossed and turned with that voice as my sole companion. Ever since my ex betrayed me, left me soulless and in the employ of a bitch goddess, that voice had been the evil twin to my optimism, the avatar of harsh reality.

You let your guard down, and you get burned, she said. *This is the consequence. You deserve this. Take your medicine.*

Terrible understanding wrenched at my stomach.

You don't belong to you. You haven't for years, and you never will again.

I closed my eyes and stopped struggling, whimpering in pain and sadness.

"Just as I thought," Marius said, smoothing my hair.

This time when his body pressed over mine, I ached not with desire but with despair. I looked away, a single phrase echoing in my mind like a dark mantra.

I am not my own.

As he rose above me, his lips pulled back in an eager grin. Every muscle in his body flexed to the firmness of steel, and he jerked. His eyes lost their green glow, pulsed with orange, then went dark. As if he were a puppet whose strings had been cut, Marius crumpled on top of me, lifeless. Behind him, stone-faced and angry, stood Flynn.

"Fucking satyrs," he growled.

Flynn grabbed Marius by the hair and tossed his body away from me. Drawing a knife, the mage sliced through the vines. Cut off from the earth and from the spell-casting satyr, the barbs fell from my skin, leaving oozing welts.

"At least I get to be the hero," he said.

I couldn't speak. I tried to say the two words racing through my entire being—*thank you!*—but the sound came out of my mouth as a choked sob. I flung myself at Flynn, wanting nothing more than to feel his comforting arms around me, to make all of this go away. He pushed me back from him and fixed my eyes with his.

"I'm bailing you out. Again. Come on," he said tersely.

Confused, I blinked.

On the floor, Marius began to gray and shrivel with age as death took him. A part of me mourned the friend I'd thought I'd had, while another quivered that he'd been so sadistic. Which Marius had been real?

Flynn hauled me off my feet and dragged me up the creaking, rickety stairs. Disorientation filled my head with a fog that seeped into my limbs. I moved sluggishly beneath that leaden weight.

We emerged in the kitchen of a decrepit house. From the looks of it, no one had lived here but maggots and mice for the last ten years. The few remaining cabinet doors hung listlessly on their hinges like the last leaves of autumn. Inside the peeling walls with its blistered paper, I heard skittering, crunching noises of rodents. Black slime formed a skin in the porcelain sink. I coughed and gagged, overwhelmed by the fetid smells of rot and shit.

"Don't be a baby, Cat," Flynn said. "We need to get out of here. Then you can collapse into a puddle, okay?"

Numb, I nodded and followed him from the kitchen into a derelict living room. The threadbare carpet was covered with stains. Some were yellowish like dried vomit, others the rusty red of old blood. Shafts of white sunlight thrust between the boards on the windows and through the bullet holes in the door.

"Open it," he said.

I lifted a hand to discover the door had no knob. Just a deadbolt with no keyhole. "I don't know how," I croaked.

His eyes rolled with annoyance. "Seriously? You can't fucking open a door? It's just a door. If you can't do this what's the point of having powers in the first place?"

My palm shook as I cupped the deadbolt. I reached out to find the tumblers, the clicking mechanisms that made up the lock, but I couldn't feel them. The cold steel was dead to me.

"Useless," Flynn said. The words bit into my heart and turned my blood cold. "You're useless. Move over."

The mage shoved me aside and stroked a single finger down the doorjamb. Instantly, the lock clicked, the door creaked open, and sunlight poured in. Flynn stepped through then turned around, blocking my path.

"I think I was wrong about you, Cat. You don't have powers. You're just a tech geek who's gotten lucky a few times."

"You can show me," I said. "You promised you would."

His laugh rang out in a peal of chilly, bitter notes. "Right. Why would I waste my time? Get yourself out of this one," he said. "Assuming you can."

Disgusted, he shut the door, leaving me alone in the shack.

"No! You can't leave me here." Silence. "Flynn? Flynn!"

Hurling myself against the door, the punctures on my arms screeching with agony, I called out his name again and again. But no one answered. No one but the voice in my head with her unwelcome truths.

He's right, you know. How many times has Flynn had to ride to your rescue? How many times have you gone crying to him when you've screwed something up or needed someone to help put you back together again? Well, Humpty Dumpty, no king's men will come for you today. If you can't get yourself out of this one, you deserve to die here. Maybe the rats can get some use out of you.

Hours or minutes—I don't know how long it went on. I could have been punching at that door for a year, and still no one came. I pounded and kicked, screaming all the while, until my knuckles bled and my shredded throat choked on my breath. Spent, I slid down to the floor in a sobbing heap. With my cheek pressed against one of the bullet holes, I sat there crying until my heart ran dry.

"I warned you," Dahlia said from behind. "I warned you to stay away from him, but you didn't listen."

Pawing at my eyes with the heel of my hand, I wiped away my tears. She didn't need to see them. She'd caused enough of my pain to have it memorized. I shifted so my back rested against the door. Even surrounded by the detritus and decay of this house, she managed to shine with her ethereal beauty. Dressed in ivory gossamer that complimented the mahogany of her skin, Dahlia glimmered with faery power. Her raven hair hung unbound to her waist.

Her oil-black eyes regarded me coolly. "And now look at you," she said. "What is left of you?"

"Not much," I rasped. I closed my eyes and tilted my head back against the door.

"Oh, you still have something? What is it?" she asked as she crossed the room.

What did I have left? Dignity? Pride? *Please.* I'd been humiliated by Marius, abandoned by Flynn, and left to become another rotting corpse in this shithole of a house. I didn't even have my unusual talent. I'd only unlocked it a few hours ago, but already the absence of my technomagic left me feeling cold and empty.

What could I possibly muster that would amount to anything now?

I lifted my hands and let them fall uselessly to my sides.

Dahlia's plump lips parted in the slightest of pouts. "Poor Cat," she said. "I expected more of you."

So did I.

"Oh, I'm sorry," I sneered, "do you feel cheated?"

She shook her head. "I had such high hopes when I met you. So did my Lord. But now, look at you. On the floor and wasted. Used and broken."

An anger born eight years ago that I'd nurtured and cosseted rose up within me. For so long, I'd left it pent up, but now I'd been reduced to so little, I realized this was the last of me. This was the final ember in the dying fire I'd become.

"You know, Dahlia," I said. "I do have something left."

"What's that?"

"Rage."

I lunged for her, knocking her back to the stained carpet. I lashed out and took her throat in my hand. Her pulse jumped beneath my thumb, quickening as her eyes widened with shock.

Hatred blazed in my belly. Her delicate face—pained and surprised—became the avatar of all the things I loathed. Every frustration, every tiny inconvenience of the past eight years flooded me.

I couldn't get a decent job. I was stuck in Las Vegas. I couldn't keep a relationship. The fact that I was forced to work for Eris, that I'd been chased by living statues and killed a shark-man in my parking lot. And Marius! If it hadn't been for Dahlia, I never would have met the bastard, would never have let myself want him, let alone give in to need and wrap myself around him. I wouldn't have needed Flynn to rescue me. Or anyone else. If not for her, I would still belong to me.

Right or wrong, in this moment all of it was Dahlia's fault. My broken heart and everything that came after. Each transgression boiled through me, distilling in my hands around her neck.

"Can't...do...this," she sputtered.

Veins began to bulge in her temples.

"Watch me," I snarled.

"He'll come...for you."

"I. Don't. Care."

Kneeling over her, I squeezed with everything I had. Her eyes rolled back into her skull, and with a sudden *pop!* I no longer held a woman's life but a pile of cinders and glimmering dust. Behind me, the door crashed open and four faery men burst in. They wore leather armor and oak-leaf brands. At the sight of the ash in my hands, the largest thrust out his fist.

"Murderess!" he cried.

What was left of Dahlia blew away through my fingers in the cool breeze along with the remnants of all that I'd once been. Carefree, hopeful, and naive Cat had died right alongside the faery.

Now that even my rage had been spent, I felt empty.

Now, Dahlia. Now there is truly nothing left of me.

The soldier barked an order to his mates. "Fetch her! We will take her to our Lord, and he will see that justice is served."

CHAPTER EIGHTEEN
"Strip My Mind"

The faery soldiers led me out of the shack and into a front yard. Years of neglect had left it dry and brittle, overgrown with weeds standing as tall as my shoulders in some places. The leader held his hands out to his sides, and the stale grass parted at his whim to clear our path. Briefly, I'd entertained the notion that faeries had been responsible for crop circles. It made sense that they'd do nothing but run around in confusing rings.

It might have been minutes after dawn or high noon, I couldn't tell. Though the sky was bright, the sun itself hid behind a veil of clouds.

"Where are we?" I asked, my voice callused and warped.

The leader glared at me over his shoulder but gave no answer.

It wasn't long before the weeds gave way to a meadow of heather and thistle. The dale spread out to the horizon where the earth rose to form a soft mound. On the hill, an enormous tree stretched her branches to the sky, leaves fanning out in a full canopy. This tree, it turned out, was our destination.

When I stood beneath it, I shook, humbled by its sheer size and grandeur. Like a birch, the bark was pale silver and gleamed in the indirect light of the sun. As the leaves rustled in the breeze, there came an eerie sound. Whispers? Was someone crying? No. Just the wind moaning through the treetop.

The leaves themselves were remarkable, too. Flat and as large as my head, they looked like black leather with veins of crimson. The roots twisted, sinking knobby knuckles into the earth. There between the roots, his legs tucked up against his bare chest, sat Puck.

Like most of the Fae, Puck appeared ageless. His face was smooth like a young man who hadn't grown his first beard, and yet his eyes—silver and black—spoke of centuries of mischief and gathering secrets. His hair, the color of spring grass, swept up and back from his face to form curling horns. He reminded me of a certain comic book bruiser, but Puck's claws were not made of adamantium. This faery's cruelty would never be so obvious.

"Welcome," he said in a musical tenor. Unfolding his legs, the faery stood. With a barrel chest and short stature I thought of bantam roosters—small, potent, and wily.

"Cat Sharp, isn't it?" he asked.

I nodded.

"Well, aren't you a fine addition?"

He circled me, those alien eyes appraising me.

"I will not serve the Fae," I said icily.

"No? And why is that?"

The smile at his lips told me he knew damn well why not. "An old grudge."

"I'm told you have collected on that debt. Poor Dahlia rides the back of the wind, and I believe yours are the hands that killed her. Is that right?"

I nodded mutely.

"Surely you know her blood must be answered for. If not with your obeisance then with your own life."

I straightened my spine and lifted my chin. "Go ahead. There's nothing left to get out of me and my stupid life."

Puck giggled and skipped to the tree. As he capered around it, his stubby fingers caressed the trunk lovingly. "It's a remarkable tree, isn't it?" he asked. "My people call her the Giving Tree, for she gives us shade, comfort, food, and life eternal. Her sap is potent as both a poison and as a medicine. A single sliver of her bark can be taken and pounded into strong armor. But it is her fruit, you see, that is most valuable."

I looked up into the branches. I don't know how I'd missed it before. The pear-shaped fruits—the color of a pomegranate with the smooth-looking skin of a tomato—sagged from the branches, plump and ripe, as if they might fall off at any time.

"They are not to be harvested en masse, as your people seem to prefer," Puck continued. "No, these are sacred. We take of them when dire times demand it, for we understand this is her greatest gift."

Above me the fruit pulsed. Not as one, but each individual orb had its own rhythm.

"Catherine Sharp," he said, voice carrying into the vastness. "Do you refuse to pledge fealty to the queens of Faery and become an emissary of the Sidhe?"

I made sure to enunciate so he'd understand. "Fuck. You."

His mouth hitched into a smirk. "Very well."

Before my eyes, the roots of the tree writhed, and a seam appeared in the trunk. The wood creaked and groaned as it shifted, and once more I could hear that eerie mewling of the wind.

"You will be executed," Puck announced. "Traitors and upstarts like yourself think they can ignore their duties, but in the end you all bend to the will of the Sidhe."

As if on hinges, the silver bark opened to reveal the inside of the tree. She bristled with splinters and spikes. The Fae—allergic to ferrous metals—had invented their own version of the iron maiden.

I gulped in shallow breaths. Who wouldn't be terrified looking into a maw of wooden stakes and quills? My heart raced. As I turned to run, two of the faery soldiers took me by the arms and pulled me forward.

And then it made sense—the leathery texture and red veins of the leaves, the throbbing, crimson fruit.

"The Giving Tree," Puck said reverently, "provides us with the elixir of life. Your blood will fertilize the land and nourish our sacred fruit."

The soldiers shoved me into the trunk. I stood as far from the spikes as I could. Puck placed both hands on the sides of the opening and leaned in, his eyes level with mine.

"So you see, in the end, you will still serve the Fae." He bowed. "We thank you for your sacrifice to the Realm."

Then, the tree moaned and popped as the trunk constricted around me, and splinters pricked my flesh. I raised my arms to my face and drew in a breath, trying to brace myself for the horror to come. As the first of the points pierced my stomach I let out a shriek. As the tree knitted itself back together, the spines drove into my legs, my back. Bones crunched beneath the pressure, and hot blood flowed out of me in gushes. The pain was infinite. Though I ripped apart, I couldn't fall, couldn't pass out. The same wood that tore at my flesh and muscles held me up and together.

I closed my eyes and screamed, begging for one of the spikes to slice my brain and end me.

CHAPTER NINETEEN
"Warped"

The searing agony of the wood in my flesh stopped abruptly, though my wailing went on until my voice was little more than a weak breath. Someone gripped my wrists and pulled my hands away from my face.

"Catherine!"

What the...? Jolted by the surprise of hearing Marius's voice, I opened my eyes. The satyr stood in front of me, fully clothed, alive and well. His face—without any bleeding cuts or abrasions—twisted not with malice but with confusion.

I pushed away and took a few wobbly steps back. The memory of his horned face and sweaty leer blazed in my mind. My feet stumbled over something. I turned to see I'd bumped into Dahlia. Also very much alive... She still wore her black leather, and regarded me with a mixture of wary hesitation and haughty triumph.

My temples began to throb, the pressure of questions and shock squeezing my head like a vice. My eyes darted between Marius and Dahlia for an explanation.

"Catherine, breathe!" Marius ordered.

I gasped and cool, evening air flushed through me. Head spinning like a deflating balloon, I doubled over and braced myself on my shaking knees. When I was mostly certain I wouldn't pass out, I looked up to get a lay of the land.

The sky was fully dark, and the light of Las Vegas blotted out the stars. A lush garden replaced the faery glade and its Giving Tree. The grass, an emerald green, had been cut short to the soil, almost like a golf course. Flowers sprang up from the earth in bursts of color. A blossom of cherry red, here. Lemon yellow, there. I even saw something like a spiraling cattail

175

thrusting up into the air in a series of black-and-white stripes. Toadstools, big enough to sit on their caps, sprouted near a wooden footbridge. A small brook gurgled in a winding path through the garden, the gin-clear water rippling with the jewel tones of the koi within. Over the sounds of water and wind, loons called into the night.

As my gaze fell onto the throne, my whole body began to quiver with horror. The chair had been carved out of silver wood. The back fanned out into a display of massive branches and a canopy of leathery, black leaves.

"Excellent!" Puck sang merrily form his throne.

The Sidhe lord bounced up and clapped his hands in slow applause. As before, his hair was spring green and his face boyishly fresh; however, instead of the tanned leathers and bare skin I'd seen earlier, he wore the clothes of a modern mortal with little to no fashion sense. His wardrobe— black-and-white striped pants, a red tee, and a long purple coat—brought to mind another comic book character, this one more appropriate to Gotham City.

Puck giggled. "Oh, it's fantastic! You really are a prize," he said. "Such passion! Such fury! And who knew you possessed such a deep well of self-loathing. Fantastic!"

"What the hell is going on?" I asked, searching the three creatures for some hint.

Puck walked to me, his steps light and graceful. "Well," he said, "when Eris put a soul into the pot, I had just intended on killing the poor mortal and taking the wind out of Eris's sails. I attended the little soiree at Caesars intent on it. But, then…" He clicked his tongue and another wicked grin split his face. "Oh, but then I saw you. And when I heard it was *your* soul— back on the market after all this time—well, Cat, I was just thrilled! It's not often in my line of work that one gets to reclaim what has been lost."

With these last words he cast a stern, pointed look at Dahlia. Like thunder, my own rage rolled in my ears.

"Naturally," Puck continued melodiously, "I had to make sure you hadn't depreciated in value during your stay with that jealous hag you call a mistress. And, oh"—he laughed, bringing his hands to his mouth in an expression of glee—"you are so much more than I expected! Like a fine wine, you've matured superbly."

"What did you do to my head?" I roared.

"I had to test you, mageling. I just went into your mind and had a bit of a stroll. Taking in the sights of all your fears." He looked Marius up and down and rolled his eyes with distaste. "Your desires. All of the deepest emotions, the most potent of buttons I can push once you are in my employ."

"I will not be your pawn," I growled.

His lips formed a thin, knowing grin. "In the end, you will still serve the Fae."

The whisper, a haunting echo of his words beneath the Giving Tree, sent shivers through me. My belly heaved, and I thought I might fall to my knees.

No. I would not give him the satisfaction.

"I'm sorry to see you've been unbound," he said. "A lot of work into conjuring that spell. We'll have to take care of it after you come home to us."

I shot a hard look at Dahlia. I was surprised to see she would not meet my eyes. She laced her fingers together and stared at the ground.

"You?" I asked.

Heat rushed up my cheeks. My thoughts churned, understanding bubbling as tears filled my eyes. "Oh god," I said, "you knew?" Her silence confirmed it all, and I nodded. "You knew what I was, even though I didn't."

Dahlia refused to look up, though I saw her eyes flicker guiltily to one side.

"And *you* laid that binding on me. I thought it was Eris, but...you?" I stalked toward her, simmering. I remembered how it had felt to choke the life out of her. Tendons popping, I clenched a fist and stopped just out of arm's reach. "As if you hadn't done enough to make my life hell, you cast a fucking binding on me?"

"To be fair," Puck said casually, "she did it under the direct order of her queen."

"Why?" I snapped, whipping around to face the Sidhe Lord. "Why would Mab or Titania give a shit about me?"

He shook his head, his features darkening. "You foolish, short-sighted mortal. You can't even see it, can you? The way you're being used? Behind the scenes, your mistress and those other thieves I call kindred are plotting. I know. It's what we do. We are creatures of habit, and immortality has given us time to hone our various crafts."

"This doesn't make any sense" I said, frustration roiling in my voice like thunder.

"Of course you don't. You don't see all of the cards, and you don't know all of the rules. Now, I can't see exactly what their game is, but I know when I'm being played. And you can tell your mistress, satyr," he hissed, "that *it won't work!*"

Reaching into the deep pockets of his purple coat, Puck retrieved the poker chip.

"Take it," he said, flipping it through the air. "Take it back to your lady and tell her that I approve of her wager. But whatever she and those other scoundrels have planned, they will lose. My hand is strong," he said. "I've already won the game. They just don't know it yet.... This will all be over in a matter of hours," he said. "With the flip of a card, Dahlia's mistake of losing you will be fixed, and we will carry on with you where we left off."

Puck returned to his throne. "I'll see you soon." He winked and the garden disappeared. The creeping ivy vanished, replaced with graffiti and piss stains. We had been dropped in a dark alley of Dumpsters and trash bins.

"Well, that was weird," Marius said.

I glared at him. Even though I'd been yanked out of Puck's illusions, I still felt the Giving Tree spearing me, still felt the sting of the satyr's hands over my body. Fresh in my mind, he'd pawed at me and my body had responded with need. I knew none of it had been real but I still shuddered with too-solid memories.

I needed clarity. I needed to shove all those damn lies out of my head and purge these phantom sensations. *It never happened. I was not executed in the faery tree. I did not kill Dahlia. And Flynn!* With a surge of relief, I realized Flynn had never abandoned me. These fledgling abilities of mine were as intact as the friendship. I couldn't fathom how Marius could be so calm and collected.

And Marius. He and I had never actually...

Then a horrible thought crossed my mind. *Had Marius seen it all?*

Had he seen me wrap myself around him? Had he felt my lust as I dove into his kisses? Worse—had he been a willing participant?

I took wary steps away from him and leaned against the brick wall of the alley. Holding my aching head in my hands, I kept my eyes trained on the ground.

"What happened?" I asked.

"What do you mean what happened? You were there."

"Marius," I snapped, "just tell me what happened. The Fae did something to my head, and I'm trying to work it out, all right?"

"Fine." He sidled over and put his back to the wall beside me. "You told

Dahlia to take you to Puck, there was a flash of gold light, and then you started screaming like someone killed your puppy. What the bloody hell was that all about?"

All of it had happened in an instant?

"You didn't…? You weren't bound in handcuffs?" I asked.

If he lied, his relaxed face gave nothing away. "Handcuffs? No. Although," he added with a grin, "I'm not adverse to the idea in proper company."

My stomach turned with a nauseating mixture of relief and anger. I'd been spared the humiliation of the satyr knowing what I'd seen, what I'd almost done with him. But I'd seen it all with such crystal clarity that I'd never be able to slough it off. The physical sensations of spike and sex dissipated like the memories of a dream, but I would never forget what Puck had forced me to see. I would never forgive myself for the way I'd reacted in those illusions.

The events were false, but my feelings had been all too real. Whatever Puck conjured came from honest places in my mind and heart. I looked at Marius, and even without the lenses of Puck's dream I caught myself wondering, *if I reached out now, would his kisses be so delicious?*

I recoiled from that line of thinking, from the revelation there: I wanted Marius. Puck pulled it out of my mind from where I'd hidden it, and he'd forced me to admit it to myself. I now had to face the fact that I'd been stupid and careless. I'd gone against my better judgment by offering myself to Marius. I'd given up and let him use me. I'd been weak and had to be bailed out by someone stronger. I'd caved and cowered like a wilting flower. And I'd killed Dahlia.

Dahlia.

Rage, white and hot, flared in me as I thought of what Puck revealed: the binding had been her doing. For eight years, I thought I knew all of the ways Dahlia had complicated my life. Now, Puck had taken my idea of the truth and shattered it like a mirror. As if he'd tossed it into the air, the shards fell to create a new picture, a new truth. What I saw there was uglier than I'd imagined.

It wasn't until that moment that I realized just how fucked I was.

And it was her fault.

"She did it again," I snarled through my teeth. "That fucking bitch, she did it to me again." I growled in frustration and kicked at one of the trash bins, sending refuse rocketing down the alley.

"What's gotten into you?" Marius asked.

"Dahlia is the one who bound my powers, Marius, or did you miss that part of the conversation?"

"So? I still don't see why you're so—" He stopped talking. His eyes went out of focus as he began to think it through. "Wait," he said, "you said 'again.'" Marius's fingers danced over his lips. As he paced back and forth I waited with dread for him to puzzle it out. "And Puck. He said he'd replace it when you came home. You belonged to the Fae before Eris, didn't you?"

I couldn't look at him. I stared at the ground, eyes brimming with tears.

"Wait a minute, I've almost got it," he said. "Yesterday…yesterday you said Eris won your soul after you'd been a git and fallen in love with the wrong person."

My whole body burned with shame. Of all the people in the world that I didn't want to know what I'd done…

"Dahlia," he whispered. "It was Dahlia, wasn't it?"

My shoulders shook with quiet sobs as a wail of anguish mutated into a hiccup and died in my throat. I thought I'd known humiliation before. Marius had saved my life. He'd seen me drunk and disarmed. He'd seen my panties! But now…now Marius knew my darkest secret. He could see me for the idiot I was.

"Bloody hell! It was Dahlia!"

"Yes," I moaned. "It was Dahlia."

I wanted nothing more than to slink away into one of the trash bins and let someone carry me off to the dump where I belonged.

CHAPTER TWENTY
"Scar Tissue"

I met Dahlia at a roulette table, I told Marius. *There was something about her face—with her high cheekbones and canted eyes—that had seemed so exotic. Madame Butterfly meets Cleopatra. I know now it was her fae heritage, but at the time I was blissfully ignorant of things like gods and faeries.*

When a round of bad bets cost me the last of my bank, she offered me a drink to take the edge off the loss. She hooked me by flashing a smile that went all the way to the corners of her painted eyes. It made her all the more radiant.

The proverbial one thing led to another. A cocktail at the hotel bar turned into shots at a nightclub down the Strip. Drinks moved to a crowded, sweaty dance floor. Hips had churned along, grinding to the bass beats, and arms had wrapped around soft curves. Touching led to kissing, to teasing, and to a night drowning in desire.

When I fell for Dahlia, I'd fallen hard. I went back to her place and made her my new home. I dropped out of school to dive into a relationship with her and live the carefree life Las Vegas offered. It was exactly the kind of reckless thing you do when you're nineteen.

One night, as we lay in bed together, I basked in more than sexual afterglow. I'd never felt that depth of affection. Dewey-eyed, taking in the beauty of her dark skin against my alabaster flesh, I told her I loved her. But that wasn't enough. A simple, "I love you," couldn't contain my feelings, so I poured my emotions into this grand metaphor.

"Heart and soul, I'm yours," I'd said.

To me, these words conveyed magnitude. But, to a faery, it was a binding agreement. I'd given myself willingly—albeit ignorantly—and Dahlia had accepted.

We'd been together for seven months the night everything changed. As I usually did, I met up with her at one of the bars at the Bellagio. The slump to her shoulders had told me she'd been having a run of bad bets.

Sliding onto the barstool next to her, I asked, "What's wrong?"

"Cat, I—I haven't been honest with you."

Of course, I feared the worst. Or what I'd thought was the worst: infidelity.

"I'm…" Dahlia had looked around to see if anyone listened and leaned in close. When she spoke again her voice had been low. "I'm one of the Fae."

Her admission had thrown me off. Relieved that she wasn't cheating on me but still confused, I'd snorted with nervous laughter. "What, like Tinker Bell?"

"Fuck Tinker Bell!" She'd knocked back a shot of Jack and turned to me, her honey eyes glazing with the drink. "You know those books you like with the vampires and the faeries in Louisiana?" When I nodded she'd added, "Like that kind of faery. It's real."

I laughed. What else would I do in that situation?

"Funny," I said. "I've never seen you leave a trail of pixie dust on the pillow."

"Cat, I'm serious," she'd pressed.

The tension in her jaw and the fire in her stare had given me pause. I looked long and hard, studying her to find the joke, but I'd found nothing except her pain.

"I don't understand," I said.

She'd reached out one perfect finger and traced it along the rim of her empty glass. Frost spread down in delicate crystals, gorgeous fractal pictures as fine as her eyelashes.

My mouth sagged in surprise and awe.

"Oh shit. You mean it, don't you?"

I drew my hands down over my face and put my elbows up on the bar. A faery? *I thought. What did it even mean? Why was she telling me now, of all times?*

"So, does this change anything? With us?"

Dahlia had flagged down the bartender. "Can I get another shot and a Rusty Nail for my lady here?"

She stayed mute until the bartender delivered our drinks. She'd knocked back the shot, and worry had twisted my stomach to see my carefree and bubbly Dahlia wilting with anguish.

"What aren't you telling me?" I asked.

She pulled me into a fierce embrace, her well-manicured nails damn near clawing me. When she pulled away, she stroked my cheek with her petal-soft hand. Her face had fallen. "Cat, you have to understand that I never meant for it to happen."

"What?"

"Do you remember the night you told me you loved me?"

Of course I had, and I'd said as much.

"You said you were mine." Her voice twisted with sadness. "Heart and soul." A single crystalline tear traced down her perfect cheek. "I lost it, Cat. I bet with your soul, and I lost it."

"Wait. My soul? How can you…" I'd groped for words and just settled on an exasperated, "What?"

"Bargains made with my people are lasting. That night…" She'd paused, eyes losing focus for a moment. "You gave me ownership of your soul, Cat. I got in deep in a poker game, and I threw your soul into the pot. I thought I had it. Four queens! You'd think four queens would win! But it didn't. I lost, and now she owns you."

I had been too stunned to be angry, too worried to feel anything clearly.

"Who?"

"A goddess. I have to take you to her tonight."

That had been my breaking point. I'd gulped down my drink. "Dahlia, what the hell are you talking about? Faeries? Souls? Goddesses? I'm an atheist, for Christ's sake!"

Her flawless face had turned to a stony mask. "Not for much longer."

Grabbing her bag from the bar, she stood up and swept away. I followed in her cold wake as we walked down the Strip in silence. She led me to the penthouse of a casino where we met a woman sitting in a sparsely decorated office.

Craggy, ugly, and bony, the stranger radiated jealousy and prickly judgment. I'd known her for a bitch the second I laid eyes on her.

For protection, I drew closer to my lover.

"Dahlia, is this her?"

"Yes, Cat. This is Eris, the Greek goddess of Discord."

I'd read the Iliad *and the* Aeneid_*in high school. I'd heard the myths of Eris and her fucking apples. But those were stories!*

I burst into a giggle fit. "Right. Okay, Dahlia. I don't know what this is all about, but you got me. So, who are you? And what's going on?"

Eris's lips had split into a grin I would come to loathe. "I like her. Headstrong, lovely, and reckless. Hers is a spirit of fire. Well done, Dahlia."

The faery had hung her head.

"Um, thanks?" I'd said irreverently.

"An excellent soul to add to my collection," Eris had said. "Yes, I can think of several fun things to do with you."

I'd narrowed my eyes. "Look, I decide who I do fun things with. And you're not on the list. Dahlia, who is she? Really," I added. This wasn't funny anymore.

"The keeper of your soul," Dahlia said out of the side of her mouth.

"I don't have a soul."

"Oh, no?" Eris asked.

"Cat," Dahlia said, her voice rising with warning. "You don't know everything."

"No, Dahlia," Eris had said, "I'm interested to hear what she thinks. Go on, Cat." She'd said my name with explosive consonants that somehow mocked me. "Please, illuminate me as to how you don't have a soul."

She might as well have asked me to explain why an apple was called an apple. Why was blue *blue?*

I stammered a bit. "That's it. I have no soul. When I die, I die. The end."

"You think so?"

Then I found myself dangling upside-down over the city. Hundreds of feet above the Strip, I kicked and squirmed, suspended from nothing more than a whim.

"What the fuck?"

Eris stood beside me in midair, finger crooked like a hook. "You still think you have no soul?"

"What are you doing?"

"Look," she said. *She pointed a long, bony finger to a nearby block of windows. I'd fallen to the floor, and my hands had gone to grip at my throat in the international symbol for, "Oh shit! I can't fucking breathe!"*

Dahlia hadn't moved. She'd stood idle, her stare cold and distant.

"Do you see?" Eris asked. "Do you begin to understand, you foolish mortal?"

"What the hell? What is that?"

"Still think you have no soul?"

"Stop this!" I screamed. "Stop!"

And then I was back in my body. As I lay there on the floor, writhing and gasping for my life, the bullet of reality hit me between the eyes.

Everything I'd believed about the world was wrong. Gods and things like faeries existed. I had an immortal soul. None of that compared, though, to the darkest, most terrifying revelation of all.

Dahlia had bet my soul away in a game of poker.

She had betrayed me.

When I could speak, I'd stood up and stared at my lover as if she were a stranger, a serpent.

"You lied to me," I'd said.

She shook her head. "I never lied to you, Cat. Everything I ever told you was true."

"How could it be? You said you lo—" I'd choked on the syllable as sadness welled. "You said you loved me, Dahlia. How can I believe you?"

"You know I love you."

As she'd tried to wrap her arms around me I shoved her away. Anger had consumed me.

"Don't say it! You don't get to say those words to me ever again, do you understand? I gave you everything I had to give, and you just played with it like it was a toy? Just bartered me away in a goddamn game? Like it was nothing more than a nickel?"

"Oh," Eris said with a snort, "souls are worth far more than a nickel."

"Fuck you, Dahlia! You either loved me or you carelessly bet me away. One or the

other. They can't both be true! So which is it?"

She had refused to look at me. She'd kept her eyes to the floor, tears clinging to her lashes like dew on a blade of grass.

"Which is it?" I roared.

She said nothing.

Eris's voice was too calm. "Well, ladies, as fun as this is, I'm afraid it's time for me to rightfully claim what's mine. Dahlia, we're done here."

That was that. Without a glance for me, Dahlia had marched out of the office and down the hall.

Simmering, I glared at Eris.

"Well, Catherine Sharp," she'd said, "let's make this official, shall we?"

She took my left arm in her hand and traced a shape with her fingernail. It burned like hell. Smoke rose from my flesh. While I cried out in pain, she'd smiled. When the act was finished, my arm had a tattoo of a golden apple with one bite taken out of it.

"Welcome to my staff," she said. "Now you can go on home. I'll call on you when I have need of you."Eris turned away with a dismissive gesture of those spindly fingers.

Go home? *I thought.* Where was home? *Dahlia's apartment. My stuff had been there. I could not—would not—show my face there again. I had no place to crash. I hadn't been able to afford gum let alone a bus ticket home or rent.* Oh shit, what the hell am I going to do?

For the first time, I felt utterly alone in a foreign place. I put a hand to my stomach as a fresh wave of nausea rolled through me. Voicing the truth to myself more than anything, I said, "I have nowhere to go."

"Oh?" The goddess had turned, regarding me with naked curiosity.

"I lived with Dahlia. I don't have a home to go to."

Once more Eris fixed me with her Cheshire grin. "Well, dear, I think I can help you with that. For a price," she'd added pointedly.

"I don't have anything. You have my soul. What do you want?"

Her face had grown wintry. "Say please."

I flopped my arms to my sides, frustrated and helpless. "Please?"

"No, that won't do at all," she said, clucking her tongue. "I want you to mean it, Cat."

"Please, help me," I growled, my words hard.

Eris grinned. "No."

"What? You just said…"

"I don't think you actually want my help, dear girl. I don't believe it."

"I do!" I said, pulling at my hair. "I do! Please, I can't do this on my own."

"Better. Pour all of the fear you have into these words if you truly want my aid."

Shaking with anger, humility, and no small amount of terror, I sank to my knees and bowed my head. "Please, goddess," I said around my tears. "Help me."

I looked into her pasty, shriveled face, and she grinned. "That wasn't so hard, was it?"

Though we both had known how difficult it had been, I bowed my head again. A stack of cash hit the floor in front of me. I'd never seen so much money in one place.

"Set yourself up with a place to live," Eris ordered. "Furnish it as you will, but manage these funds wisely, for they may be the last you see from me for quite some time. You are now in my employ. I own your soul, and I expect you to repay me for this gift."

I nodded as I got to my feet. "I'll get the money to you as soon as I can."

Her laughter was hollow and merciless. "I don't want your money, Miss Sharp. You will work off this debt to me."

"How?"

"We shall see."

That's how I came to be Eris's pawn. That's how I got into this whole mess.

Stupid, huh?

CHAPTER TWENTY-ONE
"The Power of Equality"

Marius's mouth fell open with surprise as my story settled in his mind. All of the implications and insinuations made over our years together congealed and filled in the gaps of my riddle. He knew and understood me and my darkest secret. With horror, I watched as his lips spread into a smile.

"Wow," he said with a reverence. "All this time I've thought you were a prude, turns out you're a lesbian. Now it all makes sense."

"I'm not a lesbian," I said. "Dahlia was—"

"Part of a phase?" he asked mockingly.

"A mistake," I growled. "The biggest damn mistake I ever made in my whole goddamn stupid life."

"Oh, that's even better. Experimenting with bisexuality and visions of me bound in handcuffs. My, my. I have to say, Catherine, I am thoroughly impressed."

"Shut up, Marius."

"Other than the part about falling in love." He shuddered and stuck out his tongue. "Wretched that."

The self-pity melted away with the fire of my rising anger. I didn't need him to remind me, to judge me. That anyone would discover my secret—that I'd loved Dahlia, had willingly given her my soul—was bad enough. But for Marius to throw stones...

"Shut up."

"And you've certainly learned your lesson there, haven't you?" he went on. "Lost your soul, your powers, and now they're pulling the strings to do it all again. Damn! You are fucked!"

"I said shut up!" With both hands I pushed at his chest, and the satyr fell against the wall.

The ghost of a man in jeans and a leather jacket stood in front of me, face aloof as always. But beyond him, *through* him, I could see Marius's true form.

He looked the same in some ways. For example, his black hair still hung in thick waves past his shoulders. Beneath his glamour, though, his locks lacked their signature shine. His horns, nubs on either side of his forehead, didn't surprise me—I'd seen them enough recently—but now, they reminded me of unhealthy fingernails; all yellow, ridged, and coarse.

Though burdened with weariness, Marius's shoulders were broad and his chest firm. He sagged against the wall, ashen, as I examined him. For a brief moment, I imagined what he must have looked like there in Zeus's temple the day he was cursed. His hair delightfully tousled, body full and healthy, the muscles on his arms taut and lean.

I gasped as I took stock of his glassy, jaundiced eyes. *This* wasn't Marius. This was a broken soul. The arrogant satyr I knew had been defeated and starved, and I quailed with sadness.

My gaze traveled down. Like the satyrs of myth, Marius's torso blended into the legs of a goat. Black cords wrapped around his hips, slick barbs digging into his flesh. Blood matted the fur there, particularly the tuft above his—

I jumped with embarrassment and looked back up to his face, my cheeks flushing.

Yeah. Like a centaur.

The glamour of the man I knew followed my stare. As he realized body and magic had come undone, surprise widened his eyes. Dispersing like a colorful mist, Marius's wraith blew in a light breeze and settled over the satyr's body. The cords vanished, replaced once more by the leather jacket, jeans, and T-shirt.

I understood. Like neglected fruit on the vine, Marius was dying. My stomach twisted in a knot, and bitter remorse rose in my throat.

When he looked up at me I saw my friend—assuming I could call him that. I saw the man I'd spent the last few days with running for my life, the familiar Marius. He glared at me with righteous anger and loathing.

I understood the heat behind his glare, the powerful emotions fueling it. I felt the same things: wounded and humiliated. I'd been discovered for what I truly was, and there was nothing I could do to make him unsee those things. The secret I'd kept for so long was now in the open, as bare and pale as his actual flesh. In a way, we'd both been stripped of our comfortable glamours.

I feared what he would do with this new information. I worried he would twist it to his own purposes. Hell, I already knew it would give him fresh ammunition for our rounds of verbal sparring.

I drew in a breath and prepared myself for what I had to say.

"Go on," he snarled. "Get in a gibe. I know you're dying to."

Instead of slinging insults like he expected, I said, "I'm sorry."

"What?" Guarded and suspicious he clung to the wall and eyed me.

"I'm sorry, Marius."

He bristled. "Fuck your pity. I know you want to mock me, so have at and get it over with."

"No," I said. My eyes brimmed with fresh tears.

He arched a brow. "Why?"

How could I explain? How could I tell him that in a few scant minutes in the real world, I'd seen multiple incarnations of him? I'd seen the hope of a passionate lover, Puck's illusory sadist, and his reality. Marius was a broken, weak soul trapped within himself. That Marius, the real being behind his glamour, had all but destroyed my memories of the sinister copy from Puck's dream.

I shook my head. "Let me put it in a way you'll understand. We've just seen each other naked, Marius. I won't laugh at you because I wouldn't want you to laugh at me."

Marius blinked as if baffled by the concept of mutual respect. His throat flexed as he clenched his teeth. I knew the anger and confusion he must be feeling. I felt it, too.

The world had changed irrevocably, but he pieced himself back together. We both did. As his cocksure swagger returned to his steps as we left the alley, I saw in his eyes that he'd never look at me the same way again. Marius would never forgive me for seeing him so clearly.

It was okay.

The feeling was mutual.

CHAPTER TWENTY-TWO
"If"

Coming out of the alley, we emerged onto a crowded sidewalk. We weren't on the Strip, though. Overhead, a large screen served as a roof. Colors and pictures danced, holding the crowd in awe at the spectacle of the Fremont Street Experience.

"Fremont Street?" I murmured. "We're on goddamn Fremont Street?"

"So it would seem," Marius confirmed.

Fremont joined up with the northernmost end of Las Vegas Boulevard—the Strip—and jutted off at an angle of casinos and neon. We'd been transported from the Forum Shops, central on the Boulevard, to a random spot beneath the signature attraction on Fremont. This meant we were hell and gone from my car—still parked at Caesars where I'd left it just yesterday.

Goddamn Puck for dropping us here. Well, among other things.

Marius started walking, and I followed in a stunned haze. After a few minutes, I stopped. "Wait. Where the hell are we going?"

He halted and turned in a slow circle. "I have no idea," he admitted with a weak attempt at laughter. "I don't suppose you've thought of something."

I gave it a moment's thought then slumped. Frustrated and soul-weary, I parked my ass on the curb and looked up at Marius. "I don't have a fucking clue."

"Well," he said, taking a seat next to me, "I know you're not much for making plans, but I think it might be a useful skill for you to pick up."

"That's why I have you," I said, nudging him with my elbow. "You're the professional assistant."

He laughed, and though it wasn't much, it was genuine. Something inside me felt redeemed. Maybe things would be okay. Maybe I had a friend after all.

"All right," he said, "you've got the chips from Coyote, Maui, and Puck, yes? That just leaves Loki. So, I guess the trick now is to find the bastard and convince him to give you the damn thing."

"Where would I even start?"

Marius ran a hand through his mane. "Difficult to say, really. He prefers to keep a low profile."

Marius's phone began to ring in his pocket. His eyes lit up, and he dug the cell out of the inside pocket of his jacket. "Hello?" After a pause, he added, "Yes."

The satyr stood and walked a few yards away, holding his free hand up to his ear to better hear the caller. I didn't follow him. I sat right there on the curb and tried to get a feel for my bleak situation. I still had to find a wily god and get to Eris before she would consider giving me my freedom. These tasks—along with the burden of all my time spent doing such parlor tricks for the goddess—fell on me like a lead weight. I looked up and watched the light show over Fremont Street. For a few minutes, I let my mind wipe itself clean and marveled at the colors overhead.

I had to admit, I knew I'd always seen things differently, but since Flynn and I had broken Dahlia's binding, I could pick out individual lines of power, watch the dance of electrons as they flew from atom to atom. Charges, magnetic fields, light, and power. Energy gathered into a tube, bent to form the limbs of a stories-tall cowboy. Mundane and magical all at once.

I can do this. I can fix my life.

I would find Loki and get the token from him. After that, I'd give Eris her precious chips. Maybe then I could barter my freedom away from the gods and set into this strange and lovely new world.

And Marius…

When I looked at him—the real him behind the glamour—I saw how the curse had wrapped around him. Wires and motherboards I understood, but I had no idea how to cure a man dying of an empty heart. What would he do when he realized I couldn't hold up my end of the deal? That I'd been lying? We'd come to an understanding of sorts, and soon, I would betray his fragile trust in me.

I watched the Fremont Street Experience as colors danced on the ceiling. This was the closest thing I had to a church. Sitting on the curb, I basked in the glory of technology and prayed I'd find a way out of this predicament.

Marius returned, shoving his phone back into the lining of his coat. "It was Eris," he said. "We have to go to her."

Unease prickled over the back of my neck. "Why?"

"Says it's almost time for the final card to be drawn, and she needs you and the chips there. Come on. We've got an hour and we need to find a car since you wrecked mine."

"But, what about the other chip? If I don't take it to her…" Then what? Would I be stuck with her? Passed on to whomever won? "I can't go without Loki's chip."

"We're out of time, Catherine," Marius said, his voice full of sympathy and finality. "I have to take you to her."

That was that, wasn't it? *Out of time.* Maybe there would be another way. After all, I had three of the chips. That had to count for something. Maybe I could still turn this shitty deal into a winning hand.

I stood up and dusted myself off. Finally, the aftereffects of the faery illusion had worn off. The phantom vines and quills stopped biting into me, and I felt more like myself after communion with the bright lights and circuits.

"All right," I said. "Let's go."

I followed him for less than a block when he stopped in the pool of light at the entrance to the Four Queens casino and whirled around. "You have the chips, right?"

"Of course."

"Let me see them. I want to make sure Puck didn't try to pull a fast one."

I dug the poker chips out of my pocket and dropped all three into Marius's outstretched hand. As if appraising a fine diamond, the satyr held them up to his face, scrutinizing them for flaws. Out of the corner of my eye, I caught a glimpse of a familiar face. Round and ruddy, David Tullemore lumbered past, his eyes dancing over the crowds with a look of equal parts interest and panic.

"Tully!" I called.

My friend's face went out of focus as someone sprang from the door of the casino and plowed into me. The wind blew out of me as I crashed to the ground on hands and bad knee.

But the stranger had been holding a bundle of poker chips. With the impact, he'd flung them up in a great explosion of black-and-white clay. As if in slow motion, I watched as my markers launched from Marius's hands and joined the rain of chips. Dozens of the things fell to the ground and mine disappeared into the mass.

"No!" I cried.

Pedestrians, seeing the chips, set on them like a pack of hyenas on a corpse. Crawling into the scrum, I searched through the chips for the telltale golden apple. Nearby, Marius pawed through the tokens, swearing under his breath.

All of them were plain black chips with nothing more than the casino's logo. No gold. No apples. My chips, the keys to my freedom, were gone.

I looked up to Marius, eyes pleading for a miracle. "Tell me you found them. Please, just tell me you have them."

His mustache twitched. With a contrite shake of his head, he said, "No."

Without a word, I slid my feet under me so I sat lotus style on the sidewalk. I dragged my hands through my hair and down my cheeks. I'd been so damn close to freedom I'd secretly started making plans for my new life.

In my glorious fantasy, I had a new job, one where I didn't have to mainline energy drinks or worry that I wouldn't get paid this week or the next. No, I'd finally have a stable position using all my talents and paying me well for them. By day I'd work my trade. Nights would find me at YmFy, learning from Flynn about what it meant to be a technomancer. Then, I could leave Vegas. Sure, Mrs. McIntyre would lose her maintenance staff, but maybe I could ask Flynn to look in on her from time to time. I'd see the world, take that backpacking trip through Europe I'd always dreamed of, and maybe, just maybe, I could try something resembling a healthy relationship. Well, okay, so that was probably stretching it, but like I said, it was all fantasy.

Everything I'd done—the party, putting up with Marius, fighting off creepy pig-men and ginormous birds, surviving Puck's little mindfuck test—had been working to get that life for myself. Now, it all amounted to nothing. I'd lost it. Like so many people in Las Vegas, I'd lost it all.

I kicked at the litter of chips on the ground. "I was so close!" I said through my teeth. All the work and running for my life, the humiliation, and I would still lose my soul to fucking Chance.

"We've got to get going," Marius said as he got to his feet.

I shot him a bewildered stare. "Are you fucking kidding me? I can't go in there now. Without the chips, I don't know what's going to happen to me!"

"Regardless, Eris is still your mistress and she beckons. Besides, if I don't get you there, she will have my hide." He offered me both hands. "Do it for me, would you?"

I shook my head and looked away from him. It didn't matter to Marius what happened to me when the final card dropped. Giving a shit wasn't part of our bargain. No, as soon as this was over, he'd want his payment.

I'd failed, lost this game, and gained nothing but a bedazzled thong I'd have to wear on a date with a satyr. Assuming he didn't take my head off with that sword of his for lying about breaking his curse.

I let my mind wander over what might wait for me in my nebulous future. If Eris won the game, nothing changed. Same soul-crushing shit, different day. I'd worn a comfortable groove into this version of life. I could stay there if I had to, right?

If one of the other gods won, though, what then?

Assuming our meeting at the gala was any indication, Coyote wanted me for a concubine, and I am no one's whore. Maui needed someone with tech skills to help his people. Of all of the options available, his seemed the most favorable. I'd get to go to Hawaii finally and use my talents. Maybe I'd learn to do the hula. Or maybe I'd get eaten by shark-men or thrown in a volcano. Chaos reigns when you're beholden to a trickster.

As for Puck, I'd rather die. I'd already been screwed over by faeries enough to know what sorts of twisted days to expect from them. If it meant execution in that damnable tree, so be it.

I had no idea what Loki wanted of me. He hadn't made any sort of move to claim me or test me. He was the wild card. I knew very little of him. Just a couple of myths and the smatterings I'd gotten from Marius. Asgard's lazy bastard son remained a mystery.

When all the cards hit the table, I'd know. Bitch, dead, sex-slave, island paradise, or none of the above. Those were my options.

"Come on, Catherine," Marius said. "You're not the type to just sit on your ass and let life happen to you, are you?"

I wanted that to be true, but hadn't I done exactly that for the past eight years?

No more. I failed this time, but I can always try again. It doesn't matter who owns the mortgage on my soul, my life and choices still belong to me!

With renewed determination, I took his hands and let him help me up. I might not be able to win, but I'd face the gods—and my future—head on.

"Let's go," I said. "I've got a poker game to attend."

CHAPTER TWENTY-THREE
"Turn It Again"

Marius hailed a cab and gave the driver an address somewhere off the Strip. I raised an eyebrow and twisted my face with a question.

"The game is an informal affair at her house."

We'd been on the road for a few minutes when Marius leaned over to speak into my ear. "By the by, I would appreciate your discretion if you would be so kind as to not mention anything about my impairment while we are among the others."

"Why?" I asked.

"Christ, woman, I told you before: I have a reputation to uphold. Besides, Eris already has leverage on me. I don't need to give that to other, more powerful creatures, too."

I nodded. "Fair enough. My lips are sealed."

"Thank you," he said. Marius let out a breath and sagged into the seat of the car. For the rest of the ride, he was uncharacteristically silent.

The cab dropped us off in front of a large two-story home. It wasn't a mansion by any stretch of the imagination, but with its sleek, modern construction and picture windows, I was sure it cost a pretty penny indeed. Something about its boxy style reminded me of Old Vegas and the 1960s mod look. I could imagine the decor being a mix of June Cleaver and Atomic Age flair. And yet, it seemed to flow with the flat desert, bringing to mind Frank Lloyd Wright. The place was lit up like the Strip, too. White bulbs burned in every visible room and in the entryway. Floodlights illuminated the path to the house—a mosaic of cut-granite slabs running like a river through the desert landscaping. Even the front door was a work of art. A security door made of black metal had been sculpted to form a stylized sunburst with wavy rays.

Marius rang the doorbell, and I heard a simple, muffled chime from inside the house. Moments later, the interior door opened, and the goddess smiled.

"Marius. Catherine," she sang, taking both of us in with those golden eyes. "Excellent to see you. You're even early. I like that," she added as she unlocked and opened the security door. "Please, come in."

After a courtly gesture from Marius, I stepped in ahead of him. As the goddess led me through the foyer, around a corner, and into the living room, the satyr shut the door behind us.

I'd seen Eris's office, so the house's sparse furnishings didn't surprise me. What did shock me was that damn near everything was white. The walls, the ceilings, the blanched sandstone tile floor—all white. In contrast, her couch and chairs were black. Like the sofa at Treasure Island, Eris's furniture looked flattened and modern. It could have come straight from IKEA. Glass formed the end tables, and metal rods made the lamps. What little art hung on the walls represented the more minimal works of Jackson Pollack and his creative descendants: colorful and chaotic.

The home of Discord baffled me. All at once it seemed both perfectly ordered and completely wrong. The eye had little more to latch onto than black and white, leaving everything looking like an old silent movie.

I turned in a circle. Hallways speared off into other parts of the house, a formal dining room and patio doors leading to a narrow swimming pool. What interested me most sat in the breakfast nook adjacent to the kitchen.

The table itself was a round slab of glass resting on a metal frame. Green felt had been cut to the exact measurement and placed over the top. Seven simple chairs sat around the table at regular intervals. The space before two of them was vacant. At five different seats, a pair of cards lay facedown on the felt beside piles of chips of varying sizes. In the center, four cards formed a straight line, face up and winking to the world.

The queen of spades. The jack of spades. The ten of spades. And the queen of hearts.

The first four cards in a game of Texas hold 'em.

I tried to read the tracks the gods had made in the cards and chips lying on the table. I couldn't tell who sat where, except for Eris. Her spot was the one with cards but no chips. What was it Maui had said? At the fourth card—the turn—she had slid in every last asset she had, including my soul. Sure enough, lying there on the top of the pot was a black poker chip marked with a golden apple.

Staring at the handsome pile, I couldn't help but wonder, *Is this what I've been all along? Nothing more than a game piece? Is this what the gods do with their free time—make wagers and barter away the lives of humans?*

I gazed at the single black chip longing for understanding. All I wanted to do was go back and change the mistakes that led me here—a stumble with a stranger in front of a casino, ill-chosen promises over whiskey and ebony skin, a poor bet at a roulette wheel. I reached out a shaking hand to touch the piece of me that I wouldn't get back.

Before I could, though, the *crack* of a whip filled the air, followed by the rotten-egg stench of sulfur. My fingers burned. I jumped back, pulling my hand to my chest, and looked around wildly for an explanation.

Smiling like the proverbial cat who caught the canary, Eris sat on the center cushion of her sofa. "Don't touch that, dear," she said.

"What is it? The spell, I mean."

"It's insurance." When I didn't immediately follow, she explained. "A neutral dealer comes to all our major games and acts as both line judge and referee. It doesn't happen often, but if we have to break in the middle of a game, he will place an enchantment over the table so nothing can be disturbed. Only he can unlock it."

I nodded mutely. It made sense. How else could one ensure integrity in a game amongst liars and thieves?

"Please," Eris said, motioning to the armchair in front of her, "have a seat. Stay for a bit."

The chair embraced me with as much comfort as the goddess herself. I didn't understand the trend for hard furniture.

Marius did not sit but remained a presence over my left shoulder.

Opposite the goddess, I realized why this felt so wrong. Goddesses don't wear pajamas, dammit.

Eris was dressed casually in a black cotton tank top and black gaucho pants of a fabric that flowed like silk. The darkness of her clothes blended into the sofa, making the pallor of her skin all the more stark. The tank top did not flatter her figure but instead called attention to her flat chest and protruding collarbones.

I used to think she looked like a Disney villain in her pants suits. Now, though, dressed down, she scared the bejesus out of me. In her office I could see her as a goddess, but here, in the facsimile of a human home, was a true monster in sheep's clothing. As if she read my mind, her lips spread in a lupine grin.

Reaching over the arm of the couch to an end table, Eris opened a small wooden box and withdrew a slender cigar, its end capped in a black filter. With the *ping* of a Zippo and the hiss of ignition, she breathed the cheroot to life. After indulging in a long drag, she let out a smoke ring and turned her eyes back to me.

"So, Catherine, I'm told you've had a wild couple of days."

"Something like that."

"I hear you even had something to do with the unfortunate accident with the elevator at my building. Is this right?"

I nodded. Glancing at Marius for some sort of support, I said, "We ran into one of Maui's birds."

The satyr's face was placid, his eyes totally neutral as he stared at our mistress. I followed his gaze back to her to find her exhaling another ring of smoke.

"Well," she puffed, "I'm glad to see both of you came out of this unscathed."

Unscathed? Aside from the scrapes on my hands and feet and the knock to my knee, I felt like the past hours had put me through the emotional wringer. My hope of freedom flapped in the breeze like a tattered flag. I'd fought for my life against mythical horrors and backstabbing faery bitches. Oh, and I found out my ex hadn't merely lost my soul but also bound powers I'd never known existed. And Marius had seen my underwear.

Yeah, I'd say I felt pretty scathed at that point.

Instead of listing off the many injuries to body and psyche, I gave her a superficial smile laced with all the ways she could go fuck herself.

"So, do you have the chips?"

"I had them," I said, looking at my hands. "I kept them through shark attacks and faery illusions and falling down an elevator shaft, but some guy ran into me and—"

"I wasn't talking to you," she said quietly.

Meeting her eyes, I saw when she flicked a glance over my shoulder.

"Marius?" she asked, her lips wrapping around the cigar.

Silently, Marius crossed the room and stuffed a hand in his pocket. A moment later he dropped three black tokens into her outstretched hand.

"You found them?" I asked. "Why didn't you tell me?"

The satyr didn't answer, nor did he look at me. He just stared at the goddess who let the chips cascade rhythmically from one hand to the other.

All at once an icy pain filled my stomach, and my heart fell into my toes as I understood. A random stranger who just happened to be carrying an armload of black poker chips… Marius's sudden interest in checking them for evidence of treachery…

When you're beholden to Eris there are no coincidences, no accidents. Everything is a machination.

I should have guessed it sooner.

Even with the realization that I'd once again allowed myself to be duped, my eyes refused to squeeze out even a few tears. I didn't look at Marius. I couldn't. My anger for him boiled to something volcanic, my blood flowing like molten rock as shame colored my cheeks.

With a sound of equal parts anger and sadness, I said, "I can't believe it. Even knowing you have your powers of persuasion, even knowing you're a fucking bastard, I still trusted you. I actually trusted you, Marius."

"You shouldn't have," he said, teeth grinding.

"Foolish mortals and your trust," Eris said coolly. "You all like to think it's this treasure you keep under lock and key. But with the right motivations, trust is actually free for the taking. It's one thing I find so enticing about you humans."

"Why?" I asked through my fury. "Why promise my freedom then put me through all of this?"

"Who *promised* you freedom? Or anything, for that matter?" Eris took a drag on her cheroot and let the smoke ooze out of her nose in bluish tendrils. When my eyes flickered to Marius and back, she grinned. "No, Catherine, I can't give you your freedom. Two days ago I may have been willing to part with you if someone else won the game, but that was before I knew about this glorious little power of yours. When Dahlia passed ownership to me, I knew you were a meager talent at best but had no idea she had bound you. Now that the muzzle is off, if you will, and I see what an asset you could be, I cannot let you slip away. Oh, no."

"Then why the chips?"

"At first it was exactly what you thought. You had to gather the chips in order to prove each of the players approved you as a worthy bet."

"But now?"

"Now you are far too valuable for me to lose. Without the chips, the bet is nullified."

"But they'll be here. The others—Coyote, Maui, Puck. They can tell you the truth. They gave me their chips to sign off on your stupid bet!"

Eris tilted her head to the side with pity. "Dear, do you actually think a table of liars gives a good goddamn about the truth? Please!" She clucked her tongue with disgust. "We're all in it for ourselves, and we'll do whatever it takes to win. This way, though, I get to keep you, and I have the added bonus of knowing Maui and Puck have tipped their hands. I see a bit of what they've been trying to do, and now I can make them miserable. Even if someone has a better hand, I still win."

My head spun trying to sort it all out. The levels of intrigue, the games stacked one on top of the other. I couldn't fathom the amount of backstabbing and paranoia Eris and her kith lived with. This is why I never played RISK as a kid.

"And you two!" she exclaimed, head falling back with throaty laughter. She gestured with her cigar between me and the satyr. "The way you pressed one another's buttons! Here you are, always at the other's throat, and yet you're such similar creatures. The chaos you cause one another is simply delicious. I couldn't have done it better myself."

In that goddamn uncomfortable chair, I simmered and stewed. She was so smug, so proud of the strife she had wrought in my life. My rage damn near choked me.

"But," she said rising from the couch, "enough chitchat." Motioning to the delayed game, she said, "I have guests arriving shortly to settle a small matter, and frankly, dear, I don't think you're ready to sit at the big kids' table."

As icy fear plunged into my system, my rage ebbed. "What do you mean?"

"Marius, take her to the panic room. It's soundproof, and the walls are made of iron. That should hold her nicely."

"She's a technomage," Marius said. "Is it wise to put her there, Lady?"

Eris waved this off with a flippant sigh. "It's been disconnected and is little more than a broom closet at this point. Nothing she can do there."

"Are you certain you wouldn't rather I take her back to her apartment?"

Annoyed, Eris wheeled on him. With a lightning fast motion of her clawlike hand, a *whip-crack* snapped through the air. Marius reeled back, his hair a black nimbus around his face. As he regained his balance, he brought a hand to his cheek. His fingers came away bloody.

"Stop questioning me, satyr, and do as you're told! Put her in the panic room and make sure she stays there until everyone has left."

Even as he grabbed me by the arm, Marius wouldn't look at me. I struggled, hissing insults through my teeth. I kicked his shins and feet, balled up my fists and tried to wrench myself away from him, but my strength was puny compared to his. Adding injury to insult, Marius used the momentum of my flailing to bring my bad knee to a sharp stop against his leg. I let out a yelp of pain as stars flickered in front of my eyes. Sagging into him, I let my arms go limp at my sides and tried to breathe away the fire in my leg.

We rounded a corner, and while Marius fiddled with a false wall panel, I slipped a hand into my pocket. The plastic of Flynn's gadget was warm and smooth.

A thick metal door slid open. Our reflections bounced from a wall of dark monitors. On another wall were a selection of rations and several bottles of wine—at least Eris had her priorities. Stairs of corrugated metal led up to another door. Dual access. *Smart. No sense wasting time running up or down stairs in the case of an emergency.* On the third and final wall squatted a cushy sofa that would double nicely as a bed.

Marius flung me to the couch, his face drawn tight and expression grim. Blood trickled down his cheek from a thin slice just beneath his right eye.

"Just sit there, and don't make this any harder than it needs to be," he said, voice muted and flat. He turned his back on me, put one hand on the doorframe and stuck his head out as if listening.

"How could you? Goddammit, Marius, after everything… How could you?"

He didn't answer. Marius just stood there taking my lashes on his back.

"I trusted you! I promised I'd help you, and *this* is how you repay me?"

"You don't know anything," he said over his shoulder, anger rising. I palmed my weapon and took a step toward him. "Maybe not, but I know you. I see you for the selfish prick you are."

"Did I ever claim to be otherwise?"

"You're dying. Did you know that?"

He flinched but didn't respond.

"I saw it. There in the alley? You're dying, Marius. You're nothing but a sad, empty bastard who's going to die alone without even being able to enjoy a last meal."

"Now you listen to me," Marius hissed as he whirled around and came at me. He didn't get the chance to finish. The moment he pressed himself to me the anger in his eyes bled away. I don't know what he felt physically, but I saw the sting of shock in the way his mouth fell open, the jerk of his limbs. He looked down between us and saw the black plastic of my stunner pressed to his abdomen, my hand still wrapped around it.

"Bugger," he breathed.

Marius fell to the ground in a heap of leather and denim.

CHAPTER TWENTY-FOUR
"The Righteous & the Wicked"

Stabbing someone from the front is far more difficult than stabbing a person's—or satyr's—back. I had to meet his eyes when I did it. In this case, I hadn't shanked him with a blade, or anything, but the act of betrayal cut just as deeply. Shaking, I backed away, the stunner spent of its current. Though my anger was fresh, it didn't change that I'd gotten used to thinking of Marius as a friend.

Eyes staring at me with cold accusation, he lay motionless on the floor. The effects of Flynn's stunner were temporary, so I didn't have time to linger. I had to get the chips back from Eris before the other gods arrived. They had to finish that game—I couldn't be shackled to Eris any longer. Maybe I could even get in the hand by proving that I not only had the tokens but by illuminating the others that Eris had tried to screw them and renege on her bet. I might still be able to turn this around in my favor.

Maybe. But I had to work quickly.

This being my first time in the house of Discord, I had no earthly clue where to begin. Luckily, though, I had a pretty good map of the area right here at my fingertips.

If this panic room was anything like the ones I'd helped set up and maintain for work, each of these monitors connected to a closed-circuit camera somewhere around the house. Eris said the room had been disconnected, but even if that was true, it didn't matter in the slightest. Not to me.

I laid my hands on the space between the monitors and reached out into the house's wiring as I had in the elevator. Like water filling a long, dry riverbed, current flowed into the cords and cables lacing beneath the walls. Here and there, the connections clogged with old breaks or cracks. I did my best to mend them, stitching them together with my magic. With a pulse of light, the screens winked into action and fed me images of the rest of the house.

Eris moved from one screen to the other as she slipped from a hallway into the master bedroom. She opened a dresser drawer and tossed in the three poker chips. She jerked her head as the doorbell rang, checked the clock, and then closed the drawer, leaving the chips in the bedroom as she went to meet her first guest.

I skimmed the screens until I found one broadcasting a view of the front door. Coyote stood on the doorstep. Like Eris, he'd dressed casually for the poker game in jeans and a weathered Aerosmith T-shirt. He carried himself loosely, and his smile was carefree. The Native held a small bouquet of roses clutched in his fist.

Tinny versions of their voices hissed through a nearby speaker as they greeted one another.

"Coyote," Eris said. "You shouldn't have."

"These aren't for you, hag, but for the redhead."

I blushed a bit and felt a moment of kindness toward Coyote. The enemy of my enemy and all that.

As she shut the door and led him into the living room, Eris added, "About that. There's a bit of an issue, but we'll discuss it later when the others arrive."

While Eris entertained Coyote, I scanned the rest of the screens. The images weren't arranged to imitate the floor plan of the house from what I'd seen of it, so I had to do a bit of creative thinking. It was like putting a puzzle together with no idea how it's supposed to look at the end. Every couple of minutes I glanced over my shoulder. Marius lay still and silent. I knew the stunner's effects could last as long as a half hour, but I didn't want to dally on the off chance the satyr's non-human constitution would shake it off sooner.

Sweat prickled over my forehead, and I began to feel the strain of powering the security system. My temples pulsed with dull pain, as a wave of fatigue crashed over me. The screens went dark. I swayed for a moment as the current left me, my head swimming with a warm, inky blackness that promised sweet rest. I wanted to sleep and recharge while the world spun around me.

Shaking away the temptation to hibernate, I reached back into the wiring with my thoughts. "Come on," I growled as if I might be able to intimidate the damn system back into action. Whatever wellspring I'd tapped into, though, had run dry. The wires of this room refused to connect with the rest of the power grid. The monitors remained dead, and the panic room fell into darkness.

If I could sneak up to the bedroom, the chips were mine. The best route I'd found was obvious: the other entrance to the panic room. I padded up the metal stairs and pressed myself against the door. With no knobs or handles, the door opened and closed on an electric track not unlike an elevator on Star Trek. I pushed my fingertips against the doorjamb and tried to slide the door open, but it didn't budge.

For a moment, I thought of Flynn's words in Puck's illusion. If I couldn't do something as simple as open a door, I was useless. Weary and hollow from my last attempt of turning on the power in the panic room, I opened my senses once more to the mechanics in front of me. As I explored the circuitry with my mind, I found a thick wall of plastic where copper should be. Furthermore, what wiring was left had melted and fused the door shut. Damn. I wasn't getting anywhere that way.

On the floor below, Marius groaned.

Letting go of the power left me feeling as drained and lifeless as the cables in the wall. The simplest movement of raising a hand took as much effort as pushing through Jell-O. As quickly as I could, I wobbled down the stairs, past the writhing satyr, and out the way we'd come in. It wasn't ideal—Eris could catch me at any moment—but it was my only option.

Back in the hallway, I made a left and crept toward the living room.

The easiest way to the bedroom would be to run up the stairs that emptied into the living room. Coyote and Eris, however, had a clear view of those steps. From what I'd seen on the monitors, I had one other option: sliding glass doors on the balcony. I could sneak by the gods and out the back door. Once outside I'd be able to run around the pool and mount the stairs to an upper deck. If I'd read the monitors correctly, I'd end up in the same bedroom where Eris had stashed the chips.

Holding my breath, I crouched and sort of duck-walked into the living room. Every hobble sent a fresh pulse of pain through my knee. The joint was beginning to stiffen up again. Our escapades negated any good I'd done with a night's rest.

As I lurked behind one of the chairs, I could hear Eris and Coyote in the kitchen bickering over the *fzt-pop* of bottles being uncapped and the rattle of potato chips or some other snack tumbling into a glass bowl.

The chairs formed a triangle around the coffee table, the couch running along the bottommost line. From my place behind the chair, I'd have to sneak around the sofa and cut across ten feet or so of open space to get to the patio doors. If either of the gods took a seat in one of the chairs, they would see me as I tried to make my exit. I took advantage of their trip to the enclosed kitchen and scuttled as quietly as I could toward the patio.

Still squabbling, Eris and Coyote emerged from the kitchen. I froze, pressing myself up against the back of the sofa.

"Tell me, Eris."

"I don't want to have to repeat myself when everyone else gets here, Coyote, so you'll just have to be patient."

The Native American trickster rumbled with dissatisfaction as he took a seat in one of the chairs. I couldn't see which. Eris flopped onto the couch.

Shitshitshitshit.

Cigar smoke curled through the air. For a brief moment I entertained the horrible thought that she'd be able to see me there, as if the tendrils of scented air were an extension of her senses. Maybe she had eyes in the back of her head. But if I tried to make a run for it now, Coyote would notice. And something warned me that if he saw me trying to make a break for it he wouldn't keep quiet. Pressing my palms to the floor, I reached for the house's power grid intent on shutting down the lights, escaping under the cover of confusing darkness. My head spun with the effort and I gave up. My energy fizzled and somewhere in my mind I heard the sound of a sad trombone. No powers to bank on, I sat waiting, hoping for a better chance to come along.

The glass of the end table next to me clinked against the base of her bottle. Cigars, beer, pajamas—this was getting too weird for me.

A loud noise barked from somewhere near the front of the house. I nearly jumped out of my skin then clamped a hand over my mouth so Eris wouldn't hear my frightened breaths.

"What was that? Is someone else here?" Coyote asked.

"My assistant," Eris said lazily. "Had a problem with the building today, and I had a few things I needed him to attend to. Menial work. He won't be a bother."

Eris rested her arm over the back of the sofa and more thick smoke wafted into my face. At the worst possible moment for such a thing to happen, I sneezed. I stifled it as best as I could, but Eris's head whipped around at the choked noise.

Still pressed against the back of the couch, I tilted my head up to see if the goddess was looking at me. Warily, she glanced over her shoulder, never actually turning around or peering over the back. Instead, the goddess's hand gripped the sofa in an ever-tightening claw.

Then the doorbell rang. Thank the gods for a change.

"Ah," Coyote said, "our friends have arrived."

Eris snorted, launching herself up. "I don't have any friends."

She and Coyote left the room, and as I watched the gods reflected in the patio doors, they made their way to the foyer. Once they disappeared, it was time to make myself scarce. I stood up and took to the door at a full run, unlatched it as quietly as I could, and slipped out onto the back porch.

Outside, the night was cool and uncharacteristically moist. Lit from inside, the pool gave off an eerie, green glow. Ripples in the surface cast ever-shifting webs of light onto the patio and the walls of the house. As I lurched away from the door, I saw Eris and Coyote return to the living room with Maui following close behind.

Two down, two to go.

I didn't have much time.

Skirting the edge of the long, narrow pool, I tried not to listen to the gentle lapping of the water. I was so damn thirsty I could have put a straw in the pool and sucked it dry. Ignoring my body's craving, I padded toward the wood-slat stairs that led up to the balcony. The whole backyard remained cloaked in shadows. Briefly, I worried something vicious and beaked waited there for me, but the safety offered by the darkness lured me in.

My steps went off the concrete pool deck and scuffed onto sandy dirt.

"Leaving so soon?"

Jumping, I gasped and whirled around. The stranger sat in one of the deck chairs, his feet up in front of him and hands laced behind his head. The pool made shadows dance across his face, obscuring his features. From here, the most I could see was his platinum-blond hair, square jaw, and slim nose.

"Catherine? This is your name, yes?" he asked, his voice melodic and sweet.

I nodded, willing my heart to leave my throat and return to its proper place in my chest. It could also stop beating at a trillion miles per hour. *Any time now.*

"Who are you?" I asked, my tone thinner and higher than I'd like to admit.

"Just a friend," he said.

Was this Loki? I wracked my brain but couldn't fathom who else it might be. "A friend? Then what are you doing out here? Shouldn't you be in the house with the rest of the Brotherhood of Mutants?"

His teeth gleamed in the night as he smiled. "I thought I'd work on my tan. What about you? I hope you're not running away."

I shook my head. "I can't run away. Not from them. They'd all find me eventually."

"Oh, you look too young to be such a pessimist. Where's your faith?"

"I have very little faith in gods or goddesses," I said bluntly.

"And yet, you've seen them."

"It's not a matter of believing whether or not they exist, it's about believing they are forces of good in this world. They start wars and tear people apart. They play games with humans like we're toys. I have yet to see any of the gods do something useful."

"Fair enough," he said, bobbing his head in assent. "But then that begs the question—where *is* your faith?"

I started to answer, but the words caught in my throat. Where was my faith? Machines? Order? Technology? Did I have any faith left at this point?

"I don't know," I said finally.

"Can I offer you a piece of advice, Catherine?"

I flopped my hands in the air helplessly. "Why not?"

"You need to find the answer to this question. Not tonight or tomorrow but sometime soon. This kind of knowledge has its own power. It may come in handy."

For a moment, we stared at one another. "Who are you?" I asked again.

"Go," he said. "You don't have much time. The others are almost here."

I didn't hesitate. I jogged to the stairs and began to climb them two at a time. Each step resonated in the quiet night as if it were cannon fire. I expected Eris to come crashing out of her house at any moment and find me skulking about.

But with a few more strides, I made it to a pair of sliding glass doors. The room on the other side was dark, but it should have been the bedroom according to the monitors. Inside and to the right would be the dresser. And the poker chips.

Palming the handle, I gave it a cursory tug. Locked.

I drew in a deep breath, and with a flick of my will, the lock disengaged. When I pulled the handle, the door glided open. I took a moment to be grateful Eris didn't use a Charley-Bar to keep people from doing exactly what I'd done.

In case I needed to make a quick exit, I left the balcony door open, and then I swept over to the dresser and opened the top drawer. There, precisely where I'd seen her drop them, were three black poker chips. But they weren't marked with golden apples. Staring up at me was the logo of the Four Queens.

CHAPTER TWENTY-FIVE
"Fortune Faded"

"No," I whispered desperately. "No, this isn't right! Come on!"

I turned the chips over in my hand, begging whatever gods there might be that actually like me. *Just help me this once… Please, just make this work and…*

Promises tumbled through my thoughts in the most fervent prayer of my life as I rifled through the drawer. Eris's markers didn't miraculously appear, and the chips in my hand still read Four Queens. For a moment, I entertained the thought that I'd been wrong. This wasn't the correct room.

I scurried back to the balcony and looked along the length of the deck. I didn't see any more sliding glass doors. Gazing up and down, I wondered if I'd miscounted the number of floors. I grasped at any straw I could find, and they all added up to nothing.

I thumped a fist on the railing, defeated. Once again, I'd hoped I could change things, but in the end the game was stacked against me.

Staring down at the pool, several possibilities made themselves apparent. First of all, I could jump. I doubted I'd succeed in killing myself and didn't particularly like that idea for many reasons, the least of which being that I didn't want to die. Suicide wouldn't solve any of my problems. Besides, with all the trickster gods lurking about, my luck would see me landing on my bum leg and adding a broken arm or other bones to the list of injuries. My insurance isn't all that great, either, so I'd find myself destitute or further into hock with a deity.

Option two: running. But like I'd told the blond stranger, there was nowhere I could go that these gods would not follow. And what about the bet? If I ran, would Eris keep me or would they finish the game and pass my soul on to the winner? No, running was a bad idea all around. Bailing wouldn't get my life back; it would make me a fucking coward.

I let out a peal of exhausted giggles that made me sound as if I belonged in a strait jacket. And who knows—maybe at that point I did. Because the most appealing idea I had was to walk downstairs right into the mouth of mayhem and seriously put a cramp in Eris's plan. I grinned as I imagined the surprise on her face. And what could she do about it? She had to save face with the other gods. If she let on that I wasn't supposed to be there, she'd tip her hand that she'd been about to swindle her fellow swindlers.

Yes. I'd tromp down the stairs with a smile on my face and see how the bitch liked it when someone threw a magic monkey wrench into her plans.

I might not own my soul, but I could sure as hell control my actions.

Fuck Eris and her friends.

My life. My soul. My rules.

Before I could talk myself out of it, I spun on my heel and let out a squeak as I came face-to-surly-face with a pissed-off satyr. His hard stare held my eyes.

"That," he sternly, "was a very dirty trick."

I drew a breath and laughed it right back at him. "Says the backstabbing, double-crossing son of a bitch who has to do the bidding of a vindictive harpy?"

"Oh, do shut up," he spat.

"How long has it really been, Marius? I mean, you've been Eris's minion for how many centuries? Waiting for her to decide it's worthwhile to cut your leash and lift your curse? And here in Vegas? She's torturing you and enjoying every second of it. Meanwhile, *you* can't enjoy anything. Not food, not drink. You can't even get it up to go fuck a showgirl."

He answered with cold, steely silence. It didn't stop me, though. He'd hurt me, and dammit, I wanted blood.

"And you know the best part? I don't have to do a damn thing. You're wasting away on your own. I don't have to lift a finger to score revenge on you. All I have to do is sit back while Eris pulls your strings."

Marius glared, his green eyes taking on a granite toughness. "And all I have to do is push," he said.

I felt the sting of something pricking my belly and looked down to see that Marius had drawn his sword. Its point puckered the fabric of my T-shirt, blade gleaming wickedly in the moonlight. Gulping down a ball of fear and sucking in my stomach, I pulled my eyes back up to meet his. His expression didn't waver.

"Do I have your attention?" he said with a simmer.

I swallowed another lump—this time of pride—and nodded.

"Good. Now hold out your right hand."

I complied, unwilling to take my eyes from his. I sensed movement, his left hand rising to meet mine. Then I felt a cool weight land in my palm. For an awkward moment, we stared at one another, waiting for some cue to look away. He gave an almost imperceptible nod that I took as permission.

A golden apple winked at me from the center of a black poker chip. I held the stack—the markers that could change my life.

Like a fish, my mouth worked, but no sound came out.

Marius's sword arm fell and the saber disappeared. "You're welcome," he said. The satyr whirled around and strutted back into the bedroom, leaving me on the balcony gaping after him.

My brain jerked back to life and I followed him. "How?"

He stopped short of the door. Giving me the barest of glances over his shoulder, he asked, "Does it matter?"

"Yes."

Marius walked to me, opened my hand, and dragged a finger over the poker chips. The apple disappeared, replaced by the casino's logo.

"Don't trust your eyes," he breathed.

As he removed his hand, the chips reverted to the goddess's markers.

Folding my fingers over the tokens, he leaned in close, eyes insistent. When he spoke, his voice was little more than an intense whisper.

"There is more than one game being played tonight. If you want to be rid of Eris, you need to be at the table before the last card is drawn."

Marius reached into my other hand and took the false chips, leaving me with a stack of Eris's actual markers.

"But, how did you get them? Why didn't you tell me?"

"Go, Catherine. You're running out of time."

Marius left the room, padding into the carpeted hallway.

"Where are you going?" I said after him.

He answered without looking back. "Plausible deniability."

He disappeared into another bedroom, leaving me with a head stuffed full of questions and a stack of poker chips in my hand. Most of those questions, however, would have to wait.

From downstairs I heard the doorbell ring again. Coyote and Maui had already arrived. I could safely assume the blonde by the pool had been Loki, which meant that Puck had just arrived. Any minute now the game would resume, and my fate would be decided. I could either be a part of it or sit idle and watch it all happen to me.

Fuck that.

I slid the chips into my hip pocket, and with a stomach-flopping thrill of fear and excitement, I trundled merrily down the stairs to greet the gods.

CHAPTER TWENTY-SIX
"Suck My Kiss"

I rounded a corner into the foyer just as Eris shut the door behind Puck. While the Fae lord's lips turned up in a sly smile, Eris's face fell. Like a pair of comedy and tragedy masks, the two stared at me for a moment.

"Cat," Puck said. "A pleasure as always."

I kept my face blank and my voice chilly. "Puck."

"Catherine," Eris muttered. I watched as confusion rippled over her face, followed by bitter anger. She couldn't reprimand me, not here and now. She had to go along as if nothing had happened.

"Yes?" I asked.

The goddess made a choked sound, like a song skipping. When she resumed, her tone was congenial as ever. "Have you seen Marius? I want to make sure he's finished his tasks before we start."

I shook my head and shrugged. "Haven't seen him."

Her gold eyes shimmered with hatred. "Excuse me," she said. "I need to go check on my good-for-nothing assistant."

She breezed away. Before Puck could get a word in, I turned and bounced into the living room. Coyote settled into the chair he'd sat in earlier, Maui gazed out the patio doors at the pool, and the blond hovered over the table, surveying the cards and chips as he ate a handful of pretzels.

Now that I saw him in proper light, I took a good, long look at Loki. He was big. Not body-builder or barbarian big, but his broad shoulders, barrel chest, and lantern jaw reminded me of a military man. That was it. He had the brawny look of a soldier. As he circled the table, reading the signs and portents on the felt, he hunched his six-foot frame. Like the others, he'd adopted a casual look. The sleeves of his T-shirt stretched taut over the muscles of his arms. His white-blond hair was tied in a small knot at the back of his skull, his eyes an arctic blue and cheeks round and rosy.

"Gentlemen," I said cheerfully. I sauntered into the kitchen and helped myself to one of the bottles in Eris's fridge. I'm normally not one for beer, but I was so damn thirsty, the ale might as well be the nectar of gods.

Puck meandered past me, and the others lifted their heads as I plopped into one of the armchairs. I threw my legs over one side and reclined against the other, head resting on my bent elbow.

A chorus of the gods' voices chanted variations on, "Good evening."

Maui took the last chair while Puck returned from the kitchen with his own beer in his hand. He stretched his stocky form along the sofa.

Coyote lifted a hand and caressed the air with his fingers. He looked at me, his brow furrowing with concern. "You are injured. I see a problem on the knee. What happened?"

Casually, I waved my bottle between the Hawaiian and the Sidhe. "These two tried to kill me."

The old man's face hardened and flushed with ruddy disapproval. "That was not part of our agreement," he chided. "You have broken the rules, therefore, you disqualify your claims. Very well, she is mine."

From the poker table, the blond—presumably Loki—called out, "You wish, old man."

"I had to test the merchandise," Puck explained. "Only way to be sure Eris wasn't trying to pawn off something of lesser quality."

Coyote looked at me, his cheeks drooping like a hound's. "I knew that. Hey," he barked as he rose to his feet. "Come with me, young lady, to the bathroom. I'll test you for myself."

I rolled my eyes and took a drink, pointedly staying in place.

"Sit," Loki said to the native, annoyed.

"These jokers nearly damaged my prize, but they have a point. I should get to sample Eris's offering."

"I said *sit down*. There isn't time."

Coyote begrudgingly took to his chair, mumbling, "There's always time." He sipped from a tumbler and leaned back, brooding. "Loki isn't even here yet, so we can't start."

I flashed a look up at the blond. "I thought you were Loki."

Maui snickered. "That's rich."

As the other gods chuckled, Not-Loki grinned enigmatically and popped another pretzel into his mouth.

Obviously, I was missing some inside joke here.

"All right then," I said, "who the hell are you?"

Sandals flip-flopping loudly, he padded around to the front of the table, taking his sweet time to finish his snack. The way his mouth stretched and his jaw flexed, it seemed he was doing his best not to let loose with riotous laughter. Dusting off his hands, he leaned against the table. As he crossed his meaty arms over his chest he said, "I'm the dealer."

"The dealer? What? You don't have a name?"

"Guess," he grinned.

"Rumplestiltskin?"

He snorted with laughter but refused to answer.

"Imbecile!" Eris hissed as she entered the room.

Behind her, Marius shuffled in, holding his head and looking around as if dazed. The goddess swatted Puck's legs off of the sofa and plopped her bony ass down. Glaring at me, she fumed.

Good.

The doorbell rang, and Eris shooed Marius toward the door. "Get it."

With a half-bow, Marius trotted off.

"Useless," Eris spat.

Voices drifted in from the foyer.

"Oh, you again," Marius drawled.

"Are you going to cause trouble or are you going to let me in?"

I closed my eyes and focused, trying to remember where I'd heard his voice before.

"Well," Marius said, some of the life returning to his words, "some would argue that letting you in is trouble enough, but I suppose if you're going to insist."

"Excellent. I'll see that your boss throws you a bone or two. Now run along."

The door shut, and I still couldn't place the voice. Marius returned, taking up a space behind the goddess.

As the newcomer swaggered into the room, my brand prickled with a cold wind, and it hit me. I'd seen him before. Just last night, even. Strawberry blond, his hair short and spiky, with pale, chiseled features and eyes the exact blue of a gas flame.

"You," I blurted out.

"Me?" he said pointing to himself.

"You're the guy who stopped us at the gala to check our invitation."

He regarded me with hooded eyes and mild amusement. "Good memory."

"Harassing my people, Loki?" Eris said, adding a *tsk*.

This was Loki?

He turned his words to his hostess but didn't respect Eris enough to look at her. "By the end of the night, who's to say they'll still be your people?"

"Only the girl is on the table."

Coyote slapped his knee and leaned forward. "I think this is a stellar idea. I'll have the girl on the table."

"Give it up, old man!" Maui called. "The *wahine* is mine."

"You tried to kill her."

"And I will do the same with you if you don't shut up."

"You have no fangs, fisherman."

Meanwhile, Eris and Loki bickered about the stakes of the game.

"Listen, thief, the satyr stays with me. As for the girl, you haven't won her yet. In fact, no one has. For all you know, the hand will be mine, and she'll stay right here."

"Then why are you afraid, you jealous hag?"

Puck sipped at his beer, giggling as the other gods quarreled. When voices began to rise and echo in the hollow house, the dealer whistled loudly. The deities stopped posturing, and all eyes turned to the blond man.

"I know you all have a busy schedule of bullshit and mayhem to keep, so if you don't mind, why don't we resume the game?"

Like admonished children, the gods stood up and took their places around the table. Clockwise from the dealer's space they arranged themselves; Coyote, Maui, Puck, Loki, and Eris. The dealer laid his fingertips on the table. As if he'd struck a chord on a piano, a sharp sound filled the air for an instant, a deep thrum of power pulsing. The felt, chips, and cards flashed with gold-white light for an instant, and the enchantment was lifted.

As the gods took their seats, the dealer spread his hands and shot me a quizzical look. "Would you care to come watch? You are the guest of honor, after all."

Eris stole a glance at her cards then leaned both elbows on the table. "Yes," she said around the cigar. Another drag then a puff of smoke framed her gaunt face. "Join us, Catherine. You should tell these asshats what you told me when you arrived."

Coyote craned his neck in question. The others faced me with various expressions of wonder. All but Loki. He sat there, his back to me, fiddling with the stack of chips in front of him.

I got to my feet and took slow steps to the table. With everyone seated, I could see just how desperate Eris's bet was. Any gambler in Vegas would be happy with one of the gods' seats. Maui and Puck were about even with eight stacks of colorful chips before them. Coyote trailed them, but not by much. Loki, though, had amassed quite the hoard.

The Norse trickster hunched over in his seat, feet hooked around the metal legs of his chair. With each hand, he fondled a tower, fingers deftly spreading the chips apart and shuffling them.

Coyote clutched his whiskey. A moment ago I would've testified that it held little more than melting ice, but as I watched, amber liquid rose up from the bottom as if some ghostly hand poured the ancient Native's libation. As he had at the gala, he tapped his fat, silver ring on the glass. I briefly wondered if the rhythm meant anything, if the tune in his head was sacred or just something he liked. Knowing what I did about him, it was probably the beat of song by some bubble-gum-pop princess.

Suppressing a shudder, I looked around the circle.

The islander with the sun in his smile reclined, stretching his muscular legs under the table. Beneath the fabric of his ribbed tank top, the lines of his taut abs and chest were visible. With his coffee-black stare, he held my attention then twitched his pecs. Winking, he turned back to the game.

Puck counted out his chips as if he didn't trust that his winnings had gone unmolested. Who could blame him? The beings at this table had stolen fire, snared the sun, and started wars. It would be nothing to snatch a chip or two. Puck sat several inches away from the table itself. He'd pushed his chair back so far that when he leaned forward, only his wrists touched the felt. Though he tried to maintain his arrogance, Puck's face lined with pain.

The metal, I realized. The metal frame of the table. The chair, too. Even through his clothes and at a distance his body reacted to the iron. I wondered if this was why Puck had grown so wicked since Shakespeare told of the fae's playful escapades. Since the Industrial Revolution, nearly everything had some component of iron or steel.

My eyes drifted to an empty chair between the Fae lord and Loki. There were no chips or cards in front of this one.

"Whose place was this?" I asked, resting my hands on the back of the chair.

"Anansi," said the dealer, confirming Maui's tale. "He folded early and left us. Since he has no part in this hand, he doesn't need to be at the table."

"You're stalling, Cat," Eris said, cigar held tightly between her teeth. "Tell them about your unfortunate accident."

"Tell us what, *wahine?*"

I stared at the goddess, smoldering with eight years of angst and trying to see what she was playing at. She had to know this wouldn't work, that I had the markers.

But wait…how could she?

With a flood of shocked glee, the thought flashed through my mind. *I've got her.* I had the bitch right where I wanted her. Eris had no clue Marius had given her a false stack of chips. And she didn't know I had the real ones tucked into my pocket. And she wouldn't know until I set them out for her and her demented poker buddies to see.

Keeping a straight face was a herculean task. "I have no idea what she's talking about," I said.

"Please!" A cloud puffed out of the goddess. "You came here crying tonight that you had lost the chips you were tasked with collecting. You see?" she addressed her fellow deities. "She can't keep a couple of trinkets for more than a few hours. What good is she?"

Around the table, eyebrows raised in succession as if doing the Wave. All eyes turned to me.

"Is this true?" Loki asked.

Guiltily, I stuffed my hands into my pockets and shifted from foot to foot. Eris beamed, triumph etched over every inch of her craggy face.

"Well, Catherine?" she asked. "Do you have the chips?"

I met those gold eyes and poured as much of my hate into my stare as I could muster. And believe, me, I've saved up quite a bit for her over the years. I leaned over, resting both hands on the table. "What do you think?" I snarled.

As I straightened up, my hand slid back to reveal the three black chips, each with a gleaming golden apple at its center.

I wished I had a camera. Or maybe a painter. Fuck, I'd have settled for a caveman with a chisel. I never wanted to forget her expression as she saw her signature game pieces glinting in the light.

What little color she had drained from her face in an instant. As smoke poured out of her narrow mouth, I saw her chin quiver slightly. For a split-second I thought—and hoped—she would throw up.

"How do you like them apples?" I asked.

While the others hadn't been privy to her plot, the gods knew Eris well enough to understand she'd been beaten. Laughter quickly turned into false coughing as the goddess glared at her poker buddies.

The dealer smiled with satisfaction. "All right. Now that this is settled, I think we're ready to get back to business." Sparing me a glance, he asked, "Are you familiar with hold 'em poker or should I explain so you can follow more easily?"

I knew the basics of the game. I'd even tried playing online a few times, but I wasn't so good at the bluffing, even through the interwebz. Anyway, I knew the dealer gave each player two cards for their hand. With intervals of betting, the dealer would lay out five community cards. Whoever could muster the best combination using his hand and the community cards would take the pot.

And my soul.

Pretty simple as far as rules go, but mastering the game would take me far more than a minute.

In answer to the dealer, I nodded. "I've played once or twice."

His chin dipped, and he went on in his melodious voice. "So, here's a recap for those of you just joining us. After the flop, the first three cards, Anansi folded. At the turn, Eris went all-in and included the soul of one human"—he gestured to me with his open palm—"Now, each of you gentlemen has had the opportunity to validate the bet. I will ask you all: do you approve?"

"Oh, yes," Coyote chortled. "Very much." As he turned his attention to his whiskey I heard him mutter something about his fondness for redheads.

The dealer addressed the next god. "Maui?"

"I like this *wahine*. She has moxie and a spirit as fiery as Pele's. I approve."

Puck fixed me with his eyes and leered. "The Fae would welcome her service."

"Catherine," the dealer said, "please put their tokens into the pot."

I slid the chips forward into the mass of colorful clay.

Then it was up to Loki.

For a moment, I feared he would say no. What would happen then? If I had to stay with Eris, she'd never forgive me for humiliating her. I'd pay for that one in blood and tears for the rest of my days and then some. Loki hadn't tested me as the others had. No mind fucks or quiet drinks. No giant birds and chases across the city. Did he even care one way or the other?

The Norseman's gas-flame eyes tracked up and down my body. "I like the way she handles a hammer," he said simply. His chip hit the pile with a *clack*. "I approve."

Hammer?

Holy shit. Had Loki dropped the hammer so I could kill the shark back at my apartment? I started to lift a finger, to stammer out a question, but the dealer clapped his hands.

"Okay. Moving on then."

"Burn and turn," Maui muttered.

"Catherine," the dealer called.

I jerked my attention away from Loki. "Yes?"

"Would you care to deal the final card?"

My eyes darted around, uncertain. "Why?"

"It's your soul," he said. "Don't you want to have a hand in what becomes of it?"

Struck dumb by the fact that he'd echoed my earlier thoughts, I stepped around the table and stood beside the dealer.

"Take the top card off the deck," he said, "and put it to the side. Then draw the next card and lay it out for all to see."

My mouth went dry, and my fingers shook. I discarded off the top and then stopped, fingers grazing the next card. I swallowed hard. The past two days distilled into one motion of my hand, one little playing card.

"Have faith," the dealer whispered. He placed a hand on my shoulder, and I felt empowered. I could do this.

"Come what may or hell to pay," I said.

"That's the spirit."

I flipped the last card and put it on the table.

CHAPTER TWENTY-SEVEN
"Falling Into Grace"

"Ten of diamonds," the dealer called. "A girl's best friend."

I let out a breath I hadn't realized I'd been holding. "So, now what?"

"As Eris has already wagered everything she has, she can no longer up her ante, nor can she fold. Betting will start with Loki."

He knocked his knuckles on the table to indicate he would hold without betting.

After careful consideration, Puck took half of one of his piles and set it on the felt. Sliding the stack of chips into the center of the table, Puck said, "Ten thousand."

Bug-eyed, I did a quick bit of math. I don't know if they were betting in dollars, rupees, or puppy kisses, but if half a stack equaled ten large, Puck and Maui sat with more than a cool half million. Each. By this rationale, Loki's take looked like it could easily fund a state lottery.

And that's just assuming each chip had the same value. If Puck was betting with nickels when he still had quarters, I couldn't begin to estimate how much bank these gods threw around.

Maui chucked in a handful chips. "See the ten and raise you five."

Coyote pushed a stack into the center. "Twenty."

"Loki?" the dealer asked with a flick of his icy eyes.

The Norseman added his wager mutely.

The betting swung back to Puck. He had to decide if he would call the twenty thousand now on the table or push the stakes higher. Easing up the tips of his cards, he glanced at his hand and checked it against the five community cards. Pearls of sweat glistened at his green hairline, and I wondered if it was the stress of the game or the pain of the metal table being so close to him.

"Call," he said, adding the other half of his stack.

Maui raised an eyebrow at Coyote and put on a wry smile. "You don't have anything, old man. Thirty."

Without batting an eyelash, Coyote relieved himself of another stack. "Forty."

Loki called without raising again.

Dragging his hands up over his temples, Puck sat back and sighed. "I'll call forty."

It went on this way: Puck limiting his bets, Maui antagonizing Coyote, and the Native posturing with another raise every time. Loki remained mute. As the numbers climbed and more chips rattled into the pot, I felt like I was on an auction block waiting for the gavel to fall. I wiped my damp palms on my jeans and looked around the room. Eris stared at the ever-growing pile of chips at the center, fuming. Greed wafted from her like the smoke from her cigar. Angry, salivating, she—like me—could only watch and wait.

In the living room, Marius sat on the sofa and pretended to nurse a migraine. The satyr's head fell back and rolled to face the dining room. When he met my eyes, I felt shame like a bitter, acidic tingle on my tongue. I had so many questions for him. Why had he taken the chips? If he was trying to swindle Eris, why? And why hadn't he told me? I'd have gladly helped him with the gambit.

Marius confused the hell out of me.

Two days ago, I'd hated him. He was a smug bastard with no redeeming qualities. Since then, though, I'd seen past the glamour. I'd found myself entertaining the idea that maybe, just maybe, I'd actually enjoy a date with him. Satyr though he might be, Marius was attractive, and in these past couple of days he had proven to be so much more than I thought he was: a pompous ass in a nice suit. Contrary to my beliefs, Marius was a deep well, and I'd only just dipped beneath the surface.

Eris had said Marius and I were similar creatures. Is that why I'd loathed him so much before? Because I subconsciously recognized myself in him?

He closed his eyes and looked away from me. My heart jerked with a pang of sadness, as if I'd missed some sort of opportunity.

"All-in," Coyote said. He stood up from the table and folded his arms across his chest.

The dealer did a little bit of figuring and called out the total. My jaw dropped open. There were countries that cost less than that sum. As the other gods counted out enough to match Coyote's handsome bet, I shook with anticipation. I wiped my palms again and fidgeted with my hair, my belt loops. My mouth felt cottony and dry.

The clink of ice in Coyote's glass drew my attention.

"Can I have a sip of that?"

"Of course," he said handing me the drink.

I knocked back the whole thing in one shot. I'd probably regret it later—for one reason or another—but my nerves blazed, and the thing to douse them was booze.

Coyote stared at me in awe. "Oh, I like you," he rumbled.

To my right the dealer cleared his throat. "Gentlemen?"

In turn, three voices said, "Call." The pot swelled with the addition of their chips.

The dealer pulled his lips back in a smile. "Show 'em."

As one the gods turned over their pocket cards. I looked at everyone's hands, trying to quickly parse out the best hand each could have made with the two queens, a pair of tens, and the jack sitting on the table.

A pair of pocket tens gave Eris a four-of-a-kind. My heart sank, knowing little would beat her.

To my left, Coyote had an eight-to-queen straight.

"Shit!" Puck hissed. He kicked away from his chair and stalked to the door. As it slammed behind him, Maui stared at Puck's hand. Both gods came to the table with a full house, queens over jacks.

Before I could get a look at Loki's cards, the dealer called out, "We have a winner. With a royal flush, Loki wins the hand."

Eris let both hands fall limp to her sides. "That's it," she muttered.

For an instant, I wondered if she would scowl and hand me a scathing parting line. Instead, she rubbed her hands together as if dusting them off. The brand on my arm sizzled. I sucked in a breath at the pain and stared as the apple dissolved. Fresh, pink skin appeared in its place. Without so much as a glance in my direction, she stomped through the living room and into the house.

"My luck is not so good today," Coyote said sadly. "Thank you, young lady, for humoring an old dog and sharing a drink. You've certainly put a smile on my face." The Native turned quietly, left the table and went out into the Las Vegas night. Right after he'd squeezed my ass.

Obviously disappointed, Maui shook my hand. "It was a pleasure. *Aloha oe, wahine.* Until we meet again."

I heard the doors close behind the gods. I dropped into Coyote's seat, unable to draw my eyes away from my forearm.

The brand was gone.

Gone.

Tears rolled down my cheeks as I stroked the tender skin on my wrist. After so long, I'd gotten used to seeing it there. Now it had vanished, and I wanted to dance a jig. Although Loki had won the right to my soul, for this moment I belonged to myself.

"Well done," Loki began.

Shushing him, I held up a hand. "Please, give me a second. I want..." I stifled a sob. The words stuck in my throat and more hot tears stained my face. Wiping them away, I put myself together as best as I could. "I want to feel this for a minute."

"Feel what?" the dealer asked.

"Freedom."

The dealer bobbed his head. "Come on, Loki. Let's leave her to it."

"Wouldn't dream of interfering," the Norseman muttered. The two of them joined Marius in the living room proper just a few feet away. The satyr spared me the shadow of a smile.

I was free.

Crying, I rode a wave of ecstasy. That word had dangled over my head just out of reach for years, tantalizing me and making me miserable. I knew I couldn't keep it. My freedom was on loan until Loki decided to officially claim me for Asgard. In that delicious, fleeting moment, though, I felt complete. I found myself whispering a fervent, "thank you," but I'm not quite sure to whom I offered gratitude.

My muscles relaxed. Hurt I hadn't known I'd endured released their holds, and peace flowed through me. For the first time in nearly a decade, I didn't worry about when the next shoe would drop, didn't sag with resignation. Hope sprang within me until it bubbled out of my mouth in a flood of giggles.

"You've gone mad, haven't you?" Marius asked.

He stood smiling down at me. Filled with joy as I was, I almost hugged him. I suppressed the urge, wiped the last of my tears away, and stood up with a self-conscious laugh.

"For someone who was so worried last night about walking into a room full of deities, you've certainly warmed up to it," he said.

"Was that a compliment?"

He passed me a proud smile but otherwise dropped the subject. "So," he said, "it looks like you'll be switching employers."

I punched him lightly on the shoulder. "Don't go getting all sentimental on me," I said wryly.

"I wouldn't dream of it. By the way, you realize this means professional courtesy goes right out the window. No more blocks on you, Catherine. If I decide to seduce you there will be nothing for it but for you to shag me."

"Right," I laughed.

Marius stared at me, and though his green eyes looked sad, his body practically vibrated with eagerness. He'd fulfilled his end of the bargain. Sure, he'd been a treacherous fuck there near the end and I still didn't understand it, but Marius had done exactly what he said he would do. The satyr made good on both of our bargains. He expected payment.

I opened my mouth to speak, but nothing came out. The dealer and Loki stood a few feet away, and though they were involved in their own conversation, I felt horribly exposed. I took Marius by the arm and ushered him toward the back door. "Would you gentlemen excuse us for a second?"

I turned away from their muttered responses and shoved Marius out onto the patio. Cloaked by the dark night, I felt like I could safely tell him the truth.

"About your curse." I took a deep breath, steeling myself for how much this next part would suck. "I can't lift it."

I chanced a glance up to his face. There by the pool, light and water painted him with an odd web as he clenched his teeth. "Of course," he said icily. "And why should you? I am, after all, a backstabbing, double-crossing son of a bitch."

He started for the door, but I grabbed him. "It's not that."

"Then what is it?" he snapped. "Enlighten me as to why I've risked my neck for you so you could just break your promise."

I stared at his morose face and saw myself there. He craved freedom as fervently as I ever had. What sorts of plans had he made to celebrate the day the curse finally lifted? Like me, he probably had it all figured out. Guilt slithered in my stomach.

I'm worse than Eris. At least she never promised anything. I gave my word and now I'm taking it back? Even Marius held up his end.

I searched for the words and finally settled on, "I don't know how to fix you."

"You don't know how," he said, disappointment darkening his voice. Marius narrowed his eyes. "And you're not even willing to try."

I swallowed hard, unable to respond.

Marius gazed deep into my eyes and I swear he saw my thoughts playing there. His mustache twitched with the shadow of a bitter smile. "Now who's selfish?"

With that kick in the gut, I made my decision. "Drop the glamour."

Marius changed, and I saw the broken satyr as I had glimpsed in the alley. Winding around him, the barbed cables of his curse punctured his skin. Hesitantly, I touched the barbs at his waist. Marius flinched and winced with pain. I saw naked fear streak across his eyes.

"I'm sorry," I muttered.

"Just get on with it."

Hardening my heart against the trembling creature there, I gripped the wire and pulled. His form lit up, and the curse showed itself in a language I could understand. Light danced along the path of the cords around his thighs and waist. Around his neck, glyphs formed in a peacock-blue glow.

I stroked the symbols, and they flared to life. I shielded my eyes from the blinding flash, and when I opened them I found myself in an ancient temple. Marble columns lined the walls and supported the stone ceiling. Some of the pillars were carved into the shapes of lithe maidens— caryatids—and they stared from all angles, watching.

Mist obscured the floor, and I stood in the shadow of a hulking statue.

Upon a gilded throne, a well-muscled god gripped a silver thunderbolt like a spear.

"Zeus," I whispered.

"My husband is not here," called a woman's deep voice.

I whirled around and saw her. Tall and curvaceous, she would have been quite lovely if not for her pinched, sour expression. The curls of her dark hair tumbled down around her face, and the folds of her caftan rippled as she glided through the mists.

"What do you seek, mortal?" Hera called.

I bowed my head respectfully to the Queen of Olympus. "I want to free the satyr Marius of his curse."

Bitter hatred flashed over her face. Narrowing her dark eyes, she asked, "Why?"

"I made a promise to help him."

"Not good enough."

"But it's the truth."

Her lips curled in a wry smile. "If we're speaking truth, then allow me to add my own. This creature is an abominable ass. He cares nothing for others and seeks only to enjoy himself no matter the cost. He is a liar. A selfish, foolhardy, rutting beast. Centuries may have passed, but know this: Marius earned his punishment."

"I don't disagree with you."

"Then why would you free him of this justice, mage?"

I took a few moments to ponder the goddess's question. Beyond the fact I'd given my word, why did I want Marius to get his groove back? The answer, it turned out, was simple.

"I know how he feels," I said. "I understand him—perhaps more than I'd like. I know how much it sucks to do the same damn thing day after day—enjoying none of it—while everyone around you gets to taste life."

"And?"

"And Marius saved my life."

"Because he thought he could gain something for himself," she snarled.

I nodded. "That's true, but I am in his debt. He aided me when I needed it. Regardless of his reasons, he kept his word to me. Please," I said bowing my head, "I need to free him so I can keep my promise, too."

Hera fixed me with her unyielding stare. "I will not allow you to cure him, child. The stubborn fool has not yet learned his lessons. But," she added, "I will send you off with a bit more truth."

The goddess bent, brought her lips to my ear, and whispered to me the key to Marius's freedom.

I contemplated the full weight of what held him prisoner. My heart fell and fluttered in my stomach. I felt a surge of anger on Marius's behalf, then pity. Sadness for my friend and this obstacle he might never overcome.

"Oh, shit," I said. "That's…wow. That's fucking cruel."

Proud and satisfied, Hera lifted her chin. "It gets the job done. Now you know, mage. Tell him if you will, but remember that doing so might add to his torment. I wouldn't mind, but you seem to give a damn. The choice is yours."

As the goddess walked away, the mist filled the temple. Bright blue light glowed before my eyes and once more I was in Eris's backyard. Beneath my fingers, Marius's pulse beat a shallow, quick rhythm. Dropping my hands, I stepped away from him, gasping for air as if I'd just run a marathon.

The satyr's glamour snapped back into place. "Well?" he whispered.

I shook my head. "I can't."

Marius's hair fell into his face as he sagged. "But," I said quickly.

His head shot up, the barest hope twinkling in his eyes. What Hera said was true; telling Marius the secret might add to his problems rather than solve them. If it were me, though, I'd want to know everything about the cage holding me prisoner. I couldn't keep my promise, but I could give him this.

"You can break the curse yourself."

He swallowed, letting my words sink in. I saw questions flicker over his face in the way his eyes searched mine and his lips quivered beneath his mustache. I'll never be certain, but he probably wondered how much time he'd wasted thinking Eris was his one path back to a real life. Maybe he wondered if I lied to him.

You're such similar creatures, Eris had said.

She'd been too right about that.

When he spoke, his voice was small and quiet, damn near humble. "Are you going to tell me, then?"

I steeled myself for what I had to tell him. "It will be hard, Marius. After all, you don't believe in stupid things like love."

The mention of the L-word was enough to make him flinch. He shook his head with agitation. "What are you saying?"

"You don't need Eris, or me, or anyone else to work magic to lift the spell. You need to love someone. And I'm not talking about flowers and chocolates and seduction. I mean, you have to actually *love* them. You need to care about someone more than you care about yourself." I shrugged. "That's all."

"That's all," he said, voice hoarse. Obscured by the eerie, shifting shadows from the pool, the satyr's face twisted with a wash of emotions. Anger formed harsh lines between his eyebrows. His mouth dropped open with a helpless pout. As he dragged a shaky hand through his hair, he grimaced and took a step back. "'That's all,' she says, as if it's the simplest thing in the world."

Cursing, Marius paced along the edge of the pool. "You can't know that's what needs to happen," he said. Though he tried to infuse his tone with arrogance, his face spoke of fear. "You can't."

"Marius, I have it on good authority."

"Well, fuck your authority! It's wrong! And so are you," he added as he turned his back on me.

I lifted my hands in quiet surrender.

Behind me, the door opened, and Loki stepped out into the night.

"Looks like you're done basking," Loki said. "As much as I'm sure you'd rather not, it's time to change the guard. So to speak."

I looked over at Marius. Brooding, he stared into the rippling waters.

"Okay," I said slowly, remembering my initiation with Eris, my time spent dangling over the Strip while my body suffocated. I dearly hoped Loki would be a better master.

He reached out and stroked the flesh on my arm. "Does it hurt?"

"It burns a little," I answered.

I watched as he drew lines over my skin. His touch grew cold and soothed the fever there while a shape formed. In arctic-blue-and-white light, the rune etched itself on my wrist. A vertical line with two diagonal lines coming off of it, like an *F* with its stems bent.

"Hey," I said. "That's the logo of the company I work for. Answers Inc."

Loki grinned. "The rune's name is actually pronounced *ahn-suz*. You might want to go look this one up. In fact, that's my first task for you, Catherine. You need to study. I need to know you're as smart as you are fierce."

"Fierce." I snorted. "Right."

"Hell, you've put up with Eris for this long, and you didn't kill that bastard of a satyr, so you must be quite strong. Yes, Cat, I think you and I will get along just fine."

Then I remembered something. "Wait, you said you liked the way I handled a hammer. What did you mean by that?"

"You don't really think I'd let Maui kill one of my employees without giving her a chance to defend herself, do you? No, I take care of what's mine."

Grateful as I was for his help, I took slight offense. "You hadn't won me yet."

"Cat, look at the cards. I had a royal flush from the flop. I won before your soul was even on the table."

"And so you dropped a hammer for me?"

"Yeah, borrowed it from one of my cousins. I wanted to see how you dealt with the tools at hand."

A cousin…with a hammer…from Asgard. *Holy shit.*

Stunned that I might have held Thor's hammer, I stammered. "It wasn't actually…"

"No," he said abruptly. "He never lets that one out of his sight."

I nodded quickly. "Right then."

The blond dealer approached and smacked a hand on Loki's shoulder. "Well, friends, it's time I took off for a bit. Catherine, it was good to talk with you. I hope I'll see you again."

Loki nodded to the brawny one. "I'll give you a lift." As they flip-flopped away, the trickster looked back at me. "Rest tomorrow. You've got a big day on Monday."

Hesitation wormed in my stomach. "What happens Monday?"

Loki answered with an impish grin.

As the Norseman made his way to the door, the dealer smiled and fixed me with those too-blue eyes.

"Faith," he reminded me. A quick, two-fingered salute, and he trundled away. As the door shut behind him, I realized I still didn't know his name.

CHAPTER TWENTY-EIGHT
"Hey"

I woke up sometime around noon the next day. Linux pounced on my chest and immediately started purring, giving me the head-butt of love repeatedly until I worshipped him as is his due. My cat and I spent quality time basking in the sun as it came in through the window.

I remembered, then, that two nights ago Marius had smashed through that very same window. The fight with the *kupua* came flashing back into my mind, and I hopped up to survey the damage.

There was none.

The window had been fixed. The bedroom and front doors had been mended, and there wasn't so much as a single thread out of place on my carpet. Not even a stain where the shark had bled. Briefly, I entertained the idea that I'd dreamed it all.

You had a few cocktails in you, I thought. *You probably came home and passed out. None of it ever happened.*

I looked down to my wrist. The proof that these past days had been a reality tattooed itself on my arm in a cool-blue rune. I'd been passed from Eris to Loki, and this was the souvenir.

I survived sharks and a demon bird from hell and all I got was this little tattoo.

I flopped onto my couch, laughing. I'd survived. My apartment had been trashed by monsters and repaired by tiny Hawaiian people. They'd fixed everything. Not just the stuff Maui's monsters wrecked. Everything. My bathroom door that stuck in the summertime, the leaky kitchen faucet, even the bookshelf that fell down if you breathed near it.

As I puttered around the apartment, fixing myself some toast and a frothy chai latte, I felt serene. I'd finally broken the holding pattern my life had become. But my stomach flopped at the unknown. Would Marius be okay? What would Flynn teach me about my new power? How would Loki use me? Would Eris seek revenge?

Linux reminded me what's truly important in life as he attacked my socks. While they were still on my feet. Yeah. Things would be okay.

I decided to get to work on my first assignment: learning about my new boss.

Using the wonders of the Internet, I started by reading up on a few of the more popular myths surrounding Loki. I found out he was seen as the foil to the creator gods, a mocking trickster. Like Prometheus of the Greek myths, Loki brought fire to mankind, wisdom. Answers.

This got me to wondering about his mark. The company I worked for had the same rune as part of its logo. What did it mean to him? I looked up the runes and found a picture matching my new brand. Beneath it a caption read: *ansuz*.

Clicking on the picture, I got a wall of text explaining the rune and how to read it in divination. I didn't so much care about telling the future—it would happen to me anyway, and with a trickster god running the show it was always in flux. However, the first paragraph of the explanation made me smile:

> *Ansuz: The Messenger; Norse rune associated with Loki, messages, and information. New connections and fresh starts. A new life unfolding. First Rune of Initiation in the cycle of self-change.*

I read those lines over and over again, marveling at how this rune applied to my life. A fresh start. Self-change. New connections.

My phone rang, interrupting my thoughts. I sighed at the sight of my mortal boss's name on the readout.

"This is Cat," I said.

"Sharp, I want you in the office now," he snapped. "I don't know what you've been up to for the past few days, but it sure as shit wasn't your job."

I closed my eyes and braced myself. Getting fired sure would be a great way to start my new life. I had no way to explain, no mundane excuses. It's not like I could yammer on about gods and *wakwaks*.

"I'm sorry, sir."

"I'm not the one you have to apologize to, Sharp. The big man is pissed and wants you here. Now."

"What?"

"You heard me. The owner of the damn company has been in his office with one of our top clients for the past hour, and it's not pretty. You need to get here and start groveling if you want to keep your job."

"I'll be right in, Mr. Crandall," I murmured.

I'd never met the CEO of Answers, Inc., but the rumor was that he was a shrewd, cold businessman with little interest in bullshit. Preparing to join the statistics of employee turnover, I shuffled around the apartment and got dressed in my red polo and khakis.

I'd walked halfway to the parking lot before I realized I'd left my car in the garage at Caesars a few days ago.

"Shit!" I hissed. I'd have to call a cab to get to the casino. As I fished out my keys, my thumb hit the panic button on my remote key fob. In the parking lot, my car began to wail.

Squinting with confusion I looked up to see that, sure enough, my car inhabited my usual space. On the hood, sitting lotus style, a man pressed his hands over his ears. Eyes shut tight, his mouth hung open as he howled in harmony with the car alarm. I ran across the courtyard, and his striking features came into focus. White hair, blotchy skin…

"Alfie?" I said, remembering his name. He didn't seem to hear me, but there was no mistake that the lunatic from the gala had parked himself atop my car. He'd exchanged his dapper suit for a moldy blue hoodie and grease-stained jeans. His white hair stood on end at odd angles. Even though his clothes and hair were about as couture as the average wino, Alfie's face was as clean, fresh, and smooth as a newborn's. I couldn't be sure, but I thought the pattern of his blotches had changed.

Even after I shut off the alarm, he continued to let out piercing ululations, his tongue darting about in his mouth.

I tugged at his sleeve and yelled his name again. "Alfie!"

He opened his eyes but didn't see me. Staring straight ahead he finished his chorus and slowly let his hands fall away from his ears. Alfie licked his lips and blinked. His whole body convulsed with a shiver that reminded me of a dog shaking himself dry. Even now, with his eyes and ears open, he didn't notice me.

"Alfie?" I asked quietly.

Whipping his head around, he fixed his wild blue eyes on me. "Ah! If it isn't my friend, C-C-Catherine. Fancy meeting you here. Come to enjoy the concert? I don't know if it's any good, the noise that passes for music these days, but if you don't listen you can sing along."

I shook my head, dazed by his illogic. "Alfie, did you bring me my car?"

"Mmmhmm," he said, chewing at his thumb. "Thought you'd need it."

"Okay. Um, how did you manage that?"

He wrinkled his face, thin lips twisting in a grimace. "I drove, you nitwit. What else do you think I'd do with a car? Swim in it? Maybe grow a beanstalk out of the tail pipe?"

"But I have the keys," I said, agitated. "How did you even know it was my car? And, how the hell do you know where I live?"

Alfie made a sound halfway between a snort and a chuckle. He unfolded his legs and slid off the hood. He patted me gently on the shoulder. Thankfully, this time I didn't experience the burning agony of his touch.

Shaking his head as if I were nothing more than a silly child, he wheezed with laughter.

"Oh, Catherine, much like you, the answer is simple."

"Really? Do tell."

He leaned in close and whispered in my ear. "I pay attention."

Without another word, Alfie ambled across the gravel lot and walked out into traffic. Cars swerved and honked, but he didn't seem to notice. He was too busy singing along with the cacophony. Soon, a wall of cars obscured my view, and Alfie was gone.

As I crawled into the car I spared a quick thought to hope he would be all right. I reminded myself, then, that I had other things to deal with.

***

Answers, Inc. squatted in a small industrial complex southeast of the Boulevard. The windows cast back gray reflections of the carefully manicured hedges and obscured any attempts to see in. The glass-and-concrete maze reminded me of a labyrinth for the modern age, a feeling that grew as I navigated the call center inside. Most grunts worked in pods—workstations about a quarter of the size of a typical cubicle. The phone operators handled overflow tech support from a few of our affiliate companies while mobile staff—like me—milled about between assignments.

I passed the break room and the litter of bagel crumbs on my way to my boss's office. He didn't have a door, so I knocked on the metal frame. Mel Crandall looked up, his agitation a film of sweat on his round head.

"Sharp," he barked. His chair creaked as he leaned back, and his red polo stretched over his rotund belly. "Would you like to tell me why I'm here on a Sunday?"

The whole drive into the office I'd been trying to come up with an excuse. The best I could come up with was a watered down version of the truth. "Mr. Crandall, I'm so sorry. I was in a car accident Friday night, and the on-call phone was lost in the mess."

Mel's pointed nose wrinkled. "I don't give a shit about the on-call phone, Sharp. I want to know why one of my most loyal clients is in my boss's office having a screaming match because one of my people botched a job!"

Crandall hooked his thumb over his shoulder and indicated The Boss's office. You could tell it belonged to The Boss because it was the one room in this god-forsaken building with a door. From the other side of the wood, I heard a low, wordless murmur in between the high-pitched litany of anger.

"Who's in there?" I asked.

"Tullemore. Caesars' shift lead."

"Tully?"

Mel nodded.

The cell on his desk chirped, and a cool, muffled voice filled the room. "Is she here yet?"

Crandall grabbed his phone and keyed the walkie-talkie function. "Sharp is here, sir. You want me to send her in?"

"Please."

Mel peered over his rimless glasses and gave me a pitying glance. With a shrug in The Boss's direction, he said, "You heard him. Better get in there."

Though he didn't say it, I could make out the, "nice knowing you" implied by his dour tone. I straightened my spine, and in two confident strides, I knocked on the door.

"Come in," The Boss said.

I turned the handle and went through the door.

CHAPTER TWENTY-NINE
"Otherside"

I'd expected to find Tully, red-faced and sputtering curses at a calm suit. What I found on the other side of the door, however, was one man standing behind a desk. A smile wrinkled the corners of his gas-flame eyes.

While I tried to reel my jaw up from the floor, Loki quietly said, "Please shut the door, Ms. Sharp."

My chest felt tight and cold with a breath I couldn't exhale. The door closed with a slight *click* that echoed in my ears as if I'd slammed it. I jumped at the tiny sound, and the god's smile deepened.

"Surprised?" he asked.

I looked around the office. Like Eris, the Norse avatar of Mayhem kept an immaculate space. Unlike Discord, however, Loki showed considerable taste. His desk was a heavy monolith of Old World magnificence and polished cherry. A sleek, paper-thin laptop sat at an angle facing the god's leather wingback chair. On the shelves around the room, classic literature shared space with computing manuals. Java and UNIX cozied up with Joyce's *Ulysses*.

My eyes drifted back to Loki with his strawberry-blond spikes and impish grin. "Where's Tully?" I asked.

Loki cleared his throat and when he spoke, my friend's voice flew out of his mouth. "I'm in the doghouse, Cat."

My eyebrows tried to climb over my scalp as I stared, bug-eyed. "What the mother fuck?"

Where there had been a god, plain and round Tully now stood. He rolled out from behind the desk and past me. As he whipped open the door he turned back to me, expression sad.

"I'm sorry, Cat. You're one of the best, but this is unacceptable."

Mel's head popped out of his office to watch as Tully lumbered down the hall. Mel cast a quick glance in my direction then, like a scared meerkat, ducked back into his room.

"You know people," Loki said with a sigh from over my shoulder. He closed the door and turned his palms up to the ceiling in silent surrender. "Always seeing what I want them to see."

Confused as hell, I blinked.

"Have a seat, Catherine. We should talk."

I took one of the chairs in front of his desk. To my added surprise, Loki sat in the other one, beside me, rather than the regal wingback. He didn't say anything. The god leaned back in his chair and laced his fingers together in his lap, waiting.

My eyes darted around the room without actually seeing anything as my mind whirred along, connecting the dots. "The whole time?" I whispered.

Again, Loki moved his mouth, and Tully's voice came out. "If a light bulb so much as flickers, my boss will grind me to a pulp and serve me up for tacos on the ten-dollar buffet."

"You're Tully?"

"Yes," he said quietly.

"So what?" I stammered. "He's never been real? It's been you all this time?"

Loki's chin dipped in silent assent.

I choked on words I couldn't form. I'd known Tully, at least as a colleague, since just after I moved out of Dahlia's place. Though he wasn't someone I hung out with, David Tullemore was a friend. I replayed conversations we'd had over servers and bad wiring, about his life, his complaints about his boss…

"He had a wife."

"And so do I."

My stomach rolled with a hollow pain. "This whole time it's been you," I said again. In trying to divine the god's reasons I succeeded in twisting my mind into a pretzel. "Why? I can't figure it out. Why go through all this?"

Loki stood and moved around his desk. He closed his laptop and curled it against his body. "I need you to come with me. I have a task for you."

I threw my hands up in frustration. "And here I'd hoped you'd be different than Eris. Come here. Do this. Game after game. You're exactly like her, aren't you?"

Those arctic eyes burned as he scowled at me. "That jealous bitch and I may be cut of similar cloth, but do not ever compare me to the Mistress of Discord. You know how this works. I am the keeper of your soul. Nothing much changes, Catherine Sharp. You are still my employee as you were yesterday and the day before that. Today, this relationship is more direct. Now, please come with me."

Without another word, Loki spun on his heel and breezed out into the hall. I passed Mel's office and saw him shaking his head. I wondered what it was he thought he saw. Had Loki projected some other illusion on us? Or me? Had I left sobbing?

Whatever he did, no one paid us any attention as we left the building. A car alarm disarmed with a *squawk*, and Loki opened the passenger door to a grey Ford Mustang.

"Get in," he said.

"Where are we going?"

"To work," he said.

For about five minutes we rode in silence. As he guided the car south, I stared out the window as the neighborhoods shifted by.

"Is that why you didn't test me like the others? Because you already knew me through Tully?"

"Who says I didn't test you?"

I took a breath to argue, but the words caught in my throat. My mouth hung open like a codfish.

Loki chuckled. "I didn't send colossal beasties after you or invade your mind, but I had a few questions of my own about you."

"You know about Puck's test?" I asked, face flaring with shame.

He nodded. When he spoke, his voice carried a quiet sympathy. "I don't know all of the details, but I know it happened."

"How?"

"I have my sources." Loki took his eyes off the road and met mine for a second too long to be comfortable. When his attention was once more on the light traffic, he added, "I put you through a few paces myself. For example, I thought you handled Alfie's insanity admirably. I risked a lot inviting him to my little soiree, but it was worth it. I learned a lot about you in those few minutes you spent humoring him."

Pity mingled with fear as I thought of the broken soul at the buffet. "Was it an act?"

"Sadly, no. Alfie is what he is, and there's little in this world that could heal his mind."

His words got me to thinking. I played over as much as I could remember of what Tully had told me a few days ago. A picture began to form, and I didn't like it.

"A major server goes down at Caesars the same night Eris bets my soul in a poker game. A poker game you'd already won."

"Keep working at it," he urged.

"When the backup controller kicks in, a gala mysteriously shows up on the schedule that has everyone scrambling, and I just happen to get a job handed to me that sends me to Caesars to help your alter ego fix the broken controller. Hell," I said in shock, "your fingerprints are all over this thing!"

"Beautiful, isn't it?"

"How far back does this go? I mean, are you the reason my car broke down on the way to my senior prom, too?"

His rubbery face wrinkled into a self-satisfied smirk. "Not my work, I'm afraid."

"You rigged the game, didn't you?"

"I did nothing of the sort."

"You blew the domain controller at Caesar's to cover the sudden addition of your party to the schedule, though."

Both hands sprang off the wheel, and mischief danced in his eyes. "Guilty," he sang proudly.

I shook my head, astounded by the complexity of Loki's gambit. "I still don't understand why. Why go through all of this for a soul? Why the disguise as Tully? Why all the crazy games?"

"Are you kidding?" Loki asked. "Why do you play any game? Because it's fun. As to why bother with all of it for a soul, this answer is easy, too. Because it's yours."

I raised an eyebrow. "What's so great about my soul?"

We made a right into a vaguely familiar neighborhood. The playhouses for the rich and famous sprawled on acres of desert. I'd probably fixed someone's cable or wired a panic room out here at some point.

"I think you said it best yourself, Catherine. 'It's when the gods take notice of you that you should start praying.' Well, my dear, you've been noticed."

"I'm never going to get a straight answer from you, am I?"

The Mustang jerked to a stop, and he threw the gearshift into park. "We're here."

We'd parked on the street in front of a two-story house with an iron sunburst pattern on the security door. Even in the daylight I recognized it as Eris's home. A U-Haul sat in the driveway.

"What are we doing here?" I asked, unable to keep the fear out of my voice.

"Unfinished business."

"Yours or mine?"

He let out a belly laugh and unbuckled his seat belt. Without answering, Loki got out of the car and motioned for me to follow. I marched slowly behind my new master up the mosaic path. Before the Norseman could knock, the door flew open. Marius, his arms wrapped around two cardboard boxes, shuffled out into the Vegas afternoon. He'd made it two steps before he realized he had company.

Surprise flashed over his weary face for an instant. "Ah," he said to Loki, his mask sliding back into place. "I thought I smelled syphilis on the wind." Marius slid the boxes into the back of the truck, dusted off his hands and swaggered to Loki with his hand extended. "Pleasure, as always, to see you," he sneered.

"Good puppy," Loki sang as he gripped the satyr's hand. "Make yourself useful and go find your mistress."

Marius glared. As he stuffed his hand in the pockets of his jeans I caught a flash of dull-green paper. I narrowed my eyes at him.

"Catherine," he said. "Not even a day away from Eris, and you're already looking fresh and lovely as I've ever seen you."

I blushed, at a loss for what to say to him or how to act. "Hey."

I cringed internally. *Eloquence wins again.*

Loki took in the truck, nearly filled with boxes and a few pieces of furniture. "Going somewhere, Marius?"

"The Lady tires of the desert air."

"How sad for her."

255

"Marius," Eris called from within the house. She stopped at her threshold and narrowed her eyes at Loki. "Oh, it's you."

She joined us in the front yard. Eris still wore the same clothes from last night, her hair pulled into a tight bun at the back of her head. The goddess's golden eyes glared at me, her lips curling with disdain.

"Not to be rude, Loki, but what the hell do you want?"

"Well, hag, I have two pieces of business today. First, I wanted to thank you for hosting yet another wonderful game. It's not every day I get to add a potent technomancer to my staff."

Eris clucked her tongue. "Please, she's not so talented. You should see the mess she made of the elevator at my office. I am glad to be rid of her. What good do you think she could possibly do for you?"

Loki grinned as he appraised me. "I'm sure Asgard would be able to find some clever use for her. Or maybe I'll just hold onto her for a while, see how this particular investment matures."

"Asgard? The All-father has plans for her?"

"Did I say that? My mistake. Anyhow, as I said, I have two things to discuss with you. Now that I've thanked you for Ms. Sharp here, it's time for the less pleasant matter."

"And that is?" Eris asked, face pinched and sour.

"Get the hell out of my house."

Marius choked on a laugh and covered it with a few weak coughs. The goddess's eyes widened, and her nostrils flared with anger. "What did you say to me?"

"Funny thing, Eris," Loki began. "I have been in the market for a new home for a while now, and this one came up recently as having been foreclosed. Well, I had to scoop it up, didn't I? Got it for a song! I took possession of it as of midnight. Get out."

Grinding her teeth, Eris stewed in her rage. "You cannot order me around, Loki."

"No? Can you pay me the money you lost to me along with the mage? It's not like you to skip town after a game. If the others had any reason to think you couldn't make good on your bets it might weaken your status at the table."

The goddess squinted, malice swirling in her eyes as she pondered her precarious situation. When her jaw clenched and her cheeks pinched with sour revulsion, I knew that my new boss had her over the proverbial barrel.

"Marius," Eris barked, "we're leaving."

"But I've left my jacket in the house," he whined. "Now!"

Marius scrambled to close up the cargo bay. As he passed us on his way to the cab, he pointed to the house. "I'll just get it on my way back 'round town, shall I?"

"Wait," I said. "You're going?"

What the hell was I doing? Was I about to make some scene out here in the driveway with him, our bosses watching? I shuddered, shut down with nerves.

Marius met my eyes, his smile sad. His mustache twitched, and his voice softened. "You know how she is."

As the satyr pulled himself up into the driver's seat, he peered over the door at Loki and me. Eris slammed herself into the passenger seat and fumed. Marius followed suit and started the U-Haul with a thunderous rumble.

"Anything left inside I'll consider a down payment on what you owe me," Loki called. His smile was so smug he could give Marius lessons.

The truck rumbled out of the driveway and down the street. When Marius and Eris were out of sight, Loki grabbed me by the arm. "Come on, this is the best part!"

Like a child getting private access to an amusement park, Loki bounded into the house and turned a circle in the empty living room. "What do you think?" he asked. "Pull up the carpet? Paint the walls? What would you do?"

I wasn't up for playing interior decorator. I had other things on my mind. A few of the coincidences of the past few days began to gel together and form a new mosaic.

"Marius," I said. "You bought him, didn't you?"

Loki regarded his feet. "What makes you say that?"

"Well, for starters, you just palmed him some cash."

"Good eye," he said appreciatively. "Everyone has a price, Cat, and the satyr is—as you could imagine—quite cheap."

I decided to bounce my theories off of him. "So, you set up the gala— wearing your Tully suit—so that you and the rest of the gang would have a chance to see me out and about. You met Marius and me at the door and worked some spell over the invitation. Were you passing Marius a message?"

He smirked. "She's good!"

"And last night. You were the one who was supposed to meet us at Caesars, weren't you?"

"At least I didn't destroy the place and render everyone there null and void."

I ignored him and kept going. "And the phone call when Marius and I landed on Fremont. That was you, not Eris. That's when you told him to get the chips away from me. So you distracted me by being Tully in the crowd."

Loki's expression grew serious as he leaned against a bare wall. He sighed. "I had to make sure Eris didn't try to take back her bet."

"That's when he told you about Puck's illusion."

"Yes."

"So Marius was working angles for you the whole time. And now you're using me to piss off Eris."

Loki nodded.

"I can respect that," I said. "But, if you and I are going to be working together there are a few things we should get straight right from the start."

Loki folded his arms and regarded me as if I were a precocious child. If he patted me on the head I would slug him. I drew in a deep breath. "I have free will. This means that if Coyote wants to borrow me for the weekend, or if you want to send me off on some errand to start a war, I can say no. You have my soul, but I have control of my actions and my body. Is that clear?"

"Crystal."

"Good. Also, from here on out I deal with you. Not Tully or some illusion. You want to talk to me? You want to know something about me, Loki? Fine. But I get to know when it's you. If Marius told you what Puck did to me, then you know that I do not respond well to mindfucks."

Loki nodded. "I can't promise that circumstances will not force me to use illusion and disguise. Sometimes it is necessary for me to be someone else. Even someone as insignificant and mundane as David Tullemore. However, if I cannot appear to you as myself, I will make sure that you know you are dealing with me. And your mind and body shall remain your own while you are under my care."

"Care?" I scoffed.

"As long as we're setting some ground rules for our relationship, Catherine, allow me to be frank. I am not Eris. Yes, I am using you. You are an investment with lucrative possibilities. What you are not, however, is a slave. I need your mind intact and your faculties sharp. It is not in my best interest to play tricks with your mind to find a sadistic foothold."

"If I'm not a slave, what am I?"

He sighed, weary. "What I offer is a symbiotic partnership. I give you an assignment, you carry out the work and receive payment. Like a typical day job there are other benefits to being on my payroll. First and foremost is protection. Unlike Eris, I am not some withering hack trying to claw my way back into power. My name still has meaning, and others will think twice before they cross one of my people."

Stunned, I blinked and soaked it in. I had a god as an ally.

"What if I want my soul back?" I asked. "What if I want to end our arrangement?"

Loki's hard face grew dark. "Breaking our bond is not in your best interest. You've attracted a lot of attention. Believe me, Catherine, I may not be the devil you know, but I am the lesser of the evils who would have you."

A chill skittered over my spine.

"Besides," he added. "Your soul is not mine to give."

"What are you talking about? You won it last night."

"I'm merely a steward," he said, spreading his hands. Before I could ask any more questions, Loki clapped loudly and bounced away from the wall. "Now! About the house. What do you think?"

I looked around the empty, bone-white space. With a shrug I gave a non-committal "eh."

"It's yours," he said. "If you'll have it."

I whirled around to face him. I expected to see some sadistic, lupine grin like the one worn by Eris. Instead he gave a warm, almost benevolent smile.

"Why?" I asked.

"How much have you given up, Cat, to be Eris's minion? How much did you get in return? I like to make sure my people are happy."

I thought about it. You could fit two of my apartment into this house and have room left over to park a few cars. A pool and a panic room added to the value, of course. The real selling point, though, would be that it was a kick in the face to Eris. I looked around at the white walls and white carpets. The little breakfast nook, though empty of the table and chairs, would always hold the memory of the poker game where my soul was gambled away.

"No," I said. "I will stay where I am, thank you."

Loki's forehead wrinkled as his brows climbed up. "Really?"

"Really. It's too big and cold. Not my thing. Besides, my landlady would be lost without me."

The god stood staring at me, mouth hitching up in amusement. "You are full of surprises, aren't you, Catherine Sharp?"

I shrugged. "I am what I am."

"All right, then. I suppose I'll find something to do with this place."

Loki led the way out to the driveway. When we were back in his Mustang and on our way across town, he said, "I'm sure you understand that I can't have you working such erratic hours for the company. I can't have you making excuses to managers if I need you to go on an assignment for me."

"Are you firing me?"

"No," he said, "I still want you working around the city with some of our bigger clients. You'll be on the payroll as an executive consultant. Congratulations, you've been promoted."

"Will I still be working with Tully?" I asked.

"Occasionally, yes."

While he laid out the details of my new job, I listened and watched Las Vegas fly past the car windows. It looked as it always had, but in just a few days the world had changed in so many ways. For the first time in years I didn't know what tomorrow would hold.

"What's next?" I murmured to no one in particular.

Beside me, the god smiled. "We'll have to see."

***

Crunching across the pathetic courtyard to my apartment I saw the trademark pink terrycloth of my landlady. Mrs. McIntyre stood at my door holding a colorful bouquet of flowers.

As I came up behind her I said, "Hey, Mrs. M. What's up?"

"Oh, Cathy," she said, turning around gingerly. "I wanted to talk to you."

"Is it about the water heaters? I'm free the rest of the afternoon so I should be able to have a look."

"No, dear, no," she said, that phlegmy rumble clogging her voice. "Doris had her grandkids over and do you know they pushed a few buttons and now poor Doris can't get her DVR working. You know how much she loves her shows."

"Oh, sure," I said. "That'll take two minutes to fix."

I unlocked the door and held it open for Mrs. M. She hobbled in, leaning heavily on her walker with one hand and carrying the flowers close to her chest with the other.

"These are for you," she said. My landlady put the vase down on the tile counter. "They were by your door when I stopped by. Along with this."

Mrs. M dug into her fluffy pocket and produced a smooth white box about the size of a deck of cards. I looked at the vase and realized someone had sent me half a dozen orange and red dahlias. My throat grew tight and my fingers shook as I reached for the small envelope in the stems.

"Probably from your beau," Mrs. M said. She pursed her lips in a knowing smile. "Seems he enjoyed your date."

I grinned nervously. "Friday night was...memorable."

Pulling the card from the envelope I saw a flowing hand had written a single line:

Don't think I've forgotten.

My fingers shook as I opened the box. A swath of black fabric and nothing more.

Carefully, I picked up the cloth and shook it out to find elastic strings and a small triangle of cotton. Glittery text read *Pirate booty*.

Heat crawled up my face, and I thought my hair would catch fire. I chanced a glance at my landlady. Her wrinkled lips pursed together, and her cheeks flushed to match her Muppet-fleece robe.

"Oh, my!" She patted at her cotton-candy wisps of hair and looked away. I was convinced I'd caught a wicked twinkle in her rheumy eyes first, though.

I stuffed the thong into my pocket and stammered, voice cracking like a pre-teen. "I, well, we went to...uh. He thought..."

"Don't worry a bit, Cathy. I've seen my share of thongs visiting my sister in Boca Raton. I even tried one once. Whole thing was made of pearls."

And just like that, my flaming horror was doused by a cold wave of revulsion.

"Mrs. M," I squeaked, "what was it you needed again?"

"Doris's television."

"Oh, yeah. I can get to that right now. And I'll finish up with the heaters tomorrow, if it's okay."

"Fine, dear. Just fine. If you have time, could you also look at the stove in number four? I'm getting a new tenant in there next week, and I think the burners are shot."

I nodded. "Sure thing, Mrs. M."

She patted me on the cheek and passed along an effusive, toothless smile. "You're a peach, honey."

She tottered around and made her wobbly way to her apartment. I followed and stopped by Doris's about the DVR. Sure, I'd spent the past few days running from gods and their minions. I had a new job and life had taken a strange, surprising turn. Of course I had other things I could have focused on. But Mrs. M had problems, and she'd called me to fix them. How could I say no?

I'm Cat Sharp, and I fix things.

It's what I do.

Acknowledgments

First and foremost, I have to thank my publishing rock stars: my agent, Jennie Goloboy at Red Sofa Literary; my editor, Danielle Poiesz. Without them this would still be just a Word document being passed around to my friends. I also have to thank my Attack Fish, my intrepid beta readers: Angela Leach, Lejon Johnson, Rhys McNamee, Susana LaLuz, and Inge Atkinson. Special thanks goes to Jeremy Martin—dauntless GM extraordinaire—who was kind enough to let me borrow the concept of a satyr who can't feel pleasure. To Jesse Cox, for many things, least of which is pushing me to rekindle my love of writing. My gratitude also goes to Colleen Lindsay and Gabrielle Harbowy, friends and colleagues who have helped me in ways they may not know.

Much love to the Red Hot Chili Peppers. No, they had nothing to do with making this book, but their songs provided not only the soundtrack while I was writing, but also the chapter titles.

Most importantly, though, I have to thank my family. My mother and father who always believed in me and pushed me to follow every dream. My grandmother who bought my first typewriter and recorded my first stories. My relatives and dear friends who have supported me through every peak and valley. And my husband, Sean, and our daughter, K. You put up with so much while I work and live in my head or ramble on about my imaginary friends. Words cannot express my gratitude and love, or what it means to me to know you're always in my corner.

And last, but never least, I thank *you* for reading this book and giving me the chance to share my stories with you. This is only the beginning.

About the Author

After a misspent adulthood pursuing a Music Education degree, JAMIE WYMAN fostered several interests before discovering that being an author means never having to get out of pajamas. She has an unhealthy addiction to chai, a passion for circus history, and a questionable hobby that involves putting a flaming torch into her mouth. When she's not traipsing about with her imaginary friends, she lives in Phoenix with two hobbits and two cats. Jamie is proud to say she has a deeply disturbed following at her blog. Visit and join the fun at www.jamiewyman.com.

www.ingramcontent.com/pod-product-compliance
Lightning Source LLC
Chambersburg PA
CBHW060404180626
46817CB00007B/2516